Captivating Captains

THE CAPTAIN AND
THE PRIME MINISTER

CATHERINE CURZON &
ELEANOR HARKSTEAD

The Captain and the Prime Minister
ISBN # 978-1-83943-864-6
©Copyright Catherine Curzon & Eleanor Harkstead 2020
Cover Art by Cherith Vaughan ©Copyright March 2020
Interior text design by Claire Siemaszkiewicz
Pride Publishing

THE CAPTAIN AND THE PRIME MINISTER

Dedication

CC — For the Provolone Rangers!
EH — For Frankie, who likes a floppy fringe!

Prologue

"And, of course, Gill Hart's death comes just a year into her husband's term as prime minister—it's no secret he and I have never been friends! Everyone's thoughts, though, regardless of political affiliation, must surely be with Alex Hart and the couple's infant twins. A manny might seem unorthodox, but let's see how he gets on—stranger things have been seen in Downing Street!"

—Pierce Cowell, *The Great British Morning Show*, ITV

Chapter One

Three years later

Tom lay sprawled on the beanbag between the two small beds — one shaped like a car, the other shaped like a boat. He'd almost sent himself to sleep with the twins' bedtime story, but it finally seemed, from the sound of their gentle breathing, that they'd dropped off. He sat in the quiet, dimly lit room, the elephant nightlight casting its gentle glow. And in that glow, he re-read the text from Stuart.

Hey good lookin', ya miss me? Through with Barca and heading home — you shud SEE my tan lines babe. Get ready Laaahndaaaan! x

Stuart wasn't high on the list of people who Tom wanted to talk to. Their break-up had been acrimonious, Stuart furious at one too many dates being canceled at the last minute because Tom had to look after the twins. *'You love that family more than you love me!'* And off Stuart had gone to Barcelona.

Except, apparently, Stuart was back.

And that list of Tom's was rather brief.

It'd be rude not to reply, wouldn't it?

Tom lifted his head and glanced at the children. They were both sound asleep, so Tom carefully got up from the beanbag and tapped his reply.

Hey Stuart yeah I'm still in London. Maybe I'll see you sometime? T.

They'd been through a lot—both ex-army, both gay, although Tom's career had taken an unusual turn when he'd decided to become a nanny. Or *manny*, as the press had christened him. But it worked. Captain Southwell had transformed into Tom, but he still dealt with crises before breakfast, and marshaling small children was just as challenging as directing a company in a warzone.

The reply took seconds.

Believe it manny Tom. I'll be knocking on door of no 10 and sayin' where's my man ;) xx

Tom worked on the principle that being hostile to exes wasn't the mark of a gentleman, but, equally, dealing with someone who thought Tom was his *man* after all this time wasn't a task that filled him with joy.

I thought your man's in Barcelona? T.

And his phone rang, vibrating silently in his hand as Tom heard the flat's front door opening and closing softly, so as not to disturb the sleeping children. The prime minister was home.

Tom stuffed the phone into his pocket. He wasn't going to answer it — he had a family to look after.

Before Alex had reached the kitchen doorway, Tom had poured him a glass of wine. It sat there on the worktop when Alex appeared in the doorway, his hand already loosening the knot of his tie.

"All the way from the House I was thinking about diving into a *huge* glass of red wine." Alex chuckled, widening his eyes at the sight of it. "And there it is!"

"You look like you could do with one!" Tom said.

"The thought of cuddling Al and Mad and a little sniff of red is what's kept me going through the last two hours of paperwork," Alex told him, slapping a matey hand to Tom's shoulder and letting it linger there. "As soon as I hit the bottom of the despatch box, I made for home. I don't suppose there happens to be any supper left over, or am I raiding the fridge again?"

Tom passed him the glass across the marble worktop. "There's a shepherd's pie waiting for you if you'd like it?"

"If anyone finds out about this, they'll be tempting you away with a pay rise," Alex teased. "I already have to tell them you're like the anti-Mary Poppins to throw them off the scent."

Tom checked the pie in the oven then turned it on to warm.

"I don't have a magic carpet bag, and I'm not into chimney sweepers," he said. "I have no intention of leaving, tempt me all they like!"

"If any chimney sweeps *do* come along, I want to know about it," Alex told him. Then he raised his glass to his lips and took a grateful drink. "I can't lose my shepherd's pie whisperer."

"Do you want to eat in here, or in the lounge?" Tom hoped he'd say the lounge, because if Alex put the television on in the kitchen and discovered that the last channel Tom had watched was BBC Parliament, it might be rather awkward.

It's because the children wanted to see you when they came home from preschool. Honest.

"Lounge, sofa, general couch potato of a night?" He nodded, apparently satisfied with his own suggestion. "Did you eat with the kids?"

"Well, I tried! We had sit-down dinnertime together but Madeleine wanted to draw at the same time, so I had my hands full." Tom dragged his hand back through his hair. "I think I got all the sweetcorn out of my hair, but I'm not sure!"

"I'm going to nip in and see them before I eat," Alex decided. "I hate that I missed them tonight and I know they're asleep, but it's really for me, not them. But you know that."

"I know." Tom patted his arm. "They'll know you're there. You'll suddenly pop up in their dreams."

"Oh, God help them! Then you have to be off the clock, Tom, you know that. Much as I love coming home to you and your shepherd's pie, you must be cursing my name?" He assumed a grumbling mutter to say, "Bloody Alex keeping me bloody working all bloody hours."

"It's not really *work*, though," Tom assured him as he got a tray ready for Alex. "We're like housemates!"

"I couldn't ask for a better fellow to share with." Alex laughed and brushed Tom's shoulder as he headed for the door. "I'll be back, Captain!"

Tom leaned against the kitchen cupboard, flicking through a recipe book. He heard Alex's footsteps through the baby monitor and saw the night-vision version of the prime minister on the screen. Tom should have gone back to his book to give Alex his privacy, but he couldn't resist a glance at Alex crouched beside his child's bed. He was such a kind father and it brought a lump to Tom's throat. Thank God Stuart hadn't rung again and shattered their peace. He didn't need it tonight, and Alex certainly didn't.

Tom heard Alex's voice, as gentle now as it had been commanding in the Chamber earlier, wishing his sleeping children sweet dreams. Then, as he always did on the rare nights that he didn't make it home in time for supper and bedtime with the twins he adored, Alex remained in the room for a while. He settled onto the beanbag where Tom had sat just a few minutes earlier and became part of the peaceful scene, soaking up the calm in that sometimes rather busy room that his son and daughter shared. And though the two children slept on, surely they sensed that protective presence watching over them until, with a whisper of, "I love you," Alex rose to his feet and made his careful way toward the door.

Alex was such a lonely figure sometimes, and during those moments Alex shared with his children, Tom wondered if he was thinking of his late wife.

He shouldn't ever be lonely. Gill wouldn't have wanted it, and Tom certainly didn't. Alex deserved to be loved.

"I see the permanent marker has *almost* washed off of Alastair's cheek," Alex observed cheerfully as he padded back into the kitchen. He returned to the serious business of unknotting his tie and added, "You must have magical skills that I lack!"

The sound of the silk rasping against Alex's hand very nearly sent a tremor through Tom, but he pushed it down.

You can't think those things about your straight boss.

"We had a game at bathtime—I made them beards and mustaches out of bubbles, then rubbed them off. Al didn't notice a thing—he was too busy laughing."

"See, I learned the hard way that saying *don't scribble on your face* is the guaranteed way to get a little monster like my son to scribble on his face." Alex threw his tie onto the worktop. Then he unfastened his silver cufflinks and tossed them with only a little more care atop his discarded tie. Tom knew what was coming next even before Alex rolled first one immaculate sleeve to his elbow then the other, because he knew Alex's routine as well as his own. *And his arms are to die for.* "He's joining a long line of Hart boys who never did as they were told!"

Tom chuckled. "Were you naughty, then?"

You wish he still was naughty, Tom.

"I was a terror." Alex leaned forward to peer through the glass door of the oven, his hands braced against his knees. "But I went one better—I drew on my sister's face while she was asleep. Gave her a mustache to be proud of!"

"And having met your sister—!" Tom tried not to notice how the fabric of Alex's suit trousers strained pleasingly across his bottom as he leaned down. He was a fine figure of a man—Tom would be an idiot not to notice. "Bet she was pleased!"

"Oh, she loved it, you can imagine how thrilled she was!" Alex stood straight again and turned to face Tom.

"You don't have to hang around if you don't want to, you know. Honestly, I can't imagine this is how you want to spend your off time."

"If I worked in an office all day, I'd be chilling at home just like I'm doing now, so... It's fine, honest." Tom slipped the recipe book back on the shelf. He liked being part of a family, too. In some ways it made up for the lack of his own. "I should apologize for these jogging bottoms, though. I don't think I've even jogged in them. But then...you wouldn't want to see me in my pajamas, would you?"

Although I wouldn't mind seeing Alex in his again.

"This is your home, Captain Southwell. If you have to see me bleary-eyed in my bath towel now and again, I wouldn't complain if you wanted to wear your pajamas after a long day trying to keep my children in line!"

Alex in a bath towel. That's a thought to ponder.

"I *say* pajamas, I actually sleep in—" *My boxer shorts. Oh, God, he doesn't want to know that.* "Do you want to see what the twins got up to at preschool today?"

Tom was already delving into the satchels that Alastair and Madeleine carried about as proudly as the chancellor wielded his briefcase on Budget Day. Alex gave an impromptu drumroll, pounding his hands on the worktop, and asked, "Go on, show me."

"Ta-da!" Tom produced a sheet of paper from Madeleine's bag and handed it over. "They had to draw their families, so she's done you in the House of Commons. She's even got the green seats right, although she's only given you three strands of hair."

"But what excellent strands they are." Alex laughed, brushing his hand back through his rather more generous head of *real* hair. "But who's the terrible threesome watching from the benches? Alastair's hair's looking rather bluer than I remember, but she's got Gill's curls right, and as for *you*... How is it that I look like a balding headteacher and you look like a film star?"

With a deliberately camp flourish, Tom said, "Oh, just my fabulous good looks! I suppose I'm the minister of tidying up the toy box?"

"A deserved gold star for Mads." Alex beamed proudly. He took the picture and placed it on the fridge, where it joined a gallery of his children's artistic efforts. "At least she drew it on paper, not on her brother's face."

"And that's why I suggested wipe-clean paint on the walls in this house!" Tom said. "You never know when a pen or a crayon'll go rogue. Face, walls, clothing—if it's a surface, it can and *will* be drawn on."

"The question is will Tom's shepherd's pie win a gold star of its own?" Alex peered at his reflection in the silver fridge door. "And will my hair survive the last year of its first Downing Street term?"

"You're not doing too badly. Not like some former PMs I can think of who start off with a full head of dark hair and end up with hair as white as Father Christmas." Tom peered into the oven. "That smells good, doesn't it? It's bubbling like a lava flow."

"I don't know what we'd do without you," Alex admitted, swirling the wine in his glass. "Honestly, Tom, I really don't."

Tom put on the crocodile oven gloves and brought the shepherd's pie out of the oven. So many confused feelings swirled through him at that moment, clashing with the resolutely homely image of the pie in his hands. Because he wasn't sure what he'd do without them either. Sometimes he had to remind himself that they weren't his children, and when Maddy put him in her family drawings, it made it even harder.

And that was before Tom addressed the fact that Alex was gorgeous. He shouldn't have a crush on his boss, but he did. He hadn't to begin with — Alex was handsome, yes, but he had been Gill's husband. And after Gill's death, Tom had seen him as the twins' father.

But something had changed.

One day, for no reason that Tom could identify, he'd seen Alex in a different light, and he'd realized then that he'd developed a crush on him.

Even though, in more ways than Tom could count, his crush was utterly hopeless.

"I suppose you'd eat more takeaway without me!" Tom laughed.

"That'd be the least of our worries." Alex smiled, raising his glass to his lips. He leaned back against the worktop and closed his eyes, transformed into a picture of relaxation. Switching off was a skill, Tom had to admit, and one that Alex had done well to learn.

'I don't know what we'd do without you.'

As Tom dished up, he tried his best to drive away the demon on his shoulder who wanted to read far more into Alex's words than the man must've meant.

He's straight and he's the prime minister. Dream on, Manny.

Tom passed Alex his neatly laid-out tray and put the remains of the pie in a bowl for himself.

"Dinner is served," Tom announced.

"Come on, soldier, suppertime."

They went through to the lounge, Tom angling his chair so he could still hear the occasional sigh and mutter over the baby monitor. Alex sank onto the sofa and settled the tray on his lap. He inhaled the steam rising from his plate and murmured, "God, I'm lucky to come home to this."

"My nan taught me how to make it. Never fails to hit the spot." Tom spooned some into his mouth and closed his eyes.

"A talented woman with a talented grandson," was Alex's verdict. "So, everything's been okay today? What did I miss?"

You missed watching BBC Parliament.

"Well, we were photographed by tourists, that was fun. Not. Then I collected the twins, we had lunch, and they played with Alastair's fire engine. The firefighters have moved into the dolls' house, by the way. Teatime followed by bath, followed by bedtime, followed by you coming home."

"I think we need to get on top of this *photographing* thing." Because nothing seemed to irritate the usually unflappable Alex more than his children being snapped by opportunistic passersby or tourists. "I don't know what to do. It's a tricky one because it isn't the press, so… I just don't like you and the twins being public property. You're nothing to do with the public — they don't have any right to be taking photos of you."

"As long as there's no harm in it." Tom shrugged. "But yeah, it's not good for the kids. They're not the PM, are they? Besides, imagine growing up thinking it's normal to see a bank of photographers outside your front door, even if they're not taking pics of you?"

"So if you were me," Alex lifted his glass halfway to his lips, "what would you do?"

"Pass a law and chop off their heads!" Tom laughed. "Sorry — that's not very helpful, is it? And I can't grab their cameras or their phones off them because it's not illegal to take photos if we're in a public place."

"Well, they're *my* children, so it's not really legality that's the issue. It's invasive, Tom." He took a sip of wine. "And they don't know the twins, they know you, and that's the press's fault. You should be able to do your job without being photographed by God knows who just because you live here."

"You'd think they'd have more important stories to print than *Who's the PM's Manny?* wouldn't you?" Tom sighed. "Do you remember that really stupid one in the Mail's fashion section, with arrows stuck all over the photo analyzing what I was wearing? All I'd done was go out for a coffee with a friend and someone recognized me and took that stupid photo. And people lined up to complain because my trainers cost £100. Am I supposed to wear plastic bags on my feet?"

Alex put his glass down and admitted, "I remember them all, because they're all bloody annoying. I can't help but think that if you were a woman, they just wouldn't care. You're a novelty — a good-looking man who's also a nanny."

Good-looking?

"It gets a bit embarrassing. Like when I've been out with my mates, and some random comes up and they recognize me but can't remember why. They always think I've been in an advert or on a reality TV show." Tom sipped his wine. "I can't tell them what I do — the security issue bothers me, although it's tempting to say, *you know me! I'm the one who supervised potty training in Downing Street!*"

"You could make something new up every time somebody asks." Alex laughed. "Get more and more outrageous every time until you're telling them you play for Real Madrid or won an Oscar last year?"

"It's tempting! Someone thought I was in a shower gel ad once. They were *convinced,* so in the end I said, *yeah, okay, that was me,* and they took a photo with me and that was it." Tom shook his head. "How bizarre is that? They were a bit drunk, though."

"Shower gel?" The prime minister blinked, then took a rather enthusiastic gulp of wine. "Did they ask you to take your shirt off and prove it?"

"Fortunately not — they'd definitely have realized I wasn't in a shower gel advert then!" Tom laughed, trying to distract himself from the recollection of the sight he sometimes saw first thing in the morning, of Alex, freshly dressed, his hair still damp from the shower.

"I'm trying to imagine a world in which *I* could be mistaken for a shower gel model." Alex sighed, making a pantomime of it. "I don't think that world exists, sadly. Enjoy it while it's yours, Tom!"

"It was dark and they were drunk!" Tom coughed, embarrassed. "I mean, that sounds like the start of a questionable anecdote, doesn't it! But, you know, this was at a nightclub where men in very small trunks dance in cages, so it was only my fashion spreads that made them come and talk to me. And even then they couldn't properly remember who I was."

Alex was peering at him as though he were speaking another language, amusement and bemusement struggling to win control of his expression. After a second he commented, "It was dark, they were drunk, there were half-naked men in cages. I don't remember any of *this* in your job application, Captain Southwell."

"But *I* wasn't drunk *or* half-naked in a cage, although I was wearing my — *Shock! Horror! Call a general election!* — £100 trainers!" Tom laughed. The article had been the reason for a meeting with the press secretary after someone had claimed that Tom had knowingly participated in the 'fashion spread'. He hadn't, of course, and he wouldn't have even if they'd paid him.

"God, I remember those trainers. All that bloody fuss, people telling me to make sure I didn't polish my own shoes too well because it *'doesn't look good after this'*. Shoes! Not a mink bloody coat." Alex was warming to his theme now, as he often did with the benefit of wine and a hearty meal. "When I was growing up, you polished your shoes. Is a hundred quid a lot for trainers? Probably not these days and — I can see from your face that I'm ranting." He laughed. "I'll stop."

"Oh, no, I like it!" Tom gestured to him to carry on. "Reminds me of you doing your thing at the despatch box."

Not that I watch you on BBC Parliament or anything.

"Don't get me ranting again." Alex laughed. "What a bloody shower of lunatics they rolled out today! Did you see any of it?"

"Erm…yeah." Tom nonchalantly flopped his hair into his eyes. "I can't see how *anyone* can attack a bill designed to make kids' lives better."

He shrugged. "Welcome to British politics. I look at them sometimes — my own lot, not just the opposition — and I wonder, *why are you even here*? It's like they exist purely to throw obstacles in the road!"

"*You* don't, though." Tom leaned back in his chair, pillowing his arm behind his head. "You always talk sense."

"That's nice to hear. It makes me angry and a little bit sad that fighting child poverty is enough to get some people riled up." Alex paused, a spoonful of supper halfway to his mouth. "If you can't get behind that, get out. Which apparently I shouldn't have said either."

"You looked like you meant it. I wished you'd grabbed him by the collar and dragged him to the door!" Tom found his gaze drifting to Alex's bare forearms. He had such lovely arms.

He could drag me about any time he likes.

Tom blinked.

I really must stop thinking about him like that.

"The press liked it," he confided. "And so did Twitter, they tell me. Just the honorable member for Richmond who wasn't keen."

"Honorable, my arse," Tom remarked. "Sorry. Just as well the baby monitor isn't two-way!"

"Prime ministers aren't allowed to say arse, Tom, it'd cause a constitutional crisis."

"Mannies shouldn't either—it'd be mayhem at preschool!"

Alex laughed. "And you in your hundred-quid trainers, leading the revolution."

"Oh, I didn't tell you, did I?" Tom started to laugh. "A young Picasso who I won't name has decided to decorate them. My famous trainers have been graffitied!"

The smiled vanished from Alex's face and he said, "I'm so sorry, Tom, when did—" And he swallowed, clearly catching the mirth that was glittering in his blue eyes. "I'll pay to replace them, of course."

"Don't worry, it's a manny battle scar." Tom winked at him.

Winked? What am I doing?

"Best sort of battle scar," Tom added, not winking this time.

And...was the prime minister of the United Kingdom blushing?

"I'd like to make it up to you somehow."

"Honestly, Alex, it doesn't matter." Tom shook his head. "You've got enough on your plate without worrying about my bloody shoes."

"I'll have a word with Al tomorrow," he promised. "I'll do my stern face."

"Threaten him with a cabinet reshuffle? Brrrr! That'll scare him!" Tom said. "He's being creative, bless him. I don't mind. Customized trainers, I'm so street."

"He thinks the world of you, you know," Alex told him. And Tom *did* know, because he adored them too. "We all do. I don't know how you put up with us!"

"Because you're—" *My family.* But Tom wasn't sure he could say so. Wouldn't that overstep the mark? "You're all great."

Alex leaned forward and put his tray on the coffee table, then settled back into the cushions. He extended one arm along the back of the sofa and sighed, "That was perfect, Tom, thank you."

"Don't mention it." Tom got up and collected Alex's tray. "I'm taking requests for dinner tomorrow, by the way—what would you like?"

"You and I could be really lazy and phone out for pizza? It's not quite new trainers, but it's a start." Alex waited for Tom's reply, his head to one side.

"I wouldn't say no to pizza — thanks!" Tom took Alex's tray into the kitchen and returned with the bottle of wine. "In case you wanted a top-up?"

Alex tipped his head back and smiled up at Tom, a look of lazy contentment on his face. "PMQs *always* means a top-up."

Tom poured for him. It reminded him of going to the Officers' Mess when he'd first left Sandhurst. All those confident, assured men, and Tom had to remember to call himself Captain Southwell, not Tom, if anyone asked his name. "You handle them so well. You're such a statesman."

"But I'm arguing with grown men and women about *why* we need to make sure kids have food to eat and a roof over their heads and a chance to go to school or go to the park or whatever they want to do." He drew in an exasperated breath and closed his eyes again. "Why is anyone arguing that that's not a good thing? That we need to be careful or *immigrants* and *layabouts* will exploit it, and people will be popping out children left, right and center as a result. Am I just incredibly naive, Tom?"

"If they were in power and they'd come up with it, they'd think it was the best thing ever. They're doing it down because they know it's popular, so they're pressing people's buttons to turn them against it." Tom had sat back in his chair and hugged the cushion to him. He remembered going to the shop with Gill to buy it. She'd wanted to leave the flat at number 11 cozy for her family before she left them. "Not that you need me to tell you that!"

"You know what they think in the House? They think I'm woolly. Give me my five years, I'll bob along waving the flag against child poverty and then off I'll trot, and they can all get back to the bear-pit politics and mud-slinging." Alex took a long drink of wine. "But this administration is actually achieving things. Without the bear-pit and the cockfights, we're making things better. Only in Westminster could that be thought of as a problem."

Tom watched him from over the cushion. He was so used to Alex as the -man -he -lived -in -a -flat -with, the man whose children he was helping to raise, that it was easy for him to forget the role he played.

The statesman, the man who wanted to make a difference and was frustrated by the compromises and backstabbing that made up his daily work.

"They're callous, really, aren't they?" Tom said. He curled his legs under him and, relaxed. "When you went to visit that school and there were those children who didn't have coats in the middle of winter, and people claimed those shivering kids had been put up to it. Can't they just accept that it's the truth and someone needs to fix it? And obviously that would be you, because if you didn't fix it, what's the point?"

"And of course somebody's going to exploit it, I'm not stupid. But if one person takes advantage and a thousand children get the help they need, I'm willing to write that one bad penny off." He smiled and said, "After all, the odds of people being honest are still a lot better than they are in the Commons."

"You can say that again!" Tom laughed. "D'you know what I'd be good at? The Speaker. If they didn't behave, I'd switch between my best parade ground bark, and my best *no cartoons for you!* finger wag. See, my unique skill set could come in handy."

"I wouldn't wish it on a decent bloke like you." Alex shifted in his seat and kicked his bare feet up to rest on the table. "We won't be here forever, I promise, trapped in Downing Street, herding cats. I hope you know, Tom, that *your* job isn't reliant on *this* job. You're part of this family, wherever it goes."

Part of the family.

Tom hugged the cushion more closely. "Thanks. That means a lot, Alex."

More than you'll ever know.

He glanced at Alex's elegant bare feet. How many people got to see those several times a week?

"You know, you might not always want me lurking about. When — if you found someone else, she might not like a manny around the place."

She might be like Stuart had turned out to be — jealous of two little children who had no mother.

"Then that wouldn't be the person for us." Alex shrugged, as though it made perfect sense. "Maddie and Alastair adore you, and I…you're part of our family. I know you won't want to stay here forever and when you feel like the time's right to move on, we'll miss you terribly, but you've got a place here as long as you want to stay."

"I'd really, really miss you guys." Tom rested his chin on the top of the cushion. "I'm not planning on leaving yet. Haven't a clue what I'd do anyway!"

"Well, we'd like to keep you for as long as we can, which is why I'm glad you didn't hit the roof over those trainers!"

"They're only shoes." Tom shrugged. "I remember sometimes how little he was when he was first born, and Madeleine too, and now he's running about wrecking the joint. And I'm glad he is!"

"Sometimes I look at them and I just… I can't believe they're mine. Because they're such perfect little people." He circled his head and rounded his shoulders for a moment, as though shrugging off the last cares of the day. "And a lot of that is down to all that you've done to keep this household sane."

"Takes a village to raise a child and all that." Yet Tom couldn't help but remember him and Alex, bleary-eyed in the kitchen, trying to warm the twins' milk in the middle of the night as they cried and cried. Caring for the babies had helped Alex deal with Gill's death, Tom was sure, but seeing the prime minister in a dressing gown testing milk on the back of his hand was a unique sight.

And they'd muddled through together, the four of them, and when he saw the prime minister in a dressing gown these days, there were happily no screaming babies to soundtrack the moment.

"You know, you could just accept that you're incredibly good at what you do." He tilted his glass toward Tom. "Say after me, I am very good at what I do."

Tom winced. "Come on, I'm British, you know I can't do that!"

"I am very good at what I do," Alex said again, a mischievous smile lighting up his face. "Say it."

"If you insist." Tom assumed a comedically bored tone. "I'm very good at what I do, which is make shepherd's pie and wipe other people's noses!"

"And keep the prime minister sane and his children safe and happy."

"I reckon I've got the best job in the country," Tom decided.

"You get to listen to a middle-aged man in a management job complain about his day while he eats the supper you cooked." Alex picked up the cushion next to him and threw it toward Tom. "And we're not even married!"

In a theatrically feminine voice, Tom said, "At least you put your socks in the laundry basket without being asked, oh husband of mine!"

Imagine being his husband, though.

No. Don't torture yourself.

"Well, you've got me well trained. I do as I'm told, Captain!"

"Hit the floor and give me twenty, Trooper!" Tom laughed. "Your face! Every time I do that, for a split second, it looks like you really are about to fling yourself off the sofa and do press-ups!"

"I'd never get up again if I did," Alex declared, though they both knew *that* couldn't be true. "The bloody tennis matches at Chequers are bad enough, you run me ragged!"

"Keeping you nice and trim, sir!" Tom saluted him. *Those tennis matches...those forearms...* How Tom ever managed to win he couldn't imagine, because the image of Alex in his tennis whites, panting, his face sheened with sweat, was a very distracting sight.

"What're you trying to say?" He patted his stomach and grinned. "It's all the good food I get at home."

Tom threw the cushion back at him, laughing. *Tum, indeed* – Alex was gorgeous, even though Tom would never say so to his face.

But then Tom heard a sound he recognized all too well.

Scratch, scratch, scratch against the door.

"I know who that is." Tom wandered off to the door, and when he opened it Billy slid inside, rubbing herself against Tom's legs as she passed. "Chief Mouser to the Cabinet Office has arrived for her evening fuss, sir!"

"Too late for supper, Billy," Alex commiserated with the new arrival. "Come and tell me all the gossip you've been overhearing, I know you don't miss anything that goes on around this place."

The calico cat leaped up onto the sofa and wandered round and round in a circle, *miaowing* in her creaky way until she settled against Alex's thigh. She pawed his leg, purring so loudly that she seemed to be passing into happy delirium.

Bloody hell, I'm jealous of a cat.

He wasn't saying he'd want *his* ears scratched, of course, but it would be quite something to curl up next to the Right Honourable Alex Hart MP, Prime Minister and First Lord of the Treasury. And there was a fairly good chance he'd end up purring.

"There's a mouse in your trousers, Alex!" Tom said. Then he hid behind his cushion.

No, I don't mean that!

For a moment Alex just looked at him, as though he wasn't sure what he'd just heard. Then he raised one eyebrow and asked coquettishly, "And how would *you* know?"

"I mean, Billy's found it." Tom spluttered with laughter. "Sorry—it sounds like I'm talking about something else entirely, and I... Sorry."

And Alex laughed too, though Billy barely moved from her comfortable spot. Thank God he hadn't taken it to heart or anything worse, even if Alex's unexpected wine-fueled detour into sheer flirtatious mischief had come as rather a surprise.

Hearing snuffling on the baby monitor, Tom turned, his ears pricked up. He wasn't sure which child it was, but the snuffling soon transformed into a cry, and Tom got up from his seat.

"I'll go, Alex—you stay there and chill."

"It's Mads, isn't it?" Alex listened for a moment, then held out his hand to Tom. "I'm sure she wouldn't mind us both making a fuss of her, if you can drag me off of this sofa."

"Come on, then, Dad."

It didn't matter what sort of a day Alex had, he always managed to wring out energy from somewhere for his children. Tom grabbed his hand and pulled him up from the sofa, and together they made their way through the flat to the bedroom where Madeleine was wailing and soon, both men knew, her brother would join in.

Tom grabbed Madeleine's ragdoll as they came into the room. Her little face was screwed up, but her crying had already seemed to dissipate. It had to be the presence of her father that had calmed her.

It calms all of us.

"What's going on, Trouble?" Alex whispered as he sank down onto Madeleine's bed and gathered her to his chest. "We're all here together. Even Billy's wondering if you're okay."

Madeleine appeared to be doing her best not to cry now. The wailing had stopped and instead she sniffled and hung her arms around Alex's neck. "I dreamed you were gone, Daddy."

"That's never going to happen," he promised, holding her close. "Are you going to go back to sleep if we stay with you?"

Madeleine nodded. Meanwhile, in the nearby boat-shaped bed, Tom heard whimpering followed by crying. Alastair was awake. Tom stroked the little boy's curved cheek, but Alastair rapidly wound himself up to a pitch and Tom lifted him out of the bed, holding him against his shoulder. He jogged him, trying to calm him and get him back to sleep.

It wasn't working.

"You get to bed," Alex instructed. "I'll get them settled."

"I'm the manny, remember, this is what I'm supposed to be good at." Tom winced as Alastair yelled in his ear. "Allegedly."

Madeleine pouted at Alex and told him, "Daddy, I can't sleep now. Al is shouting."

"Really, Tom, you need to get some rest too." But Madeleine's arms were still around her father's neck and the next step was inevitable, because only one thing would settle her now, Tom knew. "Well, Mads, how about you kip in the big bed? And Al too?"

"Yes, please, Daddy." Mads sniffed again.

"Al, how does that sound?"

Mention of *the big bed* seemed to have worked and Alastair was calmer now.

"Good," said Alastair. "I like the big bed best of all."

"Because Tom needs his bed, you too," Alex whispered, cradling Madeleine as he rose to his feet. He looked exhausted, Tom thought, but he knew from experience that there was no point in arguing. Alex's children came ahead of everything, as many a visiting dignitary had discovered and, luckily, found rather endearing. "Tom, would you mind bringing Al through for me? Then I promise that's it, your bed awaits."

"I've got him." Tom hugged the warm, sleepy little boy, and brought his toy duck along too.

He followed Alex into the corridor. The sleepy group made its way along to the room that Alex had shared with Gill for a scant few months, barely even a year. Now he slept here alone, though the press speculation into the prime minister's heartbreak and subsequent lack of companionship was as quietly insistent as it tried to be respectable.

Alastair glanced around the softly lit room, then burrowed his face against Tom's neck and sagged in his arms.

"I think he's nearly asleep again," Tom whispered. Alex smiled softly and drew back the covers, settling Madeleine and her ragdoll before he reached for Alastair.

As he did, his gaze met Tom's and he said, "I mean it, I don't know what we'd do."

At that moment, Tom had to fight the urge to kiss Alex on the cheek. To tell him it was all right and that he wasn't going to abandon them. He passed the sleeping child in his puppy-patterned pajamas to Alex, kissing the top of Alastair's head as he did so. Cuddled in her unicorn-print pajamas, Madeleine was watching from the enormous bed, looking far more settled now. Yet Tom knew her well enough to know that she had something to say. She was simply waiting for her moment.

"Are you going to wish Tom goodnight, Mads?" Alex asked.

"No," she replied, and Tom tried not to laugh at how frank she sounded. She shook her head so vigorously that her curls sprang into her face. "Tom's not going, Daddy."

"But I have to go to my bedroom, don't I? That's where I sleep—in my bed."

"No," Madeleine insisted. "You can sleep in this bed too."

Tom glanced at Alex. "Erm..."

Alex gave a rather embarrassed smile, but there was still a hint of mischief in his eyes when their gazes met. "I think Tom would rather go to his own bed, Mads. Just because you don't want to sleep in your room, it doesn't mean Tom doesn't want to sleep in his."

"But he can't go, Daddy! He can't!" Madeleine started to cry again.

Tom perched on the edge of the bed and brushed Madeleine's hair from her face. He had no idea if Madeleine remembered her mother, but she knew her from photographs and videos, and from the letters she received each birthday. She knew her as an absence.

"I'm not going anywhere. My bedroom's just down the corridor. You'll see me in the morning, won't you?"

Madeleine shook her head. "But what if I don't?"

"Oh, darling, you will," Alex told her, but in his tone Tom heard the helplessness of the father who had been left bewildered just as Madeleine had, cut adrift in a world where once Gill had been an anchor. "Please don't be upset, Mads, Tom won't be far away."

"I want him to stay." Madeleine pouted just as her brother woke up again beside her, his face creased into a frown, his lower lip wobbling into another cry.

"Come on, Mads." Tom pushed himself onto the bed and put his arm around her as he tried to comfort Alastair too by stroking his cheek. "You be a good sister — Alastair keeps waking up. Time to sleep."

Madeleine grabbed his T-shirt as Tom looked up at Alex. He shrugged. And that same helplessness was in Alex's eyes now, faced with his daughter's determination and the distress that was threatening with every wobble of her lip.

"I couldn't ask you to —" he murmured.

"What if…" Tom looked around the room. There was a decorative sofa, but he didn't fancy his chances of sleeping on it, as it wouldn't accommodate a man of his height. Then he glanced at the foot of the bed. "What if I lie across the bottom of the bed? I'll bring my duvet. I used to sleep in tents and ditches with loads of blokes all the time in the army. This'll be surprisingly comfortable compared to that, and there won't be as much snoring!"

"That's way beyond the call of duty," Alex replied, but Madeleine seemed a little less distressed at the merest hint that things might be going her way, and the night was ticking past. "If you don't mind a bit of indoor camping…just for tonight? Are you sure?"

"Yeah, it's fine! Does that sound fine, Mads?"

She nodded and finally relinquished her hold on his T-shirt. Alastair snuffled and was back to sleep.

Tom wasn't sure how much sleep he'd get—not from sleeping across the foot of someone's bed, but being so close to Alex. In his bed. *In Alex's bed.*

"I'm definitely going to make those trainers up to you after this." Alex reached out and patted Tom's shoulder. "Thank you, I think it might've been a challenging night otherwise."

Madeleine's large eyes began to close and she settled against the pillow.

Tom covered Alex's hand with his own. He whispered, "She's convinced that everyone she loves will leave her. I know we should've tried to put her back in her bed, but what does that tell her?"

Alex nodded, studying Tom's face. "We're lucky to have you."

"And I'm lucky to be here. Do you want to hold the fort while I get my duvet? I just sleep in shorts and a T-shirt, so..." *So that won't be awkward at all, will it?* "I'll keep my trousers on tonight, though."

"I sleep in feathers and Chanel Number 5," Alex told him. Then he grinned and admitted, "And sometimes in sensible pajamas, so don't look so worried."

"Sensible PJs are good," Tom replied.

He carefully rose from the bed, watching Madeleine as he did so. She stirred, then dropped off back to sleep again. Tom crept to his room and brushed his teeth, then he bundled his duvet into his arms and headed back to the bedroom.

The door to Alex's bathroom stood ajar and from within he could hear the prime minister cleaning his teeth, preparing to settle for the night. A few seconds later he emerged, clad in nothing but the vintage watch he always wore and a pair of dark blue pajama trousers. He froze in the doorway, apparently rather surprised to find himself face-to-face with his much-swooned over *manny*.

Tom's gaze fell automatically to Alex's bare chest. *Good God.* Living in the same home, it wasn't the first time Tom had seen Alex's chest, but they were now about to share a bed. And there was Alex with that broad, toned chest.

He forced himself to look Alex in the eye instead. "I'll just chuck the duvet here."

Tom fussed about with the duvet. Alex seemed just as unsure as Tom, and picked up a gray T-shirt from his pillow. He pulled it on then said, "They're fast asleep already. I wish it was this easy on Christmas Eve."

Tom heard the mattress shift as Alex climbed into bed and settled. The bed they were, in one way at least, about to share.

Tom went headfirst under his duvet. He had to curl up a bit so that his legs didn't dangle over the end, but it wasn't too uncomfortable.

"We should do this more often!" Tom whispered.

"You need only ask," Alex replied, mischievous again. "Ready for lights out?"

"Yes — lights out!"

Tom closed his eyes and wondered if he was going to get any sleep being so close to Alex. The room slipped into shadow and he listened to the steady breathing of the children, peaceful and content.

Tom hoped that the night would pass without interruption — without any emergency that would summon Alex from his bed. He needed rest — deserved it after the day he'd had in parliament.

As Tom lay there he heard soft paws cross the carpet and Billy jumped onto the bed. She *miaowed* then found an unoccupied patch on the already full bed and proceeded to purr loudly. But it was a soothing sound, and Tom's muscles relaxed one by one as he allowed himself to fall asleep.

Sleeping with the PM. One way or another.

Chapter Two

Tom had woken up with small people in the bed before, but he'd never woken up with toes in his chest. *Adult* toes at that. When he lifted the duvet, he realized that at some point in the night, he'd ended up under the bottom of Alex's duvet, and Alex was resting his bare toes against him as if he were a bolster. Tom peered at the feet, the toenails neatly trimmed, the skin soft.

Perfect for being tickled, Tom decided. He shouldn't, of course, but the urge was irresistible. And they were such nice toes.

From the other sounds in the bed, it was clear that the children were awake. Madeleine was talking to her doll and Alastair was humming merrily, bouncing his toy duck up and down atop the duvet as though it were bobbing on the surface of a lake. Occasionally he added a *quack* for good measure and Madeleine's doll responded with a *quack* of her own. Was Alex still asleep?

So Tom tickled the sole of Alex's foot.

At first the only response was the slightest flex of Alex's toes accompanied by a gentle murmur of protest. Then he heard the prime minister warn in a soft, sleepy voice, "Don't you dare, Captain."

Tom paused. *Did* he dare?

Why, yes, of course he did.

Tom grinned as he tickled across the base of Alex's toes, then round and round in circles on his sole.

"Stop it!" Alex laughed, snatching his foot away beneath the duvet. This got the attention of the children too and he heard laughter, with Madeleine's growing sillier when Alex told them, "Your *manny* is tickling my feet!"

"Give me back your foot!" Tom delved under the duvet and grasped it. Alex propped himself up on one elbow and peered down the length of the bed at Tom, rubbing the heel of his hand against one still-sleepy eye.

"I'm horribly ticklish," he admitted, chuckling. "Would you be so mean?"

"Tickle Daddy!" Madeleine giggled and her brother joined her, the two of them chanting, "Tick-le, tick-le," in unison as Alex implored them to show him some mercy.

Of course they wouldn't.

"Alex, your children have made their decision." Tom raised an eyebrow then pounced, tickling again.

The sight of the British prime minister, hair tousled from sleep, howling with laughter and trying to kick away the man who was tickling him wasn't one that Tom imagined many people would ever see. Alex finally succeeded in scooping Madeleine into his arms and warned, "Any more of that and Mads is getting some tickles of her own!"

Madeleine whooped. "Tickle, tickle, tickle!"

"Tickle Mads!" Alastair instructed, turning on his sister as only a brother could. "Tickle her, Daddy!"

"You asked for this, Madeleine Hart," Alex announced, tickling his daughter's foot. "Blame your nanny and your twin brother!"

Madeleine squealed with laughter and Tom went on tickling Alex's foot, moving up to his ankle.

It's all innocent fun!

Isn't it?

"Stop!" Alex howled, "I'm going to pass a law against tickling, I'm allowed to!"

"Fighting talk from the honourable member!" Tom laughed. Then laughed even harder, silently, at his unfortunate choice of words. *Honourable member? Really?*

"Are you about to mention mice again?" Alex succeeded in pulling his leg free of Tom's grasp and went for an easy win, asking, "Who wants breakfast?"

The twins cheered, the lure of food proving as irresistible as ever.

"Breakfast, then." Tom threw aside the duvet and sat up. He yawned as he ran his hand back through his untidy hair. And there against the pillows, blinking up at him, was the most powerful man in England. And probably the most ticklish. His eyes looked bluer than ever, though Tom reminded himself that he mustn't think it.

Better to think about breakfast instead.

Billy the cat ran ahead of them as they went to the kitchen, and Tom gathered the cereal and toast, leaving the marshalling of the kids to Alex.

"Tea or coffee?" Tom asked.

With a child in either arm and pausing in the middle of a spirited discussion on Alastair's toy duck, Alex decided on tea. He settled Madeleine on the cushion that allowed her to feel as grown up at the table as she believed she should, then placed Alastair carefully on his too. Phase one of breakfast was complete, at least.

Tom timed everything so that the kettle and toaster were on while he poured juice for the twins. He left the milk and cereal on the table with the twins' plastic bowls for Alex, knowing how much joy he took in looking after his children.

"So, mini-Harts, what are you up to today?" Alex asked the children as he poured cereal into the bowls. "Not drawing on Tom's shoes, I hope?"

"We're going to school," Alastair told him with the air of a grown-up. It wasn't the voice of someone who drew on other people's trainers.

"Only until lunchtime," their father pointed out. "Plenty of time for mischief this afternoon."

Alastair grinned at Tom through a mouthful of cereal.

"Although I know you and your sister want me to think that you're never anything but angels" — Alex joined Tom at the worktop — "but I'm not so sure."

"I was an angel in the Christmas play," Madeleine supplied.

"And I was a shepherd," Alastair added. "With a tea towel for a hat."

And they'd looked so cute that Tom had sat there with tears in his eyes.

"Loose leaf or tea bag?" Tom asked as the kettle reached its boil.

"Loose leaf, just don't tell the *Mail*." Alex leaned back against the worktop, watching his children. "When I was at school, I was —"

"The innkeeper," the twins chorused as one, having heard the story before. Alex sighed theatrically and looked at Tom.

"I bet *you* were Joseph?" He narrowed his eyes. "What do you think, kids? Joseph?"

"A sheep," was Alastair's considered opinion.

"Mary," Madeleine replied.

Tom opened a cupboard door and stuck his head inside, trying to hide his laughter.

Once he had composed himself, Tom emerged and said, "I was a king. Then a shepherd. Then — because they got in a young, trendy teacher — I was a devil from Pandora's Box. Because what says Christmas better than a gang of seven-year-olds in red leotards?"

"Blame whoever was prime minister at the time." Alex grinned. "That usually works — because I can be sure that it wasn't me!"

Tom made the tea and brought the toast and butter to the table. "What's lined up for you today, Alex?"

"Well, Tom, you are going to wish you were me, because I have a meeting this morning with Gregory-not-Greg, who feels that my *harebrained happy-clappy save the children scheme*, as he charmingly put it in an email, is deliberately designed to tank his budget." Alex picked up his cup of tea. "How jealous are you of me right now?"

"More jealous than you can know!" Tom laughed. "It really comes to something when your own chancellor isn't behind you. Would he like to reinstate workhouses and oakum picking?"

"It'd be just like his schooldays." Alex laughed. "He'd love it!"

"Gregory doesn't like Billy," Madeleine told them. "He shouted at her."

Billy at that moment was on her hind legs, stretching up to Madeleine for a fuss. Tom swooped in and collected up the cat.

"I bet Billy didn't care," Alex assured them. He reached out and scratched the cat behind her ears. "She told him to catch his own mice from now on!"

"If he opens up his briefcase on Budget Day and finds a mouse staring back at him, it's his own fault!" Tom stuck his front teeth out over his lower lip and squeaked for the benefit of the children and Billy swiped him across the nose.

"Good!" Alastair nodded, satisfied with that possible outcome. "He's a grump."

Alex gave Tom a look that seemed to say, *yes he is*, but he told his son, "Happily, you'll be having a good time at school, so you won't have to see him. And Billy'll be waiting for her treat when you get home."

Madeleine laid down her spoon and asked, "When are we seeing Nana and Grandpa?"

"Tomorrow," Alex told them. "Sleepover weekend for mini-Harts. And Tom will probably go to bed and stay there until Sunday afternoon!"

The thought of staying in bed all weekend was a welcome one, but Tom wished his mind wouldn't show him the image of Alex, with tousled hair and freshly awake, that he'd seen that morning.

You can't have a crush on your straight boss, idiot.

"I'm going to draw lots and lots of pictures for them," Madeleine announced.

"I'll pack your crayons," Tom said as he put Billy down on the floor.

"For trainers?" Alastair asked, as mischievous as his father could be when the mood took him.

"No drawing on anything that isn't your drawing book this weekend," Alex instructed. "And Nana's going to fill you with chocolate, don't think I don't know!"

The twins giggled as if sharing a hilarious personal secret.

"I wish Nana and Grandpa lived here too," Madeleine said.

"It might be a squeeze!" Tom started to round up the twins' school bags.

"They can sleep in your bed," Alastair suggested. "And you can sleep in Daddy's."

"And where would Daddy sleep?" asked Alex.

Madeleine rolled her eyes as if the answer was all too obvious. "In *your* bed, silly — with Tom."

Tom dropped one of the satchels and crouched on the floor, trying to gather its scattered contents. Madeleine was only little, she was thinking of friends having sleepovers, not — not —

Get a grip, Tom. And get a bloody boyfriend.

"Poor old Tom." Alex laughed, a faint flush of embarrassment coloring his cheeks. "Come on, let's get you two dressed and ready for school so *I* can get dressed and off to work."

Tom put the spilled notebooks on the table and sorted them between the two satchels. "Do you want to get off to work, Alex? I'll get the twins sorted if you like."

"It won't kill number 10 to wait," was the answer as Alex shepherded the children from the kitchen, his bare feet padding onto the hallway carpet. Tom wondered if he was right to sense a certain wind prevailing as the last year of Alex's term rolled round, but perhaps it was just what every prime minister went through. There was no way he wouldn't run again, no matter how frustrated he claimed to be with some of the more arcane bits of the job. And if he ran, he'd win, and they'd all be here for five more years, *above the shop*, as his employer termed it.

Next to the shop, really, but that's not as catchy.

Billy was *miaowing* to be let out, so Tom went to the front door and opened it. He could hear movement elsewhere in the building — the staff who came in early were already working. So was Tom.

Billy looked up at him, plainly changing her mind, but just as he began to close the door, she darted out.

Moments later, somewhere in the building, he heard the frustrated tones of Gregory-not-Greg.

"That bloody cat! If I end up with hair on another of my suits, I'll personally turn that fleabag into a hat!"

We live above somebody else's shop.

From the bedroom that the twins shared, Tom could hear the voices of the Hart family, where Alastair had joined his sister's call to arms for a change in the sleeping arrangements. At this point it sounded as though an elaborate system of tents was being brought into play to suit all the grandparents and even Tom's mum and dad, but central to it was the point that 'you and Tom have the big bed'.

If only.

Tom got himself ready, then prepared the twins' snack boxes and water bottles for their morning of school. He still remembered them as babies — still remembered being introduced to them as two blurred shapes on a prenatal scan. And now they were little people, heading off into the world.

"Right, Captain, two mini-Harts all shipshape." Alex herded the children into the kitchen, fussing with

Madeleine's ponytail ribbon even as she tried to do it herself. "Five minutes for me to jump in shower and throw on a suit and I'll come down with you, if that's okay?"

Down the stairs and through the connecting door that the twins were still convinced led to Narnia, even if number 10 was all that lay beyond it. *Narnia's a better choice.*

Chapter Three

Tom was in the middle of the ironing when his phone rang. He guessed who it was before the name on the screen confirmed it.

Stuart.

Who he didn't really want to talk to. But he couldn't ignore an old friend, so he answered the call.

"Erm...Stuart? I'm just doing the ironing." *Scintillating information.*

There was a long silence, then Stuart said, "God, I've missed that voice. You've got no idea how much."

Tom stared down at the half-ironed school gymslip in front of him. He wasn't sure what to say to that, because he couldn't respond in kind.

"My voice?" Tom laughed awkwardly. "So you didn't save that voicemail of me asking if I'd left my spotty socks at yours?"

"I've been thinking about you a lot, Tom. I knew I had to call as soon as I got back to London. So here I am. Calling."

"What were you thinking?" Tom hadn't thought about him for ages. "*Is he still polishing the PM's shoes?*"

Stuart laughed too and admitted, "I saw him on TV yesterday. Still jealous of the old bugger for stealing you!" And his laughter went on, but it sounded like a hell of an effort.

"Steal me?" *I wish.* "Alex Hart is very, very straight. Handsome — but very, very straight. He really gave the opposition what for yesterday, didn't he? He's such an excellent PM."

"So…has he let you have a boyfriend?" Stuart asked, as though he hadn't been the one to dump Tom. By text. From the airport as he waited for a plane to Barcelona. "Still got you chained to the kitchen sink?"

Tom *had* seen someone after Stuart had dumped him, but it had barely lasted a fortnight. There'd been the odd date here and there, the odd kiss and brief liaison, but Stuart was the longest relationship Tom had ever had.

"I'm not a Victorian servant, Stuart. Alex isn't, like, *I simply won't have a maid who has a follower!* I can have boyfriends if I want to, just as anyone else can."

And you dumped me. You dumped me as I was trying to deal with the death of my employer and friend, who had left two infant children and a grieving widower behind.

"When we split up… Look, dude, I'm not proud of how it all went tits, you know, but it wasn't all— I've changed a lot in Barcelona." Stuart chuckled. "And I don't just mean my tan and the amount I'm benching!"

Tom wondered if Stuart could hear him roll his eyes. "Well, it's nice to hear from you. Glad you're okay."

"You don't want to know my gym regime, I get it," Stuart assured him. "I was wondering though… I've done a lot of thinking since I got into yoga. I teach now, you know, got a studio up west, client list from here to

Notting Hill, you should *see* some of the gu— Yoga's given me a center, T-bird. And it's made me realize what's important. And yeah, I can bench three hundred, but does that matter? No. What matters is what my spirit can bench, and my spirit's pulling with some serious Zen shit now. And I want to make us right, you and me."

"Okay..." Tom drummed his fingers on the ironing board as he thought over Stuart's words. Their failed relationship had always felt like unfinished business, and maybe it would be healthy for them to meet. Maybe, if Stuart really *had* changed—maybe they could date. And maybe then Tom could get over his hopeless crush on Alex. "We could meet up. You know where I live. Soho's good, or Southbank."

"Sweet, nice one," Stuart said. There was a moment of silence and an echoing voice as though he had cupped his hand over the microphone, then he spoke again. "I'm just getting settled into my new place and I'll bell you, yeah? Old soldiers gotta stick together. Maybe make it this weekend?"

Something squeezed inside Tom's chest. A warning, was it? A soldier's instinct? Should he just say no? But it was too late now. And he could walk away—after all, hadn't Stuart?

"Yeah, this weekend's good. Give me a ring."

"Got it, throw the PM a how do from me, yeah? Catch you this weekend, Captain!"

"Will do!" Tom wasn't sure Alex would be impressed to know that Stuart had reappeared, bearing in mind the choice words he'd aired after Stuart had left. But what if he'd changed? People could. Tom always hoped that people could. "See you soon. Bye!"

Tom ended the call.

What the hell have I just done?

Chapter Four

Tom had never done yoga, so perhaps it really could work wonders for Stuart, a man who never seemed to take a moment to breathe. He was all about the experience, about being one of the men in shorts dancing in cages, about being pumped and wild and ready for anything. It wasn't his fault, he wasn't wrong—he just lived life in a different lane from Tom. And making room for grieving families and grizzling babies hadn't been something Stuart was ready for, so he'd left.

And now he was back.

And Zen, apparently.

Barcelona must be quite a place.

Stuart was in Tom's thoughts as he was ferried to the twins' school to collect them. He wondered what they'd think of having an Uncle Stuart, if Stuart's newfound Zen would allow him to accept the twins in his life when he hadn't been able to before.

Give the bloke a chance, Tom decided.

After lunch at home, the twins had a nap, then they were up again, re-energized from their exhausting morning with cartoons on the television while they ran between the lounge, the kitchen and the playroom. What a contrast to Alex's turgid meeting with Gregory about the speech that afternoon, which would see Alex visit an East End school to discuss the policies that were so dear to his heart. Meetings with Gregory were always long, Tom knew, and they could suck the enthusiasm out of even the most cheery man, yet Alex was more than a match for his colleague. And tonight there would be no chancellor, just Alex and Tom shutting out the world to share a pizza.

Then his phone buzzed. This time, though, it wasn't Stuart with a bench-press update or a report on his current Zen-like state—it was Alex.

Speech a hit AND have cupcakes for us all. Home by 6.30, told them no exceptions.

Tom smiled as he typed his reply.

Then you truly are the best boss ever!

Two minutes later his phone buzzed again.

I might even let you have two cupcakes for that.

Tom replied, *And can I lick yours?* But he deleted that before he sent it.

How would the world have changed if he had sent that? Well, he'd probably be in for an awkward night and a swift job hunt, for one.

See, Tom typed, *you *are* the best boss ever!*

"Tom." Alastair was at his side. "Can we get the paints out?"

Tom put the phone in the back pocket of his jeans. "Yes, of course! On the table or on the floor?"

"Table or floor?" he bellowed to his sister. "Paints!"

"Paints!" Madeleine came charging in as if she had been fired from a cannon, arms wide, hair wild, one slipper on, the other who knew where. "Floor!" she yelled, holding the word for as long as she could until she ran out of puff.

Then she flung herself down onto the floor, in case anyone had misheard.

"Floor!" her brother announced, dropping down beside her. "A picture for Nana and Grandpa!"

Tom hurried to get the plastic sheeting out and the old rolls of wallpaper that the twins drew and painted on. He managed to get them into their aprons and poured them out a palette of paint each.

"There you go!" Tom sat cross-legged beside them as they set to work. How proud Gill would be to see them, happy and filled with life and joy. And in a way, she was still here, each birthday bringing a new card for the children she had left behind, and teary smiles from the twins in return.

Even though they had different paintbrushes and paints, they were working on the same picture — Billy the cat, standing in vivid green grass. They rolled the paper out farther and added people now. A man with a red face, who Madeleine pointed out was Gregory, glared at the cat, who was three times bigger than him. Alastair dabbed a small mouse that sat on top of the cat's head, holding a splodge of yellow cheese, its whiskers given a flamboyant curl.

Very avant-garde.

Tom topped up the paint and wiped their faces when things got too messy, but there was something very calming about watching them work with so much focus and concentration. And it didn't hurt knowing that Alex would be home soon. Not as early as his boss *liked* to be home, perhaps, but still early. He felt giddy as a man with a date.

And he did have a date — sort of. With Stuart. A vague plan. Even though he was in two minds about it, because what if it got serious and Tom had to decide between living in and moving out with Stuart? No, he was thinking too far ahead. Instead, it was painting with the twins this afternoon, then pizza with their dad later.

And Stuart hasn't even come up with a firm plan, just maybe something for the weekend. It's hardly a date!

"Is the picture for Daddy?" Tom asked. He'd spotted a blob of red paint on the wall and had no idea how it had got there. But Alex wouldn't mind.

"For Nana and Grandpa," Alastair reminded him. Then he whispered to his sister, apparently confiding a great secret. She whispered something in return and he said, "It's for Daddy now."

"We can make lots of paintings. Like a factory," Madeleine assured them. She'd seen plenty of footage of her father visiting factories, a borrowed hard hat and hi-vis vest at odds with his suit.

"You need more green paint there, Als." Tom squeezed it out of the bottle for him. "You're doing well with that grass!"

Alastair smiled up at him then dabbed his brush in the paint and went back to his work. As he did he said idly, "Why didn't you kiss Daddy night night? We all kissed night night, but you and Daddy must've forgot to."

A lump settled in Tom's throat. "Yes, we must've forgotten."

"Never mind." Alastair patted Tom's hand, then held out the paintbrush, signaling that he should take his turn.

Madeleine looked up from the paper.

Tom took the brush. "What would you like me to paint, Als? Mads?"

"Daddy on the telly?" Madeleine suggested. Her brother nodded and rested his chin on his hand with great ceremony and care, waiting for Tom to make his mark.

So Tom set to work, drawing a large rectangle on the paper and filling it with Alex's head and shoulders. He colored in Alex's blue eyes then struggled to capture his dark-blond hair. The smile was easy, though, and for a laugh, he added a furious Gregory over Alex's shoulder.

The twins loved it and clapped their hands with unmistakable glee. Of course, this one might be too big to pin on the fridge.

But he knew that Alex would love it anyway.

Tom took his phone from his pocket and knelt up. "Right, you two—let's take a photo for Daddy!"

Well used to this routine, the twins held up one end of the length of wallpaper each, angling it just as Tom had shown them so the paint wouldn't run but the camera would capture the picture. Then they grinned, their faces filled with pride at their work.

"Say cheese!"

"Cheese!" they replied, and Tom sent the photo to Alex. For ten minutes there was no reply and they began to tidy, ready for dinner. The paints were away and hands were being washed when Tom's phone buzzed into life.

A video call from Alex.

Tom balanced his phone on the table against Alastair's fire engine and gathered the children in front of it.

Madeleine waved. "Daddy!"

"Family!" Alex waved back, an incongruous cheery figure in front of the heavy-paneled walls of his House of Commons office. "That's probably my favorite picture so far out of all of them. A team effort?"

Madeleine nodded enthusiastically. "Tom painted you. We did the cat. Come home, Daddy—you can see the painting here!"

"Darling—" Alex began. He couldn't come home, of course—being prime minister didn't work like that, even if Tom knew that Alex desperately wished it did.

"Come home!" Alastair agreed, chanting this new mantra, "Come home! Come home!"

Tom saw Alex steal a look at the red box on the desk beside him, then glance at the large face of his watch. Six-thirty was a couple of hours away, and from where Alex was sitting, it must've seemed further still. But he had a country to run, so—

"I'll be there in half an hour, how's that?"

"Yay!"

Madeleine leaned toward the phone, pouting to kiss it. Tom rescued it in time. "Are you sure, Alex? It's early, and we've got a *lot* of paint!"

"I missed their dinner and bedtime last night, I don't want to miss it again," Alex admitted. "And I can find an extra hour over the weekend if I need to while you're enjoying your weekend off!"

"Well, if the country can spare you." Tom smiled at him. If only his own parents had been like Alex and Gill. And as for his weekend off... Work didn't feel like work anyway. It was a far cry from his army days.

"I'm sure it can look after itself for the sake of an hour." Alex peered over the top of his computer at the sound of a knock on the door. "Still on for pizza?"

"Oh, yes!"

"Pizza?" Madeleine stared wide-eyed at the phone.

"Pasta for you and Al, I think?" Alex asked as the knock sounded again. "Are you going to help Tom make it?"

"Yes, I like cooking!" Madeleine replied.

"Pasta machine?" Tom suggested to the excited twins. He heard Gregory's muffled voice on the video call and winced on Alex's behalf. A day of being chased by the iron chancellor, the most ill-humored man in Westminster. And he had some serious competition for that title.

"I'd better go," Alex told them, gesturing his unseen visitor to sit down. "I'll be home in half an hour, even if it means Gregory has to come over with me. Family dinner, Gregory, or I'd invite you." Then he waved down the camera lens again. "Bye, family Hart, love you!"

"Love you," Alastair shouted. "Don't forget Tom's kiss tonight!"

What on earth will Gregory think?

Tom didn't have time to be awkward — he rescued the phone from Madeleine, who was trying to kiss the screen again.

"Daddy will be back soon." Tom pointed to the kitchen clock. "When the big hand is on the twelve. See you soon, Alex!"

"Bye!" Alex waved again, looking a little perplexed by talk of Tom's kiss. He'd explain when Alex got home, of course, and they'd have a good laugh about it over a glass of something nice.

Tom set up the pasta machine and it occupied the twins for a while as they gasped at the magic of the tagliatelle dropping out of its silver jaws. Pizza had nothing on this or on the fun to be had from creating floury clouds in each other's faces as though they were casting spells.

Tom cut up the vegetables and let the twins shred basil leaves into the saucepan. Or the caldron, as he called it. The twins peered over his shoulder from the chairs they were standing on, watching him stir the sauce.

"A magical dinner with a special sleeping draught so you'll be bright and breezy for school tomorrow."

Tom heard the front door close in that particular way that suggested the rest of Alex's day had not been quite as successful as his school visit. A morning with Gregory, then an impromptu late meeting with Gregory in the office. No wonder the door shut with just a little bit of a bang. Hopefully Gregory wouldn't be joining them for yet another meeting over supper!

"Half an hour on the dot!" Alex called from the hallway. "I ran in from the car, nearly sent poor old Gregory flying when I bolted for the door. Heaven knows what the press will make of it!"

"I'm sure they'll conjure up a horrible pun or two!" Tom replied. "You're just in time for magic pasta."

Tom's two assistants had already rushed off. Their excited shouts of "Daddy!" coming from the hallway made Tom smile.

Moments later the prime minister appeared, his children carried in his arms. He paused on the threshold to declare, "Not just any old pasta!"

Madeleine took her thumb out of her mouth to say, "It really *is* magic—Tom said so!"

"So Tom must be…" Alex's face took on a surprised expression and he lowered his voice to a whisper, "A wizard?"

Both children nodded earnestly, and Madeleine whispered in a tone that was no quieter than her usual voice, "He says it will make us sleep!"

"It's true!" Tom laughed. He watched as Alex carried the children across the kitchen toward the stove where the pan quietly simmered, then stopped to sniff the sauce, his eyes closed as he savored the aroma.

"It's tasty," Alastair informed his father. "A magic tea."

"And it's nearly ready." Tom tapped the side of the saucepan with a spoon. "Aprons on!"

"Should I be apron monitor?" Alex asked, still juggling his two children. "Would you mind doing the serving honors, Tom?"

"Of course!" Tom was glad Alex was there to keep the children busy while he dished up. There was enough left for two small portions for himself and Alex, and he laid out the table for the four of them.

As he did, Alex got the children into their brightly patterned aprons then threw his jacket and tie over the sofa. Tom was as comforted as ever by the familiar routine as the cufflinks followed, laid safely on the coffee table before Alex rolled his sleeves to the elbow.

"*A People's PM,*" as an approving headline had once noted. Yet Tom knew Alex well enough to know it wasn't a PR maneuver—it was just how the prime minister was when work was done for the day. Once the door to the outside world had closed, he was a friend and father. Business stayed next door.

And Tom really shouldn't look so admiringly at those bare forearms. The man was relaxing at home, and he certainly wouldn't be waiting to be pounced on by his manny.

I really need to find a boyfriend.

"I'll just...grate some parmesan," Tom said, dragging his gaze away.

But Alex got there before him, his fingers nimbly unfastening a couple of his shirt buttons just to complete the picture of the at-home -dad. And, of course, a third followed. A third *always* followed. "I'll do that, you've done everything else. My tiny contribution, some grated cheese."

"And running the country," Tom added, trying not to be too obvious as the triangle of chest visible through the unbuttoned shirt caught his attention. He turned away and marshalled the twins. "Table!"

"And spending not one, not two, but *three* hours trying to convince Gregory-not-Greg that taking action on child poverty isn't simply my way of making his life really difficult." Tom could hear the exasperation in his voice. "He's got this idea about my *legacy*."

Legacy. That was a word that had taken on new meaning since they'd arrived in Downing Street. When a PM started talking legacy, it meant only one thing — that he was readying himself to leave. But Alex had never alluded to it himself, even if Gregory was convinced that was the case. Wishful thinking on Gregory's part, of course, for who was better placed and prepared to step into the top job than the chancellor when the next inevitable landslide came?

"He's sure I'm going at the election next summer, you know. I think he's probably got money on it!" Alex brought the bowl of grated parmesan to the table and put it down in the middle. The twins both reached for it, stealing little pinches of cheese between their fingers and thumbs. "My legacy, according to Gregory, is to leave him with unbalanced books and, worst of all, *my* social conscience floating around making him feel bad."

"I hope he *does* feel bad," Tom remarked. "I hope he's haunted by shivering kids like Scrooge."

Tom wondered if he should've said that, but the twins were too busy making *whooshing* noises at their dinner to have heard.

"Beneath that gentle exterior beats a warrior's heart." Alex laughed, patting Tom's shoulder. "That's why we all love you!"

When Alex took his hand away, Tom could still feel its warmth on his skin. He swallowed a mouthful of pasta, telling himself again that he had to stop feeling like that about Alex. He was like a teenager.

Yet sitting here at the table together, it was hard to remember that Alex was his employer as well as his friend, and certainly no more than that. The closeness they shared was inevitable — it was the camaraderie of two men who had come through the worst of times and survived, thanks to the children they both adored. Any nanny would've been the same, Tom was sure, having cared for two infants as their mother battled the cancer that would eventually claim her life, but plenty of other nannies *wouldn't* have let that camaraderie turn into anything more. It was a hopeless, silly crush, and he had to get it out of his system.

But how could he ever hope to? Alex was perfect —
caring, fun, a man with a conscience who tried so hard
to do the right thing. And he was handsome. And
lonely.

And very straight.

"I thought I might put your latest masterpiece on the
wall of the office," Alex told the children. He smiled
toward Tom and added, "I'd really like to hang it in
number 10 just so Gregory could see it, but I'd better
not!"

"I'm sure the children would paint Gregory's
portrait if he asked nicely." Tom gave Alex a wink.

"Am I sleeping now?" Madeleine asked. She folded
her hands against her cheek and pretended to snore.
"Has the magic pasta worked?"

Alastair knelt up on his chair and put his lips to his
dad's ear. Then he whispered loudly, "Can I have
Mad's pudding?"

"Nooo!" Madeleine pouted. "I'm awake, I *am!*"

"Well, I *am* the prime minister, so maybe I should
get *all* the pudding! And it's cupcakes," Alex
announced imperiously. "What do you think, Tom? All
the pudding for me?"

"Yes, as a reward for having to work with you know
who!"

Madeleine folded her arms. "But I went to school
today and I did counting and wrote M for Mads."

"I wrote A," Alastair pointed out. "And T for Tom!"

"Well, I don't know." Alex made a show of
considering their claims. "Who's earned it the most
today? I think it's probably Tom, and he hasn't asked
for *any* pudding yet!"

"I'm leaving room in my tum for later." Tom patted
his stomach. What he hadn't bargained for was

Madeleine joining in and slapping his stomach through his T-shirt like a drum. Tom grabbed her hands and directed them back to her bowl of pasta. "Erm…thanks, Maddy. Time to stop."

"Sorry," Alex said through his laughter. "I'm not laughing."

"Fibber!" Tom teased. In reply Alex composed a very sensible expression, but his lips still twitched with the same mirth that sparkled in his blue eyes. He shook his head as though innocent, then stuck his tongue out at Tom.

"Daddy!" Alastair exclaimed, shocked.

"Naughty Daddy!" Madeleine stared at him, tight-lipped, her expression identical to one that Gill used to use on her husband. Of course, Madeleine could have had no memory of that—it was so strange what people could inherit from their parents.

"Oh, I'm terrible." Alex pouted. "The worst daddy ever! But I *did* bring you cupcakes."

Not that the children minded—they gurgled with laughter, and Tom joined in. If Alex had a legacy, this was it, Tom knew. He was dedicated to his country, but these children were his whole life.

After pudding—and Maddy didn't share hers with anyone—it was bath time.

Tom had got the routine down to a fine art, whether Alex was on hand to help or not. It was like clockwork these days, from bath to bed and usually sleep before he'd even finished their bedtime story. It was the childhood Tom had never had, and it made him so happy than he could play a part in it now.

Tom perched on the edge of Madeleine's car-shaped bed and tucked her in. The room was nice and cool even though it was a warm spring, but the children would kick their covers off before morning anyway.

"Night night, you two." He kissed Madeleine's forehead then leaned over Alastair's boat-shaped bed to kiss him.

"Night night, Tom!" Alastair smiled, lifting his head to receive his kiss. As he did, Alex was whispering a gentle goodnight to his daughter, who was busy dabbing her ragdoll against his cheek, as though she was giving some kisses of her own.

Tom headed back to the kitchen, leaving Alex uninterrupted with his children. Tonight, for no reason that he could fathom, he felt a lingering melancholy at the thought that it should have been Gill there with Alex, saying goodnight to their children together.

He shook his head. No one could bring her back—as Gill had said, they had to be happy for the time she'd had. And Tom had promised her he'd do his best to look after her children.

'You and Alex need to look after each other,' she'd told him one night toward the end. 'And for God's sake, no tears!'

There had been lots of tears, of course, and he knew that sometimes, for Alex, there still were. He'd never let anyone see the sadness that lingered, but now and then, when one anniversary or another approached, Tom would hear the prime minister stifling a sob on the baby monitor as he sat at the bedside of his sleeping children, or see him dab at his eyes with his pristine handkerchief as they watched an evening film in companionable silence.

But they looked after each other, just as Gill had said they should.

Tom unpinned the pizza menu from the corkboard and wondered what toppings to choose. And cheesy garlic bread sounded pretty good. What about a cheeky bottle of pop as well, just to remind him of weekends at the barracks?

He switched on the baby monitor and the night camera. There was Alex, saying goodnight to the twins. Tom hoped they'd sleep well tonight.

"Are you going back to work?" Alastair asked through a yawn and Alex shook his head, gently smoothing down his son's hair.

"Not a chance," he whispered. "I'll be watching safely here with Tom, listening out for you."

"And you'll come back if we're scared?" Madeleine asked.

"I promise. Quick story then off to sleep?"

"Yes, please, Daddy."

Tom heard the sound of bedclothes rustling as the twins settled. He leaned back against the worktop, ready to enjoy the warmth and playfulness of Alex's storytelling voice. And tonight, at Madeleine's request, was *Rapunzel*, but the version she and her brother had modified to remove any hint of blindness and to replace it with Rapunzel cutting off her own hair because its weight kept her from riding her bike. It was a better version of the story in some respects, and one that Alex always handled with considerable aplomb, lending the characters his own, little-heard natural West Country burr. He always gave them the most flamboyant, hootingly Cornish witch that Tom had ever heard, and the children loved it.

Who can blame them?

Maddy fell asleep before the end of the story — Tom knew the sounds of each sleeping child. He hoped that instead of nightmares, tonight she'd dream about riding her bike like Rapunzel.

Chapter Five

A few more minutes passed before he heard the sound of Alex's bare feet on the hallway carpet, then he appeared in the kitchen doorway and whispered, "Secret pizza?"

"God, yes." Tom patted his stomach and stopped. "Better not, you might drum on me like Mads did!"

"Sorry about that." He laughed. "You know Mads, she doesn't appreciate that not everyone is three-but-four-*nearly*."

"Oh yes, we're just oversized kids to her. And to be honest, she'd be right as far as I'm concerned." Tom passed Alex the pizza menu. "A classic pepperoni for me. And for the guys on duty at the gates."

"Just so you know, apparently *Tom's tummy is harder than yours, daddy*." Alex pouted. "But I'm still having pizza despite her verdict. Dads are allowed softer tums than soldiers."

"Poor old Daddy!" Tom laughed. He was tempted to pat Alex's tum as well, but as Tom wasn't a small child, he wouldn't get away with it. "Shall I open some wine?"

"Wine would be perfect, thank you. And ham and mushroom for me, I'm feeling rustic." Alex put the menu down on the worktop. "And cupcakes for dessert, I hope?"

"My tum won't be hard for long, will it?" Tom grabbed a bottle of wine. As he rummaged for the bottle opener, he said, "I like our evenings together, don't you?"

"More than you know." He took out his phone and began to tap in the order. "I just don't want you to think you're not allowed to go out and have a life. Don't think you have to sit in with me, Tom, I'm sure there are plenty of places a young man would rather be!"

"Nonsense, I've had my fair share of nightclubs and bars. I should take *you* out one night!"

But not like a date. Even if that sounded like me asking you out on a date.

Tom poured the wine, hoping Alex wouldn't notice his faux pas.

"I haven't been on a date in twenty years," Alex replied, his tone mischievous. "My mum and dad would want to be sure you were looking after me!"

"A date? Oh, no, I didn't mean—" Tom nearly spilt the wine as he passed Alex his glass. *My straight boss thinks I've asked him out on a date. And does Stuart think we're going on a date too?* Stuart seemed a million miles from number 11 Downing Street at that moment. "I mean, when was the last time you went out on the razzle? Two blokes, out on the town, and all of London is ours!"

"I'm joking, don't worry! You'd hardly be— Last time I went on the razzle?" Alex frowned, thoughtful. "God, I have no idea. Will *years ago* do?"

"You'd have to be in disguise, of course," Tom said. "The prime minister sitting outside Bar Italia at four in the morning—can you *imagine* the papers?"

"Do you know where I'd love to go, just you and me? Colette's. It'd be perfect, I've always loved it there." Alex took a drink of wine. "I'd say this weekend, but that's not much of a night off for you, is it, going out with your boss?"

It's not a date. It's not a date.

"Sounds fun. Yeah, we should." Tom touched his glass to Alex's and the crystal chimed.

"Tomorrow night? I'll get the office on it so it's all low-key. Nobody's going to be interested in one more middle-aged bloke having a few glasses of something nice!" He held up his phone. "Sides? Anything else for the gate lads?"

"Fries and Coke for the guys on the gate?" Tom grinned. "And cheesy garlic bread for us?"

"Done!" Alex tapped at his phone screen. "I'm ready for this. And a night out too, it must be my birthday."

"You work very hard, Alex. You need to take time out for you, sometimes." Tom drank some of his wine, then asked, "Do you fancy a film with your pizza?"

"Yeah, you choose." He slapped Tom's back lightly. "Something we don't have to think about too much!"

Tom wasn't going to suggest *Darkest Hour* or *The Iron Lady*, and he'd seen enough cartoons. "Erm...*Ghostbusters*?"

"Proper *Ghostbusters*?" Alex asked carefully.

"The first one, although not the TV edit. We're old enough to cope with the swearing, I'm sure."

Alex seemed satisfied with that and nodded. Then he crossed to the window and peered out into the spring evening, stretching his arms over his head. Tom looked up, watching the way the cotton of his shirt stretched across his shoulders.

And those forearms.

Perhaps, when they went out, Tom could play matchmaker for Alex. Find a nice lady who was going out for the first time in ages too, maybe a divorcée with a child. Or even just a woman who liked cats and wouldn't mind Billy coming and going in the flat. He knew that a crush on Alex Hart wasn't unusual — he'd seen the things that were said about him online. Other than the usual opposition-fueled tosh, there were so many men and women who declared that Alex was *dreamy,* or *well fit,* or *drop-dead gorgeous,* and Tom knew that as soon as Alex started to look for a partner, it wouldn't take him long to find one.

And when he did, Tom would be happy for him, of course, but how he'd wish it was him there at Alex's side. There was no point in wishes like that, he should be happy with their friendship. They were close as brothers these days, after all.

The pizza arrived and they settled down to watch the film, Tom in the armchair as ever. There was only the sound of contented sleeping coming through the baby monitor, and Tom stretched his legs out onto the coffee table and relaxed.

It wasn't the first time they'd watched the film together, and somehow Tom knew that it wouldn't be the last. It was one of Alex's go-to choices after a difficult day or a day of Gregory, which usually came under the former heading anyway. That was partially why Tom had chosen it, and he knew that nothing went so well with wine and pizza as the satisfaction that came with seeing Alex relaxed. It relaxed him too, in an odd way.

Tom fidgeted in his seat and ended up sitting sideways, his long legs draped over the arm, a large cushion behind his head. His gaze kept wandering from the screen to Alex, who was smiling and relaxed. And just like that, Tom noticed that the burn in his stomach had nothing to do with the pizza, but everything to do with his desire for Alex.

It's just a crush, a silly, hopeless crush.

Longing for a straight man.

Alex reached out with his wineglass and gently tapped its base against Tom's shin. He was watching him, that irresistible little smile of his lighting his expression, and when he asked, "Okay?", even his voice was relaxed.

"Yeah!" Tom hugged another cushion onto his lap. "Are you?"

"I'm always okay when I'm here." He smiled, rubbing his hand against the back of his neck. "I need to stop letting the misery next door get to me, don't I? He gives me a literal pain in the neck."

"That's not good. Do you want me to find you a physio?" Tom gazed at that large square hand and added, "Don't laugh, but remember I went on that baby massage course? If you like, I could give you a rub — rub your neck?"

For a long moment Alex looked at him, then he asked, "Would you really?"

"Yeah, of course." Tom levered himself up from the chair. He was already questioning whether this was a good idea or not, but it was too late now. And it was platonic, nothing more.

"How do you want me?"

The burn in Tom's stomach ratcheted up a notch.

The words *Hold me down and have me* were on the tip of his tongue, but instead he said, "Can you, sort of…turn to the side a little and I'll sit on the sofa just behind you?"

A safe seat, because then he wouldn't be able to see Alex's large blue eyes.

Just his broad shoulders and the taper of his firm back down to that trim waist in those immaculately tailored trousers.

Oh God.

Alex complied, leaning on the arm of the sofa as he turned away from Tom. "You spoil us, you know."

"I'm just doing my job." Tom placed his hands on Alex's shirt-clad shoulders, either side of his neck, and circled his thumbs.

Platonic! he told himself, but this was Alex—Tom was rubbing knots from his lovely back. He was holding Alex's shoulders.

Tom held his breath. He was sure it had hitched and that would only give him away and make life horribly awkward for both of them.

But—if he was holding his breath, then the other hitch must've belonged to Alex.

Yeah, keep dreaming.

"You've got talented hands, you know," Alex murmured, his voice low and sleepy, like a man halfway between waking and a very nice dream indeed.

Tom stroked down, rubbing his palms around Alex's shoulder blades. "You're very stiff—is this helping?"

The little sigh that Tom heard sent a shiver through him and Alex murmured, "It's definitely helping."

Tom put more effort in as he felt more give in Alex's muscles. His nose nearly brushed the back of Alex's head, and he realized how easy it would be to lean a little closer and let his lips brush Alex's nape.

But Tom wouldn't.

Even though, in his mind, the shirt was off and Alex was face down with a towel around his hips, his muscular back shining with oil. And Tom's lips gently dragging across the vulnerable hairline of Alex's nape.

He's straight.

He was married, for Christ's sake.

He's the father of two adorable children who see you as part of their family, and if you fuck this up with their dad, you'll break their hearts.

Tom found a particularly hard lump of muscle just below Alex's shoulder blade. With his other hand he reached across Alex's firm chest, holding him steady while he kneaded out the muscle with his knuckles.

"Sorry — just getting right in here and — *oof!* — ironing this knot out."

And the answering sigh, almost a moan if he let himself be fanciful, sent a shiver of forbidden excitement through Tom's body, darting heat straight down to his groin. Alex pushed back against Tom's touch just a little, just as Tom told himself not to think about the fact that he had his hand on the prime minister's chest. And as Tom flattened his palm against Alex's body he noticed something under his hand.

Not a button, no.

Alex's nipple was erect. But the flat was still warm from the spring day.

How could — ?

A rush of excitement and fear and surprise washed over Tom, and his knuckles paused on Alex's back.

Was this turning Alex on?

That would certainly explain those intoxicating little sighs and the soft sounds in his throat. It would explain the hitch in his breathing too. It would explain a lot of things.

Tom stroked his hand up Alex's back and rested it on his shoulder, the tip of his nose brushing the back of Alex's head. He waited, because if he was wrong, Alex would ask why he'd stopped, *wouldn't he*?

But he didn't ask. Instead he lifted his hand and put it over Tom's, entwining their fingers.

That strong forearm, with its masculine scattering of hair, and that classic antique watch at the wrist—Tom tightened his fingers around Alex's, his nerves alive to the heat of Alex's body and every breath between them.

It felt like a dream.

Tom lowered his head just enough for his lips to brush Alex's nape, and he gently planted a kiss.

There.

And he waited for the sky to fall.

But instead Alex tilted his head back slightly, letting his hair brush the tip of Tom's nose before lowering his head again. It felt like an invitation, like a tacit agreement, and the feeling only got stronger when he whispered, "Oh, Tom…"

Tom kissed the side of Alex's neck, drawing his lips up to Alex's jaw. "Alex…" he sighed.

From the street outside a car horn sounded, beeping a staccato rhythm, and Tom felt the magic flee the room with the intrusion of the real world, as surely as if someone had hurled a bucket of cold water over the pair of them.

"We—we probably shouldn't," Alex said quietly, carefully extricating their hands. "I'm sorry, I— God, what must you think of me?"

"I shouldn't have—" Tom backed away, but his legs had turned to jelly and he couldn't organize himself to stand. "Christ Almighty, Alex—that was wrong. I'm sorry. I'm going to go and—" *Take a cold shower and find a new job.* "Early night for me, I think."

Alex nodded and shifted a little to look at Tom. He looked mortified, though he did his best to turn the awful, wine-fueled mistake into a joke when he said, "You'd be way out of my league even if... Probably too much wine for both of us?"

Not even one whole glass, but it seems like a good excuse. Alex is offering a get-out-of-jail-free card.

"Yeah, the wine." Tom dragged his hand back through his hair. "Look—that won't happen ever again. I'm not going to make a mistake like that twice. I'm so sorry, I don't jump on people. I don't know what happened. Look—I'll..."

Finally, Tom found the strength in his limbs to stand. He went over to the door and glanced back at Alex. How could he have read the man so wrong?

"I really am sorry," Alex said. "Pretend it never happened?"

"Yeah. Sorry." Tom turned away, his eyes closed. *Idiot.*

"I'm sorry," he heard Alex offer again. "Goodnight."

"Goodnight," Tom mumbled, and he took himself off to his bedroom.

Chapter Six

A cold shower woke Tom up. Not that he'd slept. And he knew that Alex hadn't either. He'd heard him padding about the flat deep into the night. Tom had seen a line of light under his door — from the kitchen, he supposed. He'd heard the flick of the kettle as Alex made a drink, gone midnight. He'd frightened the man from sleeping.

And it's all my bloody fault.

Can't trust a Southwell.

Wasn't that what the old colonel had said in the officers' mess, loud enough for everyone to hear? As soon as he had found out who Tom's father was, that had been the beginning of the end.

'Untrustworthy, impetuous, more than fond of a tipple. That's the Southwells for you.'

Tom was merely carrying on the family tradition. By trying to seduce a straight man. And in the time-honored tradition of his family, he had managed to scupper the very best thing that he'd ever had.

"Shhh, come on." He heard Alex's voice, lowered to a whisper, as he passed Tom's room, the children's footsteps trotting with him. "Don't wake Tom just yet, he must've pressed the snooze button."

It wasn't like Tom not to be the first to the kitchen, but this morning the PM was on breakfast duty, it seemed.

Tom pulled on his clothes and hurried out to the kitchen.

A good soldier never deserts his post.

"Morning!" he said with brightness he didn't feel. Alastair hurtled across the kitchen to embrace his legs as though he'd been gone for days, while Alex, busy filling the kettle with water, glanced over his shoulder with a sheepish smile.

"Morning, Tom," he called. "We thought you might be sneaking an extra five minutes!"

"I was…" *Hoping I hadn't ruined everyone's lives.* "In the shower," he said. But as soon as the words escaped him, there in his mind were he and Alex, kissing, Alex pressing Tom's back against the cold tiles, and so much passion that —

Stop it now.

Tom dug his fingernails into his palms. No one would see — he had his hands in his pockets.

"I had a magic sleep," Madeleine told him.

I'm glad someone did.

"And today is Nana and Grandpa day!" Alastair reminded them, before taking himself off on a dance around the kitchen. "You and Daddy can have fun!"

"Yeah." Tom glanced at Alex. So they were going to pretend nothing had happened. That was fine by Tom. He picked Alastair up, tickling him as he went, and sat him down on his booster seat. "And you two have school this morning. I'll pack your suitcases, and when you get back from school, Nana and Grandpa will be here."

The children gave a cheer, filled with excitement at the promise of the weekend away. What of *their* weekend, though? The night out was off, Tom guessed, and probably the evenings in front of the telly that both men had cherished. They could move past this, though—they would have to.

"Tea?" Alex asked him. "You know my coffee's awful."

"Yeah, tea'd be great, thanks." Tom was about to pat Alex's back in their usual matey fashion but froze. *Give up, Tom.* "Have you put the toast on?"

"What do you think?" Alex smiled. "You know me, I'm basically useless. Toast, right."

"Let me sort the toast out. You're on tea duty." Tom smiled back. They could do this, it'd be fine.

I hope.

"And tonight?" Alex sounded hopeful, he noticed, rather than concerned. "Would you still—Colette's? There's usually something on and— I sound like a salesman!"

It was a cabaret—there'd be a show. At least they wouldn't have to make awkward conversation.

So Tom nodded. "Yeah—still on for that. Haven't made other plans."

"We're going to miss you two little monsters, but I want you both to have the best time with Nan and Gramps." Alex added tea leaves to the pot. "Promise?"

"Yes, Daddy." Madeleine nodded. "I'm going to draw lots and lots of pictures."

"And help Grandpa dig the garden!" Alastair added. "And throw mud around and play with the goats!"

Madeleine clapped. "I like the goats. And the donkey."

"I'll make sure you've got your wellies." Tom took the marmalade out of the cupboard. When he opened it, he saw crumbs from yesterday's breakfast—a whole lifetime ago, it seemed. Before he'd messed everything up.

His mum had been addicted to booze. And was Tom an addict too? To sex? To being wanted? To wrecking everything, that was it.

Alex crossed to the cupboard and took out two mugs. As he did he dropped his voice and asked, "Would you rather not tonight?"

"No, I'd love to go out. It'll be fun."

It'd be less awkward than sitting together in the lounge like they usually did. The sofa would loom large between them, a wagging finger in the corners of their eyes reminding them that Tom had overstepped the mark.

And Alex squeezed Tom's elbow. Just for a moment, no more, but it felt like it mattered. Like it would all be okay.

He just had to not think about the prime minister's sighs or his strong shoulders or that tightening nipple against his palm—

Stop it.

"Come on, mini-Harts," Alex said, carrying the mugs and tea things to the table. "Eat up!"

The children plowed in, just as they did every morning. Their world was just the same as it always was, and Tom clung to that. He was here for the children—he was their nanny. And he adored them.

And he didn't have to leave.

They sat at the table together as they always did, nothing having changed even though everything had. But tonight he and Alex could patch over the cracks and by Monday it would be as if the kiss had never happened.

But I'll never forget it.

Chapter Seven

Hey dude, chewing my quinoa and missing you. Got time to shoot the breeze if I bell ya? Xxx

Tom glanced up at Madeleine and Alastair, who were half-playing with the fire engine and half-watching cartoons. They were too excited about the imminent arrival of their grandparents to concentrate. But they were occupied, at least.

Was Stuart *really* missing him?

Tom replied, *Yeah got a couple of minutes if you ring now. T*

The phone buzzed a few seconds later with Stuart's incoming call.

"Hi, Stuart?" Tom backed into a corner of the kitchen, still with an eye on the children but keeping his voice low so they wouldn't overhear. There was a lot of noise behind Stuart and he recognized the unmistakable sounds of a coffee shop, Stuart's favorite place that wasn't a sunkissed beach or a gym.

"Hey, T-bird, just had a morning in heaven with a couple of brand-new *celeb* yoga bunnies. Got them hitting positions they never dreamed of," Stuart told him. "What's your morning been, fella?"

Tom wondered if this phone call was going to be clean enough for a nanny supervising small children. But clearly Stuart meant downward facing dogs or something.

No, still doesn't sound clean.

"Nanny stuff, really. Took the kids to school, picked them up again. They've had their lunch now and we're waiting for the grandparents to descend." Tom wondered if saying all that was a security risk, but it wasn't as if he'd sent Stuart blueprints of number 11's floor plan and a copied key for the back door. Besides, Stuart might not be the most civic-minded sort of bloke, but Tom couldn't see him running off with the prime minister's children any time soon.

"Sweet, sweet," Stuart murmured. "So, when we split it was pretty dark, right? I didn't do right by you, T. I was chilling on the beach in Ibiza and it punched me right between my baby blues, and I've got to put it right. So, you and me? Grab some sushi tonight? Talk about what went wrong, what's going on for us?"

"Ah, not tonight, sorry, mate! I've got plans. Last minute!" The squeezing in his chest reappeared. Tom felt guilty now. But why should he? Just because Stuart felt delayed guilt for what he'd done all those years before and wanted to *'put it right'*.

Stuart laughed and said, "Friday night plans? I'm not the only one who's changed! What's your Saturday looking like?"

With the twins at the grandparents', Tom didn't need to be at home to look after them while Alex did his constituency business. Tom had no excuse other than his reluctance to see a man who'd treated him as if he didn't matter.

But maybe he's changed?

"How about brunch tomorrow?"

"Let me just have a look." A few moments passed before Stuart said, "Yeah, for sure. Where're you thinking?"

"How about Oscar's on Dean Street? They bake their own sourdough bread—it's delicious." *Sourdough bread*—how they would've laughed at themselves when they were in the army, eating flavorless rehydrated rations out of packets.

"Sounds sweet to me. Eleven?"

"Yeah, eleven. And—" Tom was cut off by the intercom buzzing.

The twins leaped up and ran cheering to the door, knowing instinctively that the grandparents had landed.

"Sorry, mate, got to go," Tom said. "But I'll see you tomorrow then. Eleven o'clock it is!"

"Tom!" Alastair hurtled back into the room and grabbed at the knee of Tom's jeans. "Tom, come on!"

Tom almost dropped the phone before catching it and stowing it in his back pocket.

"Have you got clean hands?"

Too late now, he's grabbed my trousers.

Tom held Alastair's chin and dabbed his nose with a tissue. Then he picked him up and carried him to the door, Madeleine following close behind. He looked through the spyhole and could see Jenny and Malcolm, and behind them a Downing Street aide.

Tom opened the door and Madeleine darted out, grabbing hold of both grandparents at once.

"I love you so much!" Madeleine gasped as melodramatically as if she were in a soap opera. Tom tried not to laugh.

Jenny and Malcolm Hoyle greeted their grandchildren with a loud coo of adoration and Malcolm swept Madeleine up into a hug as Jenny and Alastair reached out for each other with a shared cheer. She peered over her grandson's head and said, "Hello, Tom. Sorry we're a bit late, traffic was a killer today! But we got here in the end, better late than not at all!"

"Is Noddy waiting for us?" Alastair asked, apparently more excited about seeing the donkey that had been his late mother's pride and joy than he was about his grandparents. Tom knew that wasn't the case though—both of the twins adored Gill's mum and dad, just as they did Alex's. "Can we feed him carrots?"

"Noddy can't wait to see you," Jenny assured him. "All of the animals have been asking when you were visiting!"

"I'm going to paint you lots and lots and lots of pictures," Madeleine told them as she rubbed her nose against her grandfather's cheek.

"Better put down the plastic sheeting!" the ever-practical Malcolm laughed.

"Do you want anything to drink first or are you keen to be off?" Tom asked. He gestured toward the animal-shaped backpacks and brightly colored suitcases in the hallway. "They're all packed and ready, by the way."

Jenny glanced back at Malcolm and asked, "Time for a cup of tea?"

"Yes, of course, but we can't stay too long," Malcolm replied. "You know how the traffic gets on a Friday!"

Tom wasn't sure he did, but he nodded anyway. "Madeleine and Alastair, you can show Nana and Grandpa what you've been getting up to at school."

Jenny put Alastair down and he tore away through the flat, followed by the rest of the happy party. Jenny and Malcolm had never been anything but friendly, yet Tom always had the same feeling of trepidation that had come with a barracks inspection back in the old days, as though Jenny was about to find a rogue speck of dust or ask him why he hadn't ironed a crease into his jeans. She had the certain officious yet plucky *something* that seemed to come with having once been a headteacher. A zeal for organization, even when it wasn't her own home.

"Let's get this kettle on," Jenny announced. She sallied forth into the kitchen and took the kettle over to the sink to fill it. "So, Tom, we saw Alex on *Newsnight* on Tuesday. He was looking rather sprightly, reminded me of Malcolm when he was on the run-up to retirement!"

Malcolm ran his hand through his thinning silver hair. "I'm still sprightly now, darling! But, Tom, what do *you* think Alex's plans are?"

Tom, in his hoodie, holding a sippy cup in one hand and a jumbo crayon in the other, would have made an unusual guest for Jeremy Paxman. He was hardly a political pundit.

"He hasn't mentioned anything to me. He's all about the anti-child poverty bill at the moment." But what had Alex said the other day? Tom's job wasn't reliant on them living at number 11. Maybe Alex was planning what he'd do come election time.

"Five years is long enough with a young family, don't you think?" Jenny pressed the kettle's switch and folded her arms over her neat pink blouse. "He and Gill were always very firm on that. Two terms as long as they were both happy with it, but—"

Jenny paused there and tucked a strand of her neat gray bob behind her ear. It felt like forever, as she sought for the right words to continue. Gill and Alex had discussed it. And Gill had died too young, leaving her mother and father to try to pick up the pieces after losing their only child. After a few seconds Jenny smiled and opened the cupboard where the mugs were kept.

"Gill isn't here anymore, that's what I mean. I worry, Tom, that Alex will stand down and be offered a wonderful job overseas or—" She glanced at Malcolm, this conversation clearly one that they had had before. "Or he continues here and misses the children growing up and turns into one of those PMs who everybody wishes had gone earlier. Hasn't he given you any clues?"

"I—" Tom put down the cup and the crayon. "I honestly don't know. I wipe noses and cook the tea— Alex doesn't talk shop when he gets home. Well, he does a bit, but he hasn't talked about the election with me. He does his best to be with the twins as often as he can—he sees his kids more often than some blokes do, because they're too busy down the pub or the golf club."

She nodded and told him, "I worry, you know that. I couldn't bear not seeing the little ones."

"I know." Tom nodded. "They're growing up so fast. Seems like only yesterday they were learning to walk, and now they can't go anywhere unless it's at a run!"

And, as though to prove it, in they ran, their arms full of toys and pictures and their faces filled with joy.

Chapter Eight

When the twins were away, Alex didn't rush home. Tom didn't expect him. And a doubting voice kept telling him that Alex was going to cancel their evening out and spend all night in his office. And Tom would be on his own.

It served him right.

Tom spent the day pottering — there was laundry, and toys to tidy, paint to scrub off the wall. But as he collected Alex's shirts, the scent of his cologne rose up from them, and when he scooped up the very one that Alex had worn the night before, Tom felt as if he'd been lanced in the stomach.

I've got to get over him.

But had Tom interpreted Alex wrongly? He thought again of the hardened nipple under his palm and couldn't understand how that could have happened if Alex hadn't been aroused.

Unless he had been thinking of a woman. That was probably it. No straight man would get turned on by the touch of another man's hand.

God, this is excruciating.

When there had been neither sight nor sound of Alex by six o'clock, Tom was certain that there was to be no night out. He checked his phone for a cancelation, but there was nothing. By ten past he was considering what he could eat that evening, then, five minutes later, the front door closed.

Tom's heart leaped with anticipation at seeing Alex again, even though his overarching feeling at that moment was one of dread.

He'll go back to number 10 and work through the night.

"I've just heard from Malcolm that the twins are safely arrived in Herefordshire," Alex called as he made his way along the hall. *Heading for the study, no doubt.* But he didn't. Instead, he appeared in the kitchen doorway. "We've got a table booked at eight. Is that okay?"

Tom sighed. "I wondered if you were—I thought you might… I'd got it into my head that you were going to cancel. That's great."

"Do we need to talk about last night?"

Tom leaned against the worktop, his hands folded behind him. "I…yeah, I think so. I misread you, and I'm so bloody ashamed."

And off comes the jacket.

"You didn't." Alex hung his jacket over the back of one of the dining chairs and approached Tom. He looked almost shy, certainly not disgusted or like a man about to sack his nanny. "Don't be ashamed, Tom, please. I shouldn't— I don't want this to change anything."

Didn't misread him?

Tom nodded and held his head a little higher. "Did you—Alex, I know you don't want this to change anything, but please, so I don't drive myself mad… You *wanted* me to kiss you?"

Alex closed his eyes for a second, then pinched his fingers to the bridge of his nose. He stood beside Tom, leaning against the same worktop, no doubt so he didn't have to actually look at his children's devoted nanny as he broke his heart.

Then he nodded. "I shouldn't have, I know —"

Tom shrugged. "You're straight, maybe we're both a bit lonely, you were stressed… It's okay to want human contact, you know. Even if it's with a bloke. Just a hug or whatever."

But Tom couldn't get past the words Alex had said. *He'd wanted me to kiss him, but he shouldn't have.*

"It wasn't just human contact." Alex turned his head, settling his gaze on Tom's face. "I — it was you. I wanted you to kiss me. I *want* you to kiss me."

Tom shook his head in disbelief. "Even now? *Right now*, in the kitchen?"

He saw the shine in Alex's eyes falter and he replied, "No — yes, I think so. You look horrified, Tom, I didn't want to make a mess of this and that's just what I'm doing, isn't it?"

"You're not. *I* am. Alex…" Tom wasn't sure what to say. Still, with his hands clasped behind his back, Tom inclined his head, resting his forehead against Alex's. The man he had thought was out of his reach *wanted* him to kiss him. "I really want to kiss you too."

"So maybe we should…" And all it took was the slightest tilt of Alex's head for their lips to meet.

Tom held his lips there, not moving, just enjoying. Tasting Alex, trying to imprint this moment in his mind forever. Because what if it never happened again?

Then Tom parted his lips, hoping Alex would want them to deepen their kiss. As Alex responded, following his lead, Tom realized that perhaps they wanted the same thing after all. Perhaps he had misunderstood his friend all these years. Because this was way beyond platonic.

Tom tentatively slipped one arm around Alex's waist, then a dam seemed to burst, because he was tangling Alex's hair with his other hand, sighing against Alex's mouth, bringing him tight to him as they kissed deeper and deeper still.

The arms that he had adored, fantasized about even, were around him, Alex's fingers tight against Tom's shoulder as though he were clinging on for dear life. He heard Alex gasp his name into the kiss before he renewed it, surrendering to Tom's embrace.

Tom circled his hips against Alex's, feeling Alex's erection hard against his own through layers of fabric. Tom unfastened the top button on his jeans and reached between their bodies to stroke over the hard, tempting curve in Alex's perfectly tailored trousers. He wanted to stroke it, kneel down and worship it.

"Tom," Alex whispered, entwining his fingers with Tom's to close their joined hands over Tom's erection instead. "Last night...how did you know?"

"Your breath hitched." As did Tom's at the sensation of Alex's hand against him. "And your nipple was hard, and the way you sighed."

"When you put your arm around me..." His hand stroked over Tom's clothed erection. "I—I knew you'd be able to tell, I thought you'd laugh at me."

"It's all right, Alex, I'd never laugh at you. Never. I want you, Alex—and I never thought you'd want me in the same way."

He saw Alex's eyes close and heard him breathe a sigh of relief. Then he asked, "Can we take things slowly? It's been a long time since I've been on a date. I'm a bit out of practice."

"Yeah, we can take things as slowly as you like." Tom chuckled. "I thought I had an impossible crush on you—I had no idea you liked guys. So you've dated men before, then?"

"Oh, you know." Alex touched the tip of his nose to Tom's. "I was young and carefree once upon a time. I wasn't always *Right Honourable.*"

Tom stroked the outline of Alex's ear. He was seeing everything anew. "Downright dishonourable Alex Hart? I like the sound of that! But I don't know how I didn't realize—my gaydar must be on the blink!"

"Does it work for men who— Is it a problem, me having been married? I mean, I'm not *gay*, as such, I guess. I don't know what the rules are." He laughed, a little awkwardly. "I'm out of practice in a lot of things, aren't I?"

"Bi men are fine by me." Tom nibbled Alex's earlobe, then stopped. That was hardly *taking it slowly*. "But...*you* are fine by me. If you want me, Alex Hart, then I'm yours."

Tom couldn't quite believe that the words he'd longed to say but never thought he'd be able to were now freely tripping from his tongue. And the man he longed to touch was in his embrace, his eyes closed and his breath quickening with even just that little nibble on his ear.

"First date tonight?" Alex breathed, fluttering his eyelids open. "You and me?"

"Yeah, first date. Holding hands *only*, no kissing in public?" Tom feathered kisses against Alex's neck. He smelled so good. Masculine and inviting.

"There'll be plenty of time to catch up with kissing when we get home, if that's all right?" Alex sighed, a happy sound. "I'd better shower and change. Don't want to let my date down by turning up looking as though I've just rolled out of the office."

Tom was tempted to invite Alex into *his* shower, but decided against it. *Another time, though…*

"I'll go and get changed," Tom said. "Make sure I look lovely for my man."

My man. Alex Hart. He's kissed me.

And Tom would almost have sworn that right then, at that moment, he was floating a foot up in the air.

Alex stroked his fingers over Tom's cheek. "I'll see you back here in a little while."

Tom chanced a peck on Alex's lips. "I'll see you soon, darlin'."

"In my best *not the prime minister, honest guv,* disguise." And with another twinkle of those bright blue eyes, he left the kitchen.

Giddy, Tom went to his own room to get dressed. He opened his wardrobe but didn't see the clothes — his mind was entirely occupied by their kiss, and Alex's arms around him. He wanted, desperately, to ring a friend and tell them, *I've met this amazing guy.* But he couldn't, could he? He couldn't out the prime minister.

How had that only just occurred to him? But it was okay. No one had to know. It was their delicious secret.

And they could still have a wonderful evening together.

He thought of Alex in the shower, rivulets of warm water rolling over his broad shoulders, then realized that he shouldn't have thought of that at all because this was a first date. But the vision was proving impossible to shift.

A date with Alex Hart.

Bloody hell.

Tom rooted through his wardrobe, trying to find the best outfit he could. Not even his smartest jeans would do, so Tom decided on a dark blue linen suit and a lilac floral shirt. He combed his hair, but the spring warmth was determined to scupper his efforts, so he swept it back as best he could, then sprayed on his best cologne. Alex had bought it for him for Christmas.

Then he was ready and wandered out to the lounge. He was nervous — *a man who'd jumped out of a helicopter in a war zone, for heaven's sake* — and paced back and forth.

"You look lovely," he heard Alex say from the doorway. "If I'm too *off-duty dad at school prize day,* I can change — "

Tom turned to see Alex in a royal blue shirt that achieved the seemingly impossible feat of making his eyes look even bluer. And those smart trousers...

"No, you're far more *off-duty dad on hot date.*" Tom crossed the room and took Alex's hand. And the prime minister looked nervous, more nervous than Tom could recall seeing him before, which somehow made him even more appealing.

"I've never done this before," Alex said with a look of apprehensive excitement. "But I'm really looking forward to our first date."

"I am too." Tom gently kissed Alex's lips. Nothing more.

"We have a tucked-away table," Alex told him. "And it's cabaret night."

Tom slid his fingertip along Alex's collar. His top three buttons were unfastened, revealing a tantalizing view of Alex's chest. "So we're on the same page, we're not kissing in public, are we?

"Just for now… Is that all right?"

"It's absolutely fine." Tom smiled.

"It's just — if you and I are going to do this, the press are going to go crazy. It's going to be a circus," Alex told him gently. "And I want all the various grandparents, not to mention the kids, to find out from us, not from the *Mirror*."

"I do too. If they can slather at the bit over my trainers then God knows what they'll be like when — " Tom stopped. If Alex was already nervous, reminding him how judgmental the press could be wouldn't help. He might put the brakes on completely and their kisses would lead to nothing.

Alex stroked the pad of his thumb along Tom's jaw. "Ready?"

Tom smiled. "If you are — *yes*."

So together they left the flat and descended through 11 Downing Street, past the closed doors and offices that, usually so bustling, were silent on this Friday evening in spring, along the labyrinth of corridors and out into the street where the car waited. Alex's familiar CPO greeted them with a smile and opened the door, watchful until his charges were safe in the car's opulent interior.

We're really doing it.

The car took them into Soho. It never ceased to surprise Tom how suddenly London could change from street to street. Up stately Whitehall toward Nelson standing sentry, then off into the busy Friday evening streets of Soho, bright with neon lights and hectic with people. Here Alex would simply blend into the crowds, the prime minister hiding in plain view with those out to celebrate the weekend.

It was like a wonderful secret.

Never had Tom supposed that Alex liked him in the way he clearly did. The thought of their kisses and the promise of going out on dates spread warmth through Tom. He was so lucky, and even though they'd have to keep it between themselves for a while, it was worth it to have a man like Alex as — Tom gulped — *my lover.*

"A cabaret night," Alex mused, watching the world through the car windows. "That'll be a first for me too. I feel like I'm skipping school!"

This was naughty, Tom knew, which made it all the more exciting.

The car pulled up outside what could have been taken for the front of a restaurant, with menus in glass cases on either side of the door. Above the door, in art deco type, it said *Colette's.* The CPO hopped out and opened the door, but somehow he managed to do it in a way that suggested there was nothing to see here, just two more gents out for a business-financed night on the vino. Alex hadn't really perfected the art of blending in, Tom knew, because he already had it. He saw no difference between himself and the rest of the world, had no sense of grandeur or otherness. He just had a job like any other.

They got double takes from some of the people on the street. Tom whispered, "It's that model from the shower gel advert again!"

Unfortunately that put an image in his mind once more of water cascading over Alex's shoulders, and he willed his body to behave.

"Lucky old me," Alex teased as he pushed open the door and, ever the gent, stood back to allow Tom to enter first.

Colette's was everything Tom had hoped for and more. It was like a time machine, transporting them to 1920s Paris. Posters filled the walls for cancan shows and champagne, sporty cars and perfumes. Huge brass palm trees arched overhead and the decor was black with gold highlights.

"You should totally redecorate like this!" Tom laughed.

"Oh, I can see it now!" They were led through the room with its buzz of conversation and gentle *chink* of classes and cutlery toward a secluded semicircular booth that offered a grandstand view of the stage — one of the perks of being on the arm of the PM, no doubt. Left alone with the menus, Alex asked with unmistakable mischief, "Should I go mad and have a cocktail?"

"We both should. I haven't had cocktails in ages." Not since his last boyfriend, but Tom didn't want the unwelcome presence of those memories tonight. "Classic Manhattan?"

"Sounds good to me." Alex opened the menu and peered at the page for a second, then lifted his gaze to Tom's. "I'm having the most wonderful time, you know. Thanks for saying you'd come."

"I wouldn't miss this." Tom was about to slide his hand over the table to touch Alex's, but he paused. "A night on the razzle with my favorite PM."

"And it's on me, so spoil yourself."

"Well, in that case, I'll order all the champagne!" Tom winked. "That's a joke, by the way."

"Am I going to have to keep an eye on you?" Alex smiled. "Carry you out of here at the crack of dawn?"

"You know what soldiers are like." Tom stroked his foot along the side of Alex's shoe, hoping no one would see under the cover of the table. "I'll get wasted, put my pants on my head, and ride a Boris Bike around Trafalgar Square at five in the morning!"

"I think even our guys might have trouble keeping the lid on that," he replied, arching his eyebrow and moving his foot just a little, just enough to signal that Tom's advances were definitely welcome. "Good though they are."

Tom struggled to rein in his gasp as Alex moved his foot in response. "I feel like I'm dreaming, honestly I do. I never imagined — "

A waitress was approaching and Tom lowered his head, engrossed in the menu once more.

"Welcome to Colette's!" The waitress beamed, trying and failing not to look just a little bit amazed that she had been selected to tend the British prime minister for his night on the town. Tom could just imagine what was going on behind the scenes, the scurry to get everything right, when all Alex wanted was a quiet evening out. A date, in fact. "Can I get you some drinks?"

"I'll have a Manhattan," Tom replied. *Please don't mention my £100 trainers.* "Alex?"

"Same for me," Alex told her, but she just nodded, staring at him.

Then she glanced over her shoulder and leaned forward, lowering her voice to a whisper to ask, "Before you go tonight, can I get a selfie?"

"Of course, we'll sort it out before we head off." Alex smiled. "Do me a favour, though, no special treatment? I'm hoping to fly under the radar."

The waitress nodded. "Gotcha, don't you worry." She looked to Tom and grinned. "Oh God, Manny too! I can't believe this. Two Manhattans, on their way!"

Manny.

"Yeah, Manny's night off!" Tom remarked. She grinned and left them to it, alone in the packed room.

"Sorry about the *manny* thing," Alex told him. "Do you cringe every time you hear it?"

"A bit!" Tom laughed. "It's okay, it could be worse. I know people find it weird, especially after I was in the army, but if they all remembered that my name's Tom, *that* would be odd. Borderline stalkery, really — knowing the name of the PM's nanny!"

"Especially when he doubles as a shower gel model?"

"I think I know what advert they meant and he *really* doesn't look like me!" Tom laughed, tugging awkwardly at his collar. There it was again, the vision of himself and Alex in the shower. *Imagine if Alex just turned up while I was in the shower? Just dropped his towel, walked in, and...* Tom shifted in his seat. Great, an erection while sitting next to the prime minister, in public.

Alex looked down at his menu, peering up at Tom from beneath his eyelashes when he admitted, "I'm pretty sure I know the one."

Tom leaned close, hoping people would assume they were talking about something confidential in relation to Alex's job. Not...not...

Tom grinned as he whispered, "Do you enjoy that advert? The way he strokes all those bubbles down his chest? And do you get annoyed when the camera cuts off just as he reaches his stomach?"

With a far too innocent blink, Alex said, "I hadn't noticed. Much."

"We're going to have fun, Alex." Tom sat back properly in his seat again. He'd been seconds from rubbing his nose against Alex's. "Sorry, maybe we shouldn't talk about that sort of thing in public."

He was on a date with the prime minister of the United Kingdom. And it felt so right. Because Tom wasn't going to let himself think about what would happen if it went wrong. He wouldn't let himself be another Southwell with a trail of disaster in their wake, not when Tom and the children meant so much to him already.

This is going to work.

"It won't always be like this," Alex told him in a whisper. "I promise, Tom, I know it's not ideal, but — we're out on a Friday night, that's not supposed to happen for respectable blokes like us!"

"Outside after dark — I'm not used to this!" Tom chuckled. The waitress was smiling too as she returned with their drinks, still no less thrilled than she had been when she left.

"I'm going to take your order in a mo but I wanted to say..." she lowered her voice, "when I was at school, I was one of those little kids you had without a coat every winter and you're right to do something about it. I'm at uni now — no small thanks to you and your grants — so, more power to you. Both of you."

Can she tell? Tom wondered. *She can't tell.*

"It means a lot to hear that." Alex nodded, his voice and smile warm. "I'm really glad it's helped."

"So I stuck an extra shot in to say thank you." She nodded toward the glasses and took out a tablet. "Now, can I take your order, gents?"

Tom glanced at the menu again. "Steak and chips for me."

"I'm just going to copy him, I'm afraid—I'm not used to being allowed out. Medium rare, please," Alex told her with a smile. "And can we get just something to nibble on first? That okay, Tom?"

"A sharing board?" she asked, looking to Tom to make the decision. "Bread, olives, just to get you started?"

"Sounds good!" Tom nodded. It would make a change from grazing from the fridge.

"And how d'you like your steak?" She tapped at the screen of her tablet and fixed Tom with that smiling gaze again. "Medium rare for you too?"

"Yes, medium rare's great—thank you." Tom watched Alex out of the corner of his eye. Had they lived together so long that their palates had aligned? Was that possible?

"Tempt you with sauce?"

She knows.

"Red wine," both men chorused as one. With a tap to the screen the waitress grinned and left them alone.

Laughing, Tom brought his foot back to rest against Alex's. As he did Alex lifted his glass and said, "To our night out?"

Tom raised his and nodded. "To nights out—when we have them occasionally!"

They took a drink, Alex's foot moving gently against Tom's. This would be their place, perhaps. And these memories of their first real date might be the start of something very special indeed.

Tom hadn't been sure what to expect at a cabaret night, although he was glad to see some boylesque, where male dancers in tight pinstriped shorts and bowties twirled their nipples tassels to big band jazz. There was even a magic show, and fantastic singers, as well as a mime act that somehow managed not to overstay its welcome. They both roared with laughter, and gasped in surprise, and Tom couldn't remember the last time he'd seen Alex look so happy and relaxed away from his children. The food was excellent, and the company even more so.

After their pudding had arrived, Tom slipped his hand under the table and tapped Alex's knee with his finger. He glanced at him, an eyebrow raised in a silent question. Alex met his gaze and smiled, then whispered, "I'd like that."

So Tom laid his hand lightly on Alex's knee. He didn't creep it up Alex's thigh, but left it there on his knee, a sign of his affection unknown to everyone but them.

"Are you having a good time?" Alex asked as they tackled their decadent desserts, another round of fresh cocktails on the table before them. "We could do this again, maybe?"

"We have to. Isn't this *brilliant?*" Tom laughed. "Even the mime act!"

"Even the mime act, and that's saying something." Beneath the table, Alex's hand settled on Tom's knee, holding him very gently.

What a first date.

Tom almost didn't want to leave, but the promise of Alex's kiss was an irresistible lure. When the bill arrived Alex paid in cash, handing what he guessed must be a very generous tip for the waitress. And she still had to get her selfie.

Tom faffed with his hair. He couldn't be Manny with rubbish hair. "Are you ready for the selfie?" he asked her.

"Can I squeeze in the middle?" she asked, producing her phone. "Oh God, I cannot believe this!"

"Yeah, come on, squeeze in!" Tom shuffled along the booth. It was only then that he realized how close he was sitting to Alex. He was almost in his lap.

And Alex didn't seem to mind.

The young woman scooted into the booth and settled between them. She held out the phone in front of her and put her other arm around Alex's shoulders.

Tom smiled into the camera. He looked so red in the face, and he tried not to look at Alex, but he could feel his smile radiating.

"Right." Their new companion beamed. "Say cheese, lads!"

"*Fromage!*" Tom and Alex said together. The shutter clicked and she peered at the screen, then glanced over her shoulder, her smile crumpling into the hint of a frown.

"Can we do one more? There was a weird-beard photobombing." With Alex's agreement the routine was repeated and this time their new friend looked delighted with the result. Still perched between them, she swept her finger back to the first photo and laughed. "Look at hair-wax man, trying to get in on our moment!"

Tom laughed, until he recognized the face. And turned cold.

Stuart.

He glanced over the booth, then at Alex. "Yeah, sorry, I know him."

"Well, you two have a lovely weekend." She kissed first Tom's cheek, then Alex's. "You've been a couple of stars."

"We'll be back!" Tom promised.

Bloody Stuart.

"Hey, stranger!" Stuart's head popped around the side of the booth, his hair waxed and his beard manicured. *Manscaped, no doubt.* His skin glowed with three years of suntan, and, when he stood, his body looked as though it had been inflated with a foot pump. The gym bunny had obviously gone all in.

"Didn't know cabaret was your thing, mate!" Tom tried to find something funny in Stuart's surprise appearance, but his ex materializing on his first date — which, to the rest of the world, wasn't a date at all — was hardly the least awkward situation he'd ever found himself in. He attempted a laugh, but it must've sounded to anyone listening like he had indigestion.

"I'm here with the friend of a friend of a — *Fucking hell.*" Stuart's mouth dropped open as he registered exactly who was in the booth beside Tom. "Fuck me. Is the Queen getting a round in next?"

Tom pasted on a smile. "Stuart, you know who this is. And, Alex, you might remember Stuart?"

"Back from…" Alex wagged his finger thoughtfully toward Tom. "Italy? Spain! Was it Spain?"

"*Barcaaaa,*" Stuart sang, nodding. He slapped his hand lightly to Tom's thigh and said, "Don't forget, T-bird, we've got a date tomorrow!"

Tom tried not wince. "It's just brunch, not a date!"

But hadn't he almost hoped it could be? To get Alex out of his system? Why the hell had he even thought that? Seeing Stuart and Alex in the same room made Tom realize just how much more attractive he found Alex than Stuart. Doubtless there'd be people far more excited by the inflatable bulges of Stuart's body, but not Tom.

"Hey, who's gonna blame an old soldier for trying? It's brunch, man, chill." He winked, seemingly oblivious to the CPO who had materialized seemingly out of nowhere. "Don't you keep him out too late, bossman."

"I'll do my best," was Alex's smooth, *professional politician* reply. It was the one he used when he had to speak to the US president. Curt, like a father addressing an errant child.

"Yeah, we're off now," Tom said. "See you tomorrow, Stuart."

The vast, shimmering room was darker and busier than ever as they made their way through the tables toward the door. Seeing Stuart had been an unwelcome surprise, but Tom told himself that there was no need to feel awkward, even though he did. There was no dishonesty. There was certainly no *date.*

Alex's ever-vigilant CPO looked uncharacteristically relieved when his charge was finally safe in the armored car, the doors closed and the engine purring as they pulled away from the curb. Only then did Alex say, "That was bloody good fun, wasn't it?"

Tom leaned against the seat. "It was fantastic! The food and the entertainment—the decor! And..." Tom wondered if the driver and the CPO were listening in. "And it was great seeing you relax for once!"

"I might get a taste for it," he mused, settling into the leather seat. Jenny would certainly be interested to hear that, but Tom wouldn't be the one to tell her. "I think the kids'd love it there too, though maybe for lunch rather than dinner — some of the show wasn't really child friendly!"

"What's not child-friendly about a man twirling his nipple tassels?" Tom laughed.

Alex laughed too, and from the front seat, the CPO stifled a snigger and called back, "You don't get that on trips to the palace!"

"It's a form of dance, that's all!" Tom told him. He really wanted to hold Alex's hand, but that would have to wait until they were behind closed doors.

"Soon to be on *Strictly*, no doubt," Alex told the car at large. The streets were busy despite the lateness of the hour, and from somewhere a police motorcycle glided alongside them. All this fuss for a first date, Tom thought mischievously. "Don't say I didn't warn you!"

"You never know!" Tom smiled at him. "But yeah, we definitely need to take the kids for lunch one day."

"It's a date." Alex smiled, but only Tom knew just how true that was. The gates of Downing Street were free of tourists and photographers alike and the car swept through into the peaceful road, carrying them home. They left the driver and CPO at the door of number 11 and, with a bright greeting for the police officer who stood there, made their way inside.

They headed up to the flat, and once they were inside, the door safely shutting out the world, Tom looped his arms around Alex's neck.

"Thank you for a wonderful date, Alex."

"Does that mean you'd say yes to a second?" Alex slipped his arms around Tom's waist. "I had a fabulous time."

"I did too." Tom brought himself nearer, until his body was against Alex's and their foreheads were touching. Alex's eyes were so intensely blue and Tom couldn't look anywhere else. And as their lips met again, that affectionate little smile Alex wore for him turning so easily into a kiss, Tom found that he didn't want to.

Tom crossed his arms behind Alex's head, holding him close. Their kissed deepened, and Tom sighed against Alex's mouth. He could happily have invited Alex back to his room there and then—he wanted nothing more—but Alex had asked to take things slow and *slow* probably didn't include tumbling into bed after the first date. Yet the kiss was so hungry that it was hard to remember that *taking things slow* had even been discussed.

Tom stroked one hand down Alex's back and cupped his buttock. It was heavenly—firm, but with just enough softness for Tom to squeeze it, and push their bodies closer together still.

He heard Alex's breath catch and he whispered Tom's name before kissing him again. Then Alex's hand shifted just a little from where it rested on Tom's back and he hooked his thumb into the waistband of Tom's trousers, his fingers fluttering at the top of his buttocks.

For some reason that Tom couldn't pin down, Alex's fluttering fingers were sending arrows of desire through him with more intensity that if he'd merely grasped him. But then, Alex was a refined sort of chap—Tom was a former soldier who got straight to the point.

"Tom." Alex gasped, kissing his jaw. "God, you're making this hard."

Tom chuckled. "Hope so, or I'm not doing it right!"

For a moment Alex was silent, no doubt reaching through the fog of Manhattans to realize exactly what he'd said. Then the moment passed and he laughed, dropping his head to rest on Tom's shoulder.

"Well, yes, you're making other things hard as well," he admitted.

It wasn't as if Alex's erection was easy to miss, but Tom kept that quip to himself. He loosened his grip on Alex's buttock. "Am I going too fast?"

"I think I'm probably going too slow, aren't I?" He drummed his fingers lightly where they rested just beneath Tom's belt. "Will you wait for me?"

"Don't you worry about slowing me down, okay?" Tom combed his fingers through Alex's hair. Was he close to wrecking everything, being so impetuous? "I just can't believe my luck, that's all. And I want to enjoy every second…at your speed. I'm greedy—and I'll slow down."

Alex kissed the tip of Tom's nose. "Thank you. And it's not my business but…be careful with Stuart. I remember how upset you were when— You're such a good man, Tom. I don't want him to hurt you again."

"It's just brunch. Don't worry—I'm not going to let hurt me again." Maybe Tom should cancel the brunch. "And there's definitely nothing going on in that department, by the way—I'm a one-man kind of guy."

"Hey, it's fine." Alex brushed Tom's face with the tips of his fingers. "You don't have to explain anything. And you two have history, way before you were a couple."

"Yeah, and don't worry, I won't breathe a word about *us* to him. Strictly off limits." Something tightened in Tom's chest. Alex was so understanding, and Tom wasn't all that sure he deserved him.

"Tomorrow… I'm knocking on constituency doors all day." And Tom knew that Alex wouldn't have it any other way. Being PM was one thing, but being MP to his constituents was as important as it had always been, a duty he never shirked. "But if you're not doing anything in the evening, after I've Skyped the twins…could I cook you supper?"

"I'd really like that. Do you want me to grab anything from the supermarket?" What a conversation to have while he still had his hand on the man's bottom.

"It's your day off. I'll nip to the shops while I'm out, you don't have to do anything at all."

"I get to be your kept man for the day, then?" Tom moved his hand up to rest on the slightly less dangerous territory of Alex's back. "Let me get the wine, though."

Alex nodded. "Deal. Now, much as I don't want to, I ought to get to bed, or I'm going to be no use to anyone tomorrow."

"Okay." Tom patted Alex's shoulder. What he wouldn't have done to invite Alex to his bed — just to sleep beside him, nothing more. But that'd terrify the man. Tom kissed his cheek. "Good night. And if you have nightmares, give me a shout and I'll tickle your feet."

"I'll probably be tramping the streets before you have to get out of bed, you lucky thing." Alex kissed Tom's cheek in return. "If I don't see you in the morning, have a lovely brunch."

"I'll be thinking of you the whole time. Hoping your feet don't get sore." Tom edged away. *Oh, Alex, Alex, Alex…*

Alex's elegant feet, in need of a massage of their own.

"Sleep tight." Alex took a step toward his own bedroom, the door standing ajar. "And thanks again for tonight. It was very special."

"It was, wasn't it?" Tom smiled. "Goodnight."

He wandered to his bedroom. He wasn't sure he'd get much sleep, but he'd have happy thoughts to keep him company until morning.

Chapter Nine

Tom set off for brunch with a note in his jacket pocket. Written in Alex's careful handwriting, and left on the worktop by the kettle, it read, *Have a lovely brunch – leave some room for supper!*

Oscar's was bustling and Tom grabbed a table and ordered his food before looking for Stuart. Based on yesterday's performance, Stuart would no doubt bounce up like the world's worst jack-in-a-box as soon as he saw him.

Tom could already taste the thick slices of sourdough bread, and he checked his phone as he waited for his order.

He scrolled idly through a few sites to pass the time, almost on autopilot as pictures and headlines whizzed past beneath the pad of his thumb. It seemed like a slow weekend for anything worth reading, but at least a slow weekend meant that Alex wouldn't be called away to sort out some outrageous political drama or other.

Then he saw a photo of a street he recognized, and two men he knew very well indeed.

Great.

The *Mail* had a photo of Tom and Alex getting into the car. The headline didn't seem too bad — *Night out for PM and Manny.* But Tom's stomach started to churn at the thought of what they were going to say about his outfit. The linen suit was creased, but linen was supposed to be. Would they question his housekeeping skills and speculate whether he adequately ironed the twins' school uniforms?

He should know better, he told himself, but still he scrolled down to the user comments, looking for the supportive flurry of green arrows and the accusing volley of red. With a deep breath he clicked on the top rated, and waiting for the moment of truth.

Alex has earned it — those blue eyes get my vote & OMG Manny you're a heartbreaker — I'd go out with him ANY night.

Did he want to know what the trolls were saying? No, but he clicked on the worst rated anyway, because he never could resist a challenge.

Tax money spare to be spent on a night out but not on an iron, I'd hate to see the top of their kitchen cupboards.

Tom blew a raspberry at his phone. "It's called linen, you moron."

"Hey, T-bird!" A heavy hand slapped against his shoulder. "What's cooking?"

"Morning, Stuart!" Tom looked up at him. He looked even more pumped this morning, unless he was wearing a tighter shirt than he had been last night. "Here's the menu — no *churros con chocolate*, I'm afraid!"

Stuart lifted his T-shirt for a moment to give Tom a flash of his tan stomach, every muscle defined beneath hairless, taut skin. It looked like he'd molded it from plastic.

"Does that look like it ever gets chocolate?"

Tom wrinkled his nose. "Nope."

"Don't I get a hug after three years?"

Tom stood reluctantly. It was a hug, he'd get it out of the way, and that'd be it.

"All right, mate?" Tom opened his arms to Stuart. The hug felt awkward, hardly surprising given the fact that they were former lovers with virtually nothing in common beyond that and their years in the military together. But now? Now they could've been from different planets.

When they parted Stuart stepped back and dropped into a seat, exclaiming, "So, look at you now!"

"Yeah, still the Manny." Tom slid the menu to him across the scrubbed wooden table. "So Barcelona didn't work out then?"

"Barcelona was…" He sighed, as though searching for the words. "A wild ride. Good times, bad times… But it was time to come home."

"Sounds like you're doing okay, though, with the yoga business," Tom said. "Stuart the Zen master — never thought *that'd* happen!"

Stuart nodded, looking at the menu as he said, "Aaaand you're out with your boss on Friday night? Jesus, man, get that guy a woman! I hope he paid you overtime!"

"He's a busy man!" Tom moved his phone off the table as the waiter arrived with his food. "And we had such a good time. What were you up to there? Is cabaret particularly Zen?"

"You ordered without me?" Stuart's scowl was as dark now as it had been when they were together. "That's a bit out there after three years, mate. You couldn't wait?"

"I'm hungry." Tom grinned as he unwrapped his cutlery from the napkin.

And you don't own me.

"So you got here early and ordered food? What's up, boss got the meter running?" He threw the menu down and told the waiter, "I'll get a superfood smoothie."

"It's always busy in here, so I grabbed a table as soon as I found one free. I couldn't just sit here farting about on my phone, could I?"

Although if anyone's going to be farting, it'll be Stuart after that smoothie.

Stuart scowled, letting his disapproval fester. "When I saw you last night, I thought you had some hot hunky sugar daddy hidden away in your secluded little booth." He grinned, showing a row of perfect white veneers. "I was all ready to meet the hubby!"

Tom shrugged as he poured his tea. "He is pretty hunky, but sadly unavailable..."

"Dude," Stuart laughed, "Believe me, I came through hunky to end up at ripped. He's not hunky. Cute ten years ago, maybe, but...nah."

You wouldn't say that if you'd had the pleasure of gripping his arse.

A very pleasant flush ran through Tom at the memory and he fanned himself with his napkin. "Stop it, Stuart, I'm coming over all unnecessary. *Hunky* this and *ripped* that...blimey!"

"I'm jealous, mate," he admitted with a good-natured shrug. "Because I binned off the best thing I ever had and I'm going to make it right."

He was hardly going about it the right way with that scowl within seconds of arriving. Tom slurped his tea.

"And how are you going to make it right?" Tom asked.

"I'd say by winning you back, but I've a feeling you might not be into that." Stuart glanced up as his smoothie arrived, green and glutinous in a tall glass. "So by making a go of the studio, being the best Stu Donnelly I can be, and proving to you that this old soldier has got what it takes to be worthy of the *manny*."

"Look, I think maybe I should be clear about this, Stu. I don't want to hurt you, but I think we're at cross purposes." Tom's brunch was suddenly unappealing, the egg yolk hardening where it spilled onto his plate, the smoked salmon an unpleasant shade of pink. "I'm not here on a date. I don't see any romantic future for us. I'm sorry if you do, but I can't give you what you want."

But Stuart held up his hand, instantly placating. "All I want is your friendship again, mate. Remember back in the day? Soldiers stick together. All I want is the laughs we used to have. Romance is something else, that's cool."

"That's great! You can never have too many friends, right?" Tom sawed into his food, his appetite returning. "We did have a laugh, and…yeah, let's do friends."

Tom relinquished his cutlery to offer Stuart his hand. Stuart took it and they shook, a friendship renewed.

Hopefully.

But he knew Stuart well enough to know that with him, things were rarely this easy.

Chapter Ten

Tom hadn't expected to be the first one home — the flat was empty when he arrived. He laid the table with a fresh sourdough loaf from Oscar's on the breadboard and flowers in a vase. Big, bright gerbera daisies.

Then he felt a bit lost, and changed his shirt three times in anticipation of Alex coming home.

The Skype with Alastair and Madeleine was booked for five o'clock, as was the routine when the twins visited either set of grandparents, so whatever Alex was up to on his crusading afternoon of campaigning, he would be back in Downing Street by then. Tom couldn't help the thrill of anticipation at the thought of his return, nor the night to come. The memory of their kisses and Alex's fluttering, uncertain fingers just below his belt were as fresh as ever today, and tonight they had the whole evening to themselves. In private.

"Tom!" Alex called as the flat door opened. "Are you home?"

"I am! Waiting for my—" Tom stopped. What if someone was lurking by the door with him? "Waiting for a hungry MP!"

"Excellent, because dinner won't be long!" Alex closed the front door and Tom paused for a second, assured now that they were alone. "It's been a busy afternoon for my shoe leather. How was brunch?"

"Not too bad. Stuart wants to be friends, so I'm happy with that. I'm just relieved he's all in one piece, really." Tom went to the hallway and smiled as soon as he saw Alex in his sensible jacket and jumper, his shirt unbuttoned at the neck. He was just the right side of windswept too. "And you're looking particularly handsome."

God bless the changeable weather.

"In my layers?" Alex asked with a smile. In one hand he carried a shopping bag that was filled to the limit of every seam while the other, mysteriously, was held behind his back. "You look lovely, the nicest sight I've seen all day. I left you a note, because I had to work while some people got to sleep!"

Tom stroked his cheek. "I got it! I walked there and back so I've got plenty of room for supper. But I doubt I've walked as far as *you* have today."

Alex put the shopping bag down on the carpet and, with all the extravagance of a magician producing a rabbit from a top hat, held out a bright bunch of flowers that had been concealed behind his back. Then, as if there could be any doubt, he said, "For you."

"Flowers? No one's ever bought me flowers!" Tom took them and was about to sniff them when he was overcome with affection for Alex. He flung his arms around him, kissing Alex's neck. "They're so lovely! *You're* lovely! Oh, Alex…"

And Alex enfolded him in those gorgeous arms of his and kissed Tom's hair. "They're so bright and colorful that they just jumped out at me. I always think of you as someone very cheery. So I thought...*these*."

"I try to be cheery! They're gorgeous. Thanks so much for thinking of me." Tom hugged him. He didn't want to let him go. "I missed you today."

"I've been distracted as a schoolboy with a crush! I'm going to win your affections with a boozy spag bol of my own making and a vast and decadent trifle of somebody else's making." He kissed Tom's cheek. "How does that sound?"

"Amazing. Almost as amazing as being with you." Tom rested his head on Alex's shoulder. "I got us a loaf of Oscar's amazing bread. You'll love it. I should take you there sometime! I'm sure no one'll mind if the PM keeps being seen hanging out in Soho."

"Ohh, bread!" Alex stroked his fingertips down Tom's back. "I forgot bread. Which is lucky because now I get special bread instead. Can we have a kiss?"

"Yes we bloody can!" Tom brought his lips to Alex's in a rush, hungry for his kiss. First flowers, now the sort of kiss guaranteed to knock a chap off his feet, if that chap wasn't being held in the very masculine arms of the most powerful man in the country. Yet it wasn't power that had quite unwittingly seduced Tom, it was the person behind the public face—gentle and silly and...well, yes, gorgeous too.

Tom had missed him today—had felt lost without Alex around. Here they were on the cusp of something that in some respects would change their lives forever, but in other ways only shored up what they already had. Closeness and friendship, and now that went deeper.

"You have no idea how much I needed this," Alex murmured, resting his cheek against Tom's. "I need to shed some of these layers and get the kettle on. After a bit more hugging."

"I've always been here for you," Tom replied, loosening his embrace. "But now…you get kisses, too."

"And at the end of a six-day week, I need all the kisses I can get." He smiled. "I was starting to get worried I'd miss the kids when they called."

Tom dropped his arms from Alex. "Then you'd better get on. Can't delay you with kisses!"

"Well, we've got twenty minutes to fill," Alex teased as he took off his jacket. Next came that very sensible jumper, and he dashed his hand through his hair. "Let's get unpacked. Forget tea, I *think* you mentioned wine yesterday?"

"I did indeed." Tom walked backward, beckoning with his finger. "I have a very nice red waiting for us in the kitchen."

With the stuffed shopping bag safely in his hand again, Alex followed Tom. At the sight of the table, laid and ready and bright with flowers, he laughed. "Snap."

"Couldn't resist!" Tom settled the flowers Alex had bought for him in the kitchen sink, then took wineglasses from the cupboard. "I'll find a vase for those in a minute."

"And Stuart behaved?" Alex began to unpack the shopping. "I'm not going to interfere, I just— I remember how badly he treated you, I'm bound to fuss."

"Yeah…yeah, he behaved. Well, he didn't seem too pleased that I'd ordered before he arrived, but you know what those places are like—or maybe not. But they're so busy, you can't just sit there and not order anything." Tom bit his lip. "Sorry — I sound a bit ranty, don't I? We're going to be friends, though. I'm glad he wanted to make his peace with me — he's changed. I think."

Alex nodded. "Old army pals too. I'm not surprised you look out for each other."

"He seems to be doing okay for himself. Yoga instructor, celebrity clients." Tom nudged him playfully. "You could sign up if you're in the mood for getting bendy!"

"Hmm." Alex put his arm around Tom's shoulders. "I think I'll stick to wine and pasta — *bendy* isn't an ambition of mine."

"Good. I like solid." Tom patted Alex's stomach. "Firm. Manly."

"Forty-five," Alex teased. "I'm in my prime!"

Tom kissed his neck. "You are — you're a very attractive man, Alex. But I'm sure you know that!"

"You're going to spoil me, you know." Alex tipped his head back with a sigh. "I'll have to get used to it!"

"Yes, you will! I like looking after you." Tom occupied himself opening the wine, then he filled two generous glasses. He passed one to Alex.

"To a peaceful Saturday night?" Alex raised his glass.

Tom raised his in answer. "Yes, to a peaceful Saturday night."

Five minutes and plenty of kisses later they were sitting on the sofa, Alex's tablet propped up on the coffee table ready for their video chat with the twins. It all felt wonderfully domestic, curled up here with a glass of wine as Saturday afternoon deepened into the evening.

Tom removed his hand from Alex's knee. "I'm sure they wouldn't understand, but..."

Alex pecked a kiss to Tom's cheek as the incoming call blared from the speakers. He leaned forward to touch the screen and a moment later there were Madeleine and Alastair, sitting at the scrubbed pine table in their grandparents' homely kitchen.

"Hello!" Alex called, his happiness at seeing them sending a dart of affection straight to Tom's heart. "You look like a happy pair of mini-Harts!"

"Daddy!" Madeleine waved. "We're having fun!"

"We've been feeding the animals." Alastair grinned. "And riding on donkeys and eating a little bit of chocolate."

Alex sat forward and asked, "A little bit?"

Madeleine giggled behind her small hand. "Maybe lots, Daddy!"

"That's grandparents for you!" Tom laughed. He could hear Jenny and Malcolm in the background somewhere, the clatter of pots and pans and occasional cheery asides as they prepared supper lending to a picture of perfect domesticity. There was no wonder that Alex and Gill had grown up so confident and assured, with families like this. Alex's mum and dad were just the same. Accomplished, loving, solid. *A family*. Everything that Tom's upbringing had never been, everything that Madeleine and Alastair were now wonderfully able to just take for granted.

Everything that he and Alex could be.

"I did drawings, Daddy!" Madeleine clapped her hands. "Look!"

She held something up to the screen, so close that it blurred.

"Excellent!" Tom said. A moment later her drawing was unceremoniously shoved aside and replaced by another, this one held by her brother. Alex gave Tom a little nudge and grinned, pointing wordlessly to a blurred figure with blue hair.

It's becoming a trend.

"So when I ask Nan and Gramps, they're going to tell me you've both been behaving?" Alex asked.

Madeleine nodded, her lips pressed together. It was her *Honest, I am behaving* look. Alastair looked at his sister, then said, "We *always* behave, Daddy."

"They do!" Jenny appeared in the shot behind them, wearing a no-nonsense pinstripe apron and wielding a ladle. "Tickled toes if they don't!"

"Tom tickled Daddy's toes!" Madeleine giggled. "Tom tickled Daddy in bed!"

Tom stared at the screen, his grin fixed. *Oh my shitting bloody God!*

"Tom tick—" He saw Jenny glance away from the camera toward where he assumed Malcolm stood. Her brow furrowed, then she said, "I'm sure he didn't."

"He *did*!" Alastair exclaimed. "They were in bed and Tom was tickling Daddy."

Malcolm's voice, quiet and strained, sounded off-screen somewhere. "Time to wash hands in a minute…"

Alex, of course, was used to such matters of diplomacy. He held up his hand toward the screen and said, "Believe me, Jenny, it's not half as shocking as you think it is. I'll explain tomorrow, but you don't need to look so worried, okay?"

She tossed her bob and assured him, "Oh, I'm very open-minded. But yes, a quick chat tomorrow perhaps!"

"Red or white, Jenny?" Malcolm asked, still off-screen. Then he wandered into view, clearing his throat, his face red.

Tom gripped the edge of the sofa. This did not bode well.

And Alex was still doing his best to pretend that this was nothing worth a moment of concern, because now was clearly *not* the time to tell them. He waved toward Malcolm.

"Look, the kids had a nightmare and wanted to come into my bed and wouldn't settle unless Tom was there too," Alex explained, perfectly reasonable. *But Malcolm and Jenny don't look convinced.* "Poor bloke had to sleep at the bottom of the bed like a bolster!"

"And when I woke up..." Tom wafted his hands, but he realized too late how camp it must look. "Alex's feet were just *there,* so I tickled them." Tom placed emphasis on his last words which he hoped would make sense to the grown-ups and fly far over the children's heads. "His feet—I *only* tickled his feet."

Jenny's ladle landed in her palm with an audible *slap.* She smiled, though, *thank God.* "Well, that all sounds very *Boy's Own.* It's a different world, Malcolm, I suddenly feel terribly old."

"You and me both," Malcolm replied, and cleared his throat again.

"Tickle, tickle, tickle!" Madeleine giggled, waggling her fingers at the camera. "Tickle Daddy! Ha ha ha!"

"Billy sends a big kiss," Alex told the children, deftly changing the subject. "She's chasing mice at the moment, but she can't wait to see you tomorrow."

Tom nodded. *Safer territory by far.* "She said she hopes you're having a great time, and she wants to hear all about the donkey when you get back."

"Come on now," Jenny told the children. "Time to wash hands for supper. Say night night to Daddy and Tom."

Alastair waved. "Night night, Daddy and Tom! Don't forget your night night kiss!"

Madeleine pressed her ragdoll's face to the screen. "Kissy, kissy, kissy!"

Tom nudged Alex's toe. He would rather have held his hand or outright said, *It's all right, honest, don't worry.* But he didn't want to give anything away.

"Night, night, kids!" Tom waved.

"Night, love you." Alex pressed his fingers to his lips and blew a kiss toward the screen. The children returned the gesture and, a moment later, the call was ended. As the screen went dark he looked at Tom. "I'm going to tell them, but the time has to be right. Mum and Dad are off on their latest trek around Nepal or wherever... I want everyone to know at roughly the same time. I don't want Gill's folks to know tonight and my Mum and Dad to read it when they get off the plane. Is that all right?"

"Of course. *More* than all right." Tom rested his head on Alex's shoulder, his arm around Alex's waist. "Coming out isn't easy, and I didn't even have to do it in public."

Alex kissed Tom's hair, then put his fingers to Tom's chin, easing his head higher. He placed a soft kiss on his lips and whispered, "I don't deserve you."

"I don't deserve *you*." Tom kissed him in return. "Darling, if you'd rather this was kept quiet, I don't demand everyone know. I'm not like that. I'm so lucky—this is more than I ever hoped for. If a secret's easier for you, then...then that's fine."

"Only for now, not forever." He touched his nose to Tom's. "Do you want to choose some music? Keep me company while I make supper?"

"If you like. How are you feeling? Classical or poppy? Or big, loud guitars?"

"Oh, big, loud guitars, I think?"

"Good choice!" Tom took out his phone and scrolled through to the albums. "Here we have my big, loud guitars playlist!"

"Right!" With another kiss, Alex rose to his feet. "Let's attack supper!"

Chapter Eleven

Tom did his best not to interfere as Alex cooked, there being nothing more annoying than a back-seat driver in the kitchen. But he did occasionally have to intervene when Alex couldn't find the colander or the cheese grater.

Alex didn't do too bad a job of the bolognese, but to Tom it was the best pasta he'd ever tasted. Cooked by his boyfriend, and eaten at a table that had not one but two vases of flowers. And this time, they didn't have to worry about anyone spotting a stolen touch or an affectionate smile, because there was nobody here *to* see. It was perfect.

After dinner, Tom abandoned his usual spot on the armchair and sat beside Alex on the sofa.

"A kiss for the chef?" Tom asked. Alex cocked his head to one side and put his wineglass down on the table, as though considering the question.

"At least one."

Tom ran his fingertip up and down Alex's bare forearm. "Two?"

"Let's start at two," Alex decided. He reached up and skimmed his fingertips down Tom's cheek. "And see where we end up?"

"Let's see." Tom wrapped his arms around Alex and brought their lips together. It felt great to be so close to him. It felt great to feel Alex's answering embrace too, and to feel the way his hands slid over Tom's shirt, trailing tingling heat through the fabric. There was a hint of a groan in Alex's throat as his tongue explored the kiss, more confident now than he had been before.

As their kiss went on, Tom covered one of Alex's hands with his own and guided it to a button on his shirt. He did nothing more, leaving it to Alex to decide if he wanted to take it further. Tom hoped Alex wouldn't find it too much—it was up to him if he wanted to unfasten the button or not.

Alex's hand slid down Tom's back to rest on his hip. For a few seconds his fingers lingered unmoving on the shirt button, then, without breaking their kiss, he popped it from the buttonhole.

Tom gasped. He kissed Alex with more heat now, a groan in his throat as he hoped Alex would touch him. Another button followed, and another, then Alex's hand slipped beneath Tom's shirt, caressing his chest. Tom could hear the change in Alex's breathing, the hoarse tremble of excitement as he explored his body.

Tom thought he was about to float up off the sofa and moaned in pleasure. "Alex... Alex..." He brushed his hand over Alex's chest, his nipple hard under Tom's palm. Would he mind if Tom unfastened one of his buttons?

"God, Tom," Alex gasped, nuzzling kisses to his throat. He stroked his fingertips over Tom's nipple, as though daring himself to go further. "Is it all right if—"

Tom arched his back into Alex's touch. "Yes... Alex, please..."

The kisses were fiercer now, filled with heat and hunger, and Alex tweaked Tom's nipple between his finger and thumb, teasing him.

Tom moaned again. He'd wanted Alex for so long but had never thought it would be like this — his touch sent shudders through him.

"Alex, can I sit closer?"

Alex blinked at him, then nodded. "God, yes. Yes, you can."

Tom slipped his arms around Alex's neck then levered himself up to sit astride him. He brushed his forehead against Alex's. "Are you sure? Like this?"

"Like that," was Alex's breathless reply. He rested his hands on Tom's hips and whispered, "You're absolutely gorgeous, you know. I must seem dreadfully inexperienced to you."

"You're perfect, Alex." Tom kissed his neck and lowered himself against Alex. He was careful not to press himself to him, even though he could feel the hardness of Alex's erection against him. "You know what to do...you know what feels good, right?"

He gasped an acknowledgment, arching his neck against Tom's kiss. He could feel Alex's pulse racing beneath his lips, the heat of his skin even more evidence of his desire — not that Tom needed further proof. Yet since Gill's death, Tom knew that there had been nobody intimate in Alex's life, so his sweet shyness was hardly surprising.

"Whatever you want to do or try or touch, ask me, that's all." Tom nibbled Alex's earlobe, then whispered, "Don't feel embarrassed."

"I don't know where to start," Alex admitted softly, drawing one fingertip down Tom's chest until he reached the next fastened button. He popped it free and murmured, "But I don't want you to stop."

Tom held Alex's hand and entwined their fingers. "Tell me if I'm going too fast. I'm like a kid in a sweetshop with you!"

He laughed and admitted, "No one's ever said *that* before."

"Well, I have, and I mean it. You're one big delicious treat and I—" *I want to lick you all over.* Now *that* would send him running. But he *was* irresistible, his blue eyes blinking up at Tom, those three tempting buttons unfastened on his shirt.

And I do want to lick you all over.

"I think I'm shy," Alex confessed through a bashful smile. "But… I think I just need to get past that, Tom. It's been a long time for me."

"It's all right, really." Tom bumped the tip of his nose against Alex's. "How about— Would you like me to undo another button for you?"

"I'd love it," he whispered.

So Tom undid the next button down and he smiled to see how louche Alex looked with it open. He leaned down and pressed his lips to the skin that had appeared, the hair on Alex's chest tickling Tom's cheek. Alex gasped Tom's name and as he did, his hand slipped down to rest on Tom's buttock. There it stayed, the fingertips circling gently, as he arched his back toward Tom's lips.

Take it slow, Tom reminded himself.

"Can I undo another button?" Tom murmured.

"As many as you like," Alex told him. "On the understanding that I'm in my forties, I didn't follow your lead and serve Queen and country, and I've never studied yoga in my life."

Tom took the next button, but before he unfastened it, he asked, his voice catching with excitement, "All the way down?"

"Oh bloody hell, why not?" He grinned. "You've only got a couple left, but...can I?"

"Please do." Tom sat back a little and deliberately peacocked for Alex, tensing his pectorals as he let a ripple run through his muscles from his chest down to his stomach. He saw Alex's gaze follow the ripple and heard the trembling breath that met his little display, the prime minister debauched and smiling there beneath him. Alex's eyes finally lifted again and he drew in a long breath before sighing it out again.

"So... I have the army to thank for you?"

"And lifting toddlers!" Tom laughed gently. "Funny thing is, we've seen each others' chests before, but never close up. Never like *this*." Tom didn't hold back now and unbuttoned Alex's shirt, never pausing until all the buttons were open. He swept the fabric of Alex's shirt aside and stroked him from the base of his neck down to his stomach, where Tom rested his palm over Alex's navel. "Alex, you're so hot."

"I'm not at all..." he murmured, shaking his head. "But you're sweet to say it."

"Of course you are." Tom leaned forward and kissed Alex, trailing his hands over Alex's chest. He stroked both nipples, then, sensing that Alex approved, tweaked them. The reaction was instantaneous and about as far from the 'collected, unflappable statesman' version of Alex Hart as it was possible to get. Alex's back arched again and he gave the most impossibly erotic groan that Tom had ever heard, his hand flying up to Tom's shoulder as he did.

"Alex…" Tom broke from the kiss then ran his lips down Alex's neck to his chest. He kissed around Alex's nipple then asked, "Can I kiss you here?" He didn't feel he could plunge in—it seemed too intimate to do without asking.

Alex nodded, looking down at him with something like wonder when he whispered, "Yes."

So Tom took the hot, hard nub between his lips, teasing it with his tongue as he stroked Alex's back. Quite by instinct, Tom suspected, Alex's fingers suddenly tightened, grasping his bottom. He just about managed to whisper an apology before another moan stole the words, but for Tom, no apology was needed.

Tom moved across to Alex's other nipple, nibbling a little now.

"God, that's good," he breathed, his other hand grasping at Tom's back. "Oh God, Tom…"

Tom would've happily kissed his way down Alex's torso, but he held back. This seemed to be having the desired effect for now as it was, if the little shivers and groans of pleasure were anything to go by. So Tom went on, giving Alex all the time he needed to enjoy sensations that he hadn't felt for years.

"What can I do"—he gasped—"for you, Tom? I want to make you happy…"

Tom decided to be honest. He could've said *kissing is fine,* but he needed Alex to know that he wanted him. And was willing to wait. "Is it…is it too much if you unzip me? I understand if it's a no at the moment, though."

"No, it's not a no. I want to." He combed his fingers through Tom's hair. "It might take me a little longer to dare to ask the same, though, is that okay?"

"Ask when you're ready." Tom rolled Alex's nipples between his fingers, admiring the view of the near-shirtless politician. "If it's too much, and you're happy staying on the sofa, that's fine, but...would you be more comfortable in bed?"

Clearly battling to form any sort of coherent thought thanks to Tom's dexterous fingers, Alex took a moment to consider that before he asked almost timidly, "Would you mind if we went to bed?"

"Not at all. Your place or mine?"

"Mine's bigger — the bed, I mean!" Alex laughed then, and it seemed as though some of the nervous tension deserted him when he did. "I'm only talking about beds."

"But you're certainly not small, Alex. I am very much looking forward to unwrapping your present!" Tom leaned forward and kissed him, then said, "*Your* bed, then."

"I'm sorry I'm making you wait," Alex told him, brushing another soft kiss to his lips. "I'm just...this is wonderful, Tom, honestly."

"You're right, it *is* wonderful." Tom kissed him as he rose from Alex's lap. The kiss didn't end until both men were on their feet, but before they could make their way from the room, Alex reached for Tom again, bringing him close for another kiss.

They kissed their way along the corridor to Alex's bedroom. By the time they reached the door, Tom's shirt had vanished completely, but he didn't care.

On the threshold Alex paused, glancing back at the bed, but there was no reticence in his expression, only happiness.

"So… I hope you won't sleep along the bottom of the bed tonight?"

"And not just because you don't want me to tickle your feet again?" Tom toyed with the button at the top of his trousers.

"Oh, you were merciless." Alex chuckled. "I probably shouldn't admit it, but I was so aware of you that night. In my bed, but not."

"I didn't think I'd sleep being so close to you!" Tom held Alex's hand. "But I will tonight, though. I want you to hold me while I sleep."

Alex studied Tom's face then lifted his hand kissed it with such tenderness that it almost stole his breath. "I promise not to let you go."

"You've got such lovely arms for hugging." Tom stroked Alex's bare forearms again. Firm, strong, masculine.

"Good for carrying the shopping," Alex said teasingly, then he drew Tom into his arms and held him, as gentle now as they had been heated before.

Tom stroked his hands through Alex's hair, nuzzling his neck and breathing him in. The scent of him, and the moment itself.

"Come to bed?" Alex eventually whispered, kissing Tom's cheek.

Tom nodded. "Have me," he replied. As soon as he said it he saw Alex's expression change, the faint suggestion of timidity returning. Had Alex taken that as an invitation to ravish him? Or maybe even a command?

"However you'd like to," Tom added, and brushed the pad of his thumb across Alex's lips.

"You're very sweet." Alex took his hand and together they walked toward the bed. "And very patient."

Tom stopped, resting his knee on the bed. "Would you like me to undress for you?"

The reply was a nod, though Alex's expression was still a far too appealing mixture of desire and bewildered wonder, which was hardly a surprise. The man had been widowed three years ago and married to the same woman for a decade before that. This was hardly territory he was familiar with. Yet he seemed to be more than keen to navigate it.

"Lie down, get comfy," Tom whispered. So Alex, a picture of semi-debauched decency, settled against the pillows. He stretched his legs out before himself and crossed them at the ankle, then pillowed his hands behind his head. Less a prime minister, perhaps, more a decadent emperor.

Tom's breath hitched at the sight. Was he really worthy of a man like Alex?

"You're so handsome," Tom said. And he felt embarrassed, presumptuous. Did he belong in this man's bed?

"And you're perfect, Tom, in case I hadn't mentioned it." He smiled. "You really are."

"If you're sure." Tom's gaze didn't leave Alex's as he slowly drew down the zip on his jeans and edged them down his hips. He pushed them down farther and farther until all he was left with was his shorts, then paused, his thumb under the waistband. Tom's erection was all too obvious now with only his thin shorts to restrain it. "Would you like me to...?"

Alex followed the path of Tom's hand, then swept back up to his eyes. "Would you like to?"

How long had it been since Alex had last seen another man's erection? "I would, but only if you'd like me to."

Has he ever *seen another man's erection? Maybe he's never done any of this before at all.*

"I'd like you to," he whispered.

Tom nodded. They couldn't go back from here. But could they have gone back from him kissing Alex's neck the other evening? "Just so you know, you're the most wonderful man I've ever known."

And Tom pulled down his shorts. He kicked them away and, with one hand awkwardly combing back his hair, newly naked, Tom stood before his lover.

Alex held out his hand to Tom and asked, "Come here?"

Tom took his hand and climbed onto the bed. Aware of every inch of his own body and Alex's, Tom lay down beside him. "I'm not too scary, then!"

"I've never done this before." And perhaps, now it had been said, those last shreds of timidity might fall away. "I wanted to, but... Can I touch you?"

"There's nothing I want more."

Alex kissed him almost reverentially, stroking his hand down Tom's torso. When his fingers reached Tom's stomach his touch lingered. As he dropped his lips to Tom's shoulder, he finally let his elegant fingers encircle his erection. Tom tried to stop his hips from rising up off the bed. It was the most erotic touch he'd ever felt, and he sighed as he caressed the line of Alex's jaw.

And Alex, it seemed, was getting more confident with every passing second. He eased Tom back onto the bed, dotting heated kisses along his shoulder, nuzzling at his throat and nibbling at his earlobe. All the time Alex's hand was moving, his wrist jerking against Tom's body.

Tom moaned, his pleasure building by the moment. He slipped his arm around Alex's waist, underneath his opened shirt, and stroked his skin, matching Alex's rhythm. He wanted to feel Alex's warmth and closeness as they lay together. In reply, Alex's fingers grew tighter, the movement of his hand faster and his kisses, when their mouths met again, were filled with a delicious heat.

Even if Tom was more experienced when it came to men, it had been a long time since he'd been to bed with anyone like this. Alex seemed to respond to Tom's every moan and every buck of his hips, and Tom sighed, "I'm on the edge... Oh, Alex, you're amazing!"

Experience didn't come into it when a man had Alex's inspiration, it seemed, and Alex ducked his head to Tom's chest. He drew Tom's nipple between his lips and grazed it with his teeth, then circled it with the tip of his tongue. All the time his hand moved, driving Tom on.

Murmuring his lover's name, Tom slipped his hands up to Alex's shoulders, holding on as his climax rocked through his body. There was nothing in his mind beside desire and pleasure and Alex. He gazed at Alex through half-open eyes as his climax wore itself away through Tom's trembling limbs.

Alex's smile was soft, his gaze tender, and he whispered, "Was that all right, darling?"

"Yes..." Tom stroked Alex's hair. He looked so sexy all ruffled up. "Just...just want to lie here and look at you."

He kissed the tip of Tom's nose. "Sounds perfect."

So in the soft light, Tom gazed at Alex, at those large blue eyes and his gentle smile, and that ruffled hair. And at the tempting view of his chest that showed through his opened shirt.

How long had they both wanted this? And how long had they not dared to say? *Thank God for that shoulder massage.*

Tom raised an eyebrow. "Are you going to wear this shirt all night?"

"I don't usually go to bed in my shirt and trousers," Alex told him with a smile. He sat up and stroked his hand along Tom's arm. "Do you mind if I lose a few more layers?"

"Fine by me! I'll give you a hand." Tom tidied himself up, then kissed the base of Alex's neck. He traveled his lips toward Alex's shirt-clad shoulder and slowly edged the fabric away. With a trembling breath, Alex tipped his head back. He rolled his broad shoulders, the shirt sliding down over his biceps.

Tom chased the shirt with kisses, his lips at last brushing Alex's arms. They were so strong, so sculpted, like the arms of a classical statue hewn from marble.

It took only the slightest movement to send Alex's shirt whispering onto the bed and there was that little smile again, playful and affectionate.

"I don't suppose you fancy helping with the trousers too?"

Tom couldn't imagine what it had taken Alex to ask him that question. He nodded and said, "It'd be an honor."

Tom feathered his lips against Alex's neck as he unfastened Alex's trousers with all the care he could muster. He could hardly fail to be aware of his lover's erection, but he knew this was one step at a time and they'd already taken a *lot* of steps tonight. More than he could have expected or hoped for. When Alex lifted his hips and slid his tailored trousers down and off, Tom could sense his apprehension, but he hid it by asking, "Will I do?"

Tom's breath caught in his throat at the sight of Alex, clothed only in his shorts. He took Alex's hand and entwined their fingers. "You are so handsome, I..." Raising their joined hands to his lips, he whispered, "I'm so happy this has happened, Alex. You can't imagine how much I..."

"I can," Alex admitted. "The difference is, you were brave enough to do something about it."

"I wasn't brave, I was reckless." Tom smiled at him. "I could've lost everything, could've ruined everything."

"Maybe you sensed that wasn't likely to happen?" He drew the covers over them and took Tom into his arms again, every movement gentle. "It's not as if we don't know each other pretty well already, after all. Perhaps I wasn't as good at hiding how I felt as I thought I was."

Tom cupped Alex's face. "I really care about you, Alex. And I suppose, over the years — you care about me too?"

"We've done the most difficult part first — we've found out if we can live together." Alex kissed the side of Tom's hand. "I didn't think I'd ever get past losing Gill and I don't know if I ever would if I'd been on my own, but...I wasn't on my own. And me and you and the twins, we've made it through, all of us together. And I don't know exactly when it happened, but one evening we were watching TV and I suddenly realized — *Tom's wonderful. And I can never tell him.*"

Tom sighed. "Did you think I wouldn't want to know? Oh, Alex, I've had this crush on you and it just seemed so impossible. I mean…you're into guys, too, and I didn't know. The way you touch me — it's just so perfect. *You're* so perfect."

"I thought you'd laugh at me and worse still, I was worried that you might leave." Alex smiled and set his watch aside. "But we already know all of each other's annoying little foibles — you know that I rant at *Newsnight*, can't cook and leave ties and cufflinks wherever I happen to drop them, and so far you haven't throttled me."

"I love it when you come in and take off your tie and your cufflinks. It's like a nightly striptease." Tom chuckled. "And you know my irritating habits. I fidget, my hair keeps falling into my face, I always sit in the armchair which should really be your *seat*…"

"Now you've moved into my bed too!" Alex drew Tom to his chest and hugged him. "And you're absolutely lovely to cuddle."

Tom moaned with happiness. "Your arms — how are your arms so amazing?"

"I always thought they were a bit chunky, but I'll take amazing instead." And they could hardly be closer than they were, their bodies pressed tightly together, legs entwined.

"I've always liked your arms." Tom grinned at him. "Is that a terrible thing to admit to? You come home, roll up your sleeves and I just stare at them and think, *Now* those *are a pair of arms. Manly arms.*"

"Consider them at your disposal." He kissed Tom's nose. "Whenever you need them."

Tom blinked up at him. "I need them now," he whispered. With another kiss, lingering and deep, Alex tightened his embrace, holding Tom safe in the arms he adored.

Chapter Twelve

When Tom awoke the next morning, he was still in Alex's arms. He lay there for a while, just enjoying the sensation of being held by him, and the deep sense of peace he felt as they lay there together. He could tell by the steady rhythm of Alex's breathing that he was still sleeping and sensed his lover waking as the rhythm changed, but his embrace went on. Eventually Alex moved just a little, just enough to rest his cheek on Tom's hair, peaceful and tender.

"Morning," Tom whispered. He stroked Alex's bare arm from his shoulder down to his wrist.

"Hello," Alex murmured. His lips brushed Tom's forehead and he asked, "Did you sleep all right?"

Tom nodded. Alex looked adorable, his features all soft from sleep, his hair tousled and his eyelids heavy. "And you?"

"Wonderfully." He smiled and said, "You're impossible to let go."

Then never let me go.

But Tom couldn't say that. Not yet. If he ever could. He stroked Alex down the side of his body, stopping at the top of his shorts where he rested his hand at his waist. When Alex was ready, they'd go as far as he wanted. For now, this was more than he had dared to dream of. Tom was in Alex's arms, in his bed. And he was naked.

And unless Alex wasn't paying attention, surely he hadn't missed Tom's erection.

Tom giggled as he lifted the covers to look down. Alex's chest caught his eye first, but there it was, Captain Southwell's morning salute. "What can I say? I'm keen!"

"You certainly are," Alex agreed, following his gaze. "So, Captain, what can I do about that?"

"Would you like to help me sort it out?" Tom pillowed his arm behind his head and closed his other hand around his erection. He gave it a stroke, while forcing himself to ignore the maddening hardness of Alex's erection that pressed against him.

Alex drew his fingertip down Tom's chest and murmured, "I'd love to." He closed his hand over Tom's, letting him lead. "I could get used to waking up like this."

Alex's large, square hand was surprisingly gentle and Tom was glad to lead the way. He kissed along Alex's jaw then whispered, "When you're ready for me to touch you, do you want to do it like this? You can show me what you like, how you want to be touched."

"It's been a long time since anyone touched me," he said, his smile rather bashful again. "But I'd like to do that. And I think we'd both enjoy it. And if I do anything wrong, or there's anything I should do differently, will you tell me?"

"Yes. You've done everything right so far, though." Tom grinned at him. "You've got such a lovely grip, by the way. Just right."

"Last night, I know I sort of... God, I don't know how to say it." He kissed Tom's cheek and whispered against his ear, "If you'd rather be... I sort of kissed you into the pillows like you were Scarlett O'Hara, didn't I?"

"You did, and I *loved* it!" Tom chuckled. Alex laughed then, perhaps spurred on by Tom's approval, kissed him into the pillow again, tender and heated all at once. At that moment, Tom couldn't have asked for more. *Have me*, he'd asked, and Alex most certainly was.

Their hands moved together on his body as Alex kissed him again and again, every soft sigh and hitched breath further proof of his desire. His arm was around Tom's shoulders, holding him tight, the embrace as protective as it was fierce. And just as he had last night, Alex brought Tom to his climax. Tom didn't break their kiss as pleasure darted through him, spreading through his limbs and shuddering along every nerve. He'd never felt so close to a lover before, never wanted someone as much as he did Alex.

"Oh, Tom." Alex sighed happily. "You gorgeous bloody man. What did I ever do to deserve you?"

Tom grinned lazily. "One glance from those big blue eyes and I was yours."

"You should be in the press office. Just imagine *that* party political broadcast." Alex laughed. "Breakfast in bed before the whirlwind returns?"

Tom snuggled happily against Alex, curling his body to his. "Oh, yes. Toast and marmalade?"

"Or we *could* have the extremely-bad-for-you-and-I-don't-care croissants I picked up yesterday? It wasn't only flowers and spaghetti, you know."

"I'm going to send you shopping more often!"

Tom couldn't remember a time in his life when he had felt more cared for than he did now. Alex was already a wonderful friend and a better employer than anyone could ask for, but as a lover, he was irresistible. The breakfast was decadent and rich, everything Tom suspected it would be, and they whiled away the morning with croissants and kisses as, outside, London went about its business.

With one eye on the clock, Tom stretched his arms and said, "I'm going to hop in the shower. Do you fancy one as well?"

He'll say no. He's too shy to say yes.

"I'd love one."

"With…" Tom glanced off toward the en-suite bathroom, then back at Alex. "Do you want to share?"

He took a deep breath and said, "Yes, if you don't mind me getting in your way?"

"You won't be." Tom scrubbed his hand back through his hair. "Shall I get started, and you can join me when you're ready?"

He thought again of that out-of-reach fantasy, of Alex Hart letting his towel fall and stepping into the shower with him. Perhaps Alex intuited it somehow, because he nodded. "That sounds good to me."

Tom winked at him. "Can I borrow your soap?"

"Help yourself." Alex kissed his cheek. "I'll be two minutes."

Tom climbed out of the bed and, completely comfortable in his nudity, headed into the bathroom. He sighed as he stood under the jet of warm water in the shower, and smoothed on the shower gel, which he recognized at once as one of the smells that made up Alex's scent.

As he showered, he kept one ear tuned to the bedroom, wondering whether Alex would really join him. A couple of minutes passed, then another, before he saw a shadow fall across the tiled bathroom floor, and there in the doorway stood his lover. For just a moment Alex paused, then he padded into the bathroom and asked, "You sure you weren't in that shower gel ad?"

Tom turned down the shower and opened the glass door. He smoothed his hand down his wet chest, teasing. "Well, okay, I was bored one afternoon and thought, *why not?*" But Tom's heart was racing. Alex was going to get in the shower with him. Just as he'd dreamed of. And for Alex to get this far—was he going to wear his shorts? Whether they were on or off, Tom would try his best not to glance down.

"Why not?" Alex repeated, his voice low with desire, a slight tremble evident in the words. Then he hooked his thumbs into the waistband of his shorts and slid them down.

Tom fixed his gaze on Alex's eyes. "Would you rather I didn't look?"

"I'm just shy." There was a bright twinkle in Alex's gaze, a faint flush on his face. "You can look if you want to."

"Guess what my answer is to that?" Tom reached out through the shower's partly open door and stroked Alex's arm, then he glanced down. And here was Alex as he had never seen him before— bare, aroused, and shy. Tom was moments from cracking a joke involving loofahs, but instead he said, "You really are one hell of a man, Alex."

Alex caught Tom's hand and stepped into the shower with him, making another of those unreachable dreams come true. Standing beneath the shower's cascade, he closed his eyes and tipped his head back, letting the warm water run over him. Tom combed his fingers through Alex's dampening hair and kissed his neck under the stream of water.

It was Sunday, the one day in the week that Alex really allowed himself time off, and here they were spending it in a steamy shower. One of those strong arms was around Tom's waist and as Alex lowered his chin and kissed Tom in return, his hand was massaging through the decadent bubbles on Tom's back. Tom wanted so much to stroke Alex's erection, but instead he contented himself knowing that Alex would enjoy feeling the warm water against it, and hoping he'd like the frisson of it pressing against him.

They barely spoke, devoting themselves instead to kisses, to stroking the heady shower gel over their warm skin and there, when Tom cared to look, were Alex's shoulders with the rivulets of water he had dreamed of.

Tom lost track of time, entirely wrapped up in the most sensual experience of his life. And the sweetest, too, as they kissed and caressed under the warm water.

But the day was ebbing away, he reminded himself, and soon the twins would be home and with them, the already somewhat flustered in-laws. There was to be tea and a light snack and excited children racing around, but through it all, there would be this memory. And the thought of what else was to come.

Chapter Thirteen

The bed linen was turning in the washing machine by the time the knock sounded on the door.

"I'll get the kettle on." Tom nodded to Alex. He patted his arm. "Don't worry, we've got this."

"We have." Alex smiled. He pecked a kiss to Tom's cheek then disappeared along the hallway. Seconds later the sound of cheering children filled the apartment and the peace was wonderfully shattered.

And we wouldn't change it for the world.

"Daddy!" Madeleine shouted, her ragdoll under one arm and her drawing notebook under her other. She promptly dropped them and flung herself at Alex's legs. He stooped and deftly lifted both of the children, one in each arm. The three clung to one another as Malcolm and Jenny followed along, carrying the weekend bags.

"Hello, darling." Jenny smiled as she kissed Alex's cheek. "Hello, Tom!"

"Hiya!" Tom came through from the kitchen. "Just getting the kettle on. And juice for the kids. Take a seat."

How different the sofa looked in daylight, without him and Alex embracing.

Stop thinking about it.

The in-laws sank down onto the sofa as Alex carried the twins over to Tom, both of them reaching out to give him a hug.

"Tom," Alastair said, "did you have a nice time?"

Tom hugged them, trying to avoid hugging Alex at the same time. "Yes! Your daddy and I went out on Friday for dinner, and yes, we had a lovely time."

"Out for dinner. Sounds lovely," Jenny said, but Tom could hear the effort in her voice. She had her suspicions, and no wonder given all that talk of tickling and shared beds. Then she peered down at the sofa and murmured, "What's this?"

From behind the sofa cushion Jenny produced a quantity of striped fabric, her brow furrowing with confusion. As Tom watched, his heart plummeted into his stomach because he realized now exactly where his discarded shirt had ended up.

In Jenny's hands, basically.

"It's a shirt!" she declared, as though the very concept of it was alien to her.

"Yeah, I must've lost it yesterday when I was doing the ironing." Tom did his best bland smile as he came over to retrieve it. "Thanks for finding it."

"I'm sure that's it." But her smile was fixed as she handed it over. Then she rose to her feet and asked, "Alex, could I borrow you for five minutes? Just a quick mum-in-law chat before tea?"

Alex darted a glance to Tom, but his tone betrayed nothing but helpfulness when he said, "'Course you can, Jenny. Come through to the office?"

He put the children down on the sofa beside Malcolm and led her from the room. This didn't look good.

"Erm… So the donkey's doing okay, then?" Tom resumed his spot on the armchair and Madeleine thrust her drawing pad at him, excitedly pointing out her renditions of Jenny and Malcolm's menagerie.

Malcolm talked Tom through the ins and outs of animal husbandry, but Tom took nothing in. What the heck was Jenny saying to Alex?

"Where did you and Daddy go?" Alastair climbed up into Tom's lap. "For your dinner?"

He brought with him a waft of talcum powder and sweets, and Tom hugged him.

"We went to a restaurant in Soho, but it looked like it was in France," Tom explained, knowing that Alistair only had a vague grasp of what *France* might mean. "We'll all go there for lunch soon. You'll love it."

"Sounds…interesting," Malcolm said. "Soho."

"Soho's *amazing*," Alastair assured him. "We've found all of the noses!"

Malcolm looked even more perplexed by that, the smallholder from Herefordshire unsurprisingly not overly familiar with London's art installations. Tom was just wondering whether to explain when Jenny's and Alex's voices could be heard, friendly and chatting as ever, as they made their way back to the kitchen.

"Right." Alex stood in the doorway and clapped his hands together, his smile just a little strained. "Who wants tea?"

Malcolm raised his hand. "Milk and two sugars, you know how I take it, thanks."

Tom rose from the chair but he couldn't quite bring himself to approach the kitchen, as if it were surrounded by a forcefield. He had seen that fixed smile on Alex's face before, painted on for more challenging Downing Street visitors, unmoving when he was forced to do unwanted press calls by the party's media machine.

What did Jenny say?

"It's okay, Tom, it's your day off," he said. "And you don't have to run around waiting on us anyway. Let me."

"No, it's no bother, honest!" Tom gathered all his gumption and headed into the kitchen, which at that moment was as inviting as a vat of warm acid. He glanced up at Jenny, his bland smile still in place, but waves of displeasure rolled toward him from her, which nearly tripped him up.

"Good drive up?" Tom asked as he spooned out the tea leaves.

"Uneventful," she replied, smiling. "Just how we like things to be, Tom. Nice and uneventful."

"Great. No traffic jams, no dicky tums?" Tom pointed toward the twins and laughed. "You're a brave woman, traveling with the monsters!"

Her smile grew warmer then and she assured him, "Oh, we don't mind any of that. We adore them and we talk Gill all the time. It's very important to us that she's a big part of their lives, even if… Well, Alex won't be single forever, will he? Good luck to whoever takes him on though, I can only imagine the microscope the press will turn on her!"

Her. And in that word was the warning bell, the veiled reference to Gill being replaced and forgotten — something Alex would never allow and Tom would never want. They had been friends long before he and Alex were anything more than professionally polite — *partners in crime*, as Alex had once called Gill and Tom when they returned from one of their long, laughter-filled lunches. He had no intention of *replacing* Gill or elbowing her out, and the press could go hang.

"Nobody's going to replace Gill," Alex said, his tone uncharacteristically snappy. "I don't want to hear you say that again, Jenny, all right? Whatever happens, she's part of our lives."

"Well, let's hope it stays that way." She looked Tom up and down and swept from the kitchen toward the sofa, where her smile was transformed into a beaming grin for the children.

Tom sagged against the worktop. He wanted to hug Alex, there and then, but he knew it would only make matters worse. With a wan smile for him, Tom finished making the tea.

Jenny wouldn't make him choose between the memory of Gill and finding new happiness, he told himself.

Would she?

Chapter Fourteen

Malcolm had been in a voluble mood, and Tom had done his best to engage, but once he and Jenny had left, he felt nothing but relief. The twins had their tea, then it was bathtime.

"*Why* do I have to have bath time?" Madeleine held on to her crayon with an iron grip as Tom tried to get her down from the table. "I'm not smelly!"

"Because all children have baths on Sunday night," Alex told her with admirable parental logic. "I had to, Tom had to, now you have to. Come on, Mads, crayons down."

"I don't want to," Madeleine whined, on the edge of tears, as if she were being forced to run a marathon through the snow in flip-flops. "I *don't*, Daddy."

Tom crouched down on the floor next to her chair. "Come on, you can play in the bath. You've got those soap crayons — you like those. And then bedtime."

Madeleine shook her head. "I hate my bed. I'm not going to bed."

"If she's not going to bed, I'm not going to bed," Alastair informed them. He folded his arms, challenging Alex and Tom to disagree.

Alex raked one hand through his hair and told them, "You're both going to have a bath, then a story, then bed. And you can choose any story you like, how's that?"

"I don't want to, I don't want to!" Madeleine wailed. All the hallmarks of a tantrum were brewing.

"Now listen." Tom pulled out her chair and crouched again, holding Madeleine's hands. And the crayon. "When I was out in the desert, I still had to have a bath and go to bed. And I was told when to go to bed by a man who shouted a lot if I didn't do as I was told. Would you like me to invite him round and send you to bed? No, you wouldn't. Everyone has baths and bedtime — if you didn't go to bed you'd fall asleep in your chair, wouldn't you?"

"Mads?" Alastair asked, reaching up to take Alex's hand. "If you fall asleep in your chair you'll fall on the floor."

Madeleine widened her eyes in horror and shook her head. "No, no, I don't want to fall on the floor! But I don't want to have a bath."

"Why don't you fancy a bath?" Alex stroked her curly hair. "What's the problem, darling?"

Madeleine blinked at him. "Because after bath I go to sleep and what if I close my eyes and I don't wake up ever, ever again?"

For a moment there was complete silence, then Alex knelt beside the chair and asked gently, "What do you mean, Mads? You'll wake up and be just as loud and curly-headed as ever."

"But I might not, and then I'd never, ever see you again." Tears were rising in Madeleine's eyes now. In a whisper, she added, "Like Mummy."

And Tom knew then that *something* had been said during their trip. Some helpful little chat about Gill that had succeeded only in terrifying her daughter. He saw that Alex knew it too, registered the swallow in his throat and the flicker in his gaze before he said, "Do you want to come and sit with me and we'll have a talk about it all?"

Madeleine swung her legs back and forth and sniffed. "Yes please, Daddy."

He picked her from the chair as he stood, with Alastair seemingly happy to trot across and bounce onto the sofa under his own steam. As Madeleine clung to Alex, he met Tom's gaze and asked, "Will you sit with us?"

Tom had started to tidy away the twins' crayons, but he stopped. "Yeah...yeah, of course."

He headed over to the armchair and sat down.

Safely gathered on the sofa, Alex offered Tom a brief smile then asked the twins, "Have you been talking about Mummy this weekend?"

"Yes," Madeleine replied. "Nana showed us photos."

"And said that Mummy went to sleep and never woke up," her brother added. And it was true, Tom knew, just as he knew that Alex had done his best to explain to the children what had happened to their mother and why she was no longer there to care for them. It didn't sound as though Jenny's efforts had been quite as well planned, perhaps.

"We've talked about Mummy a lot," Alex told them, his voice measured, containing all that sadness that he and Tom had faced as they tried to care for two infants between them. "And you know she was very poorly. It was nobody's fault, nobody did anything wrong, but she was too poorly to get better. Mummy *did* go to sleep, darling, but she was sick and very tired. That won't happen to you or Al or Tom. I promise you it won't."

Madeleine gripped his shirt sleeve with her fist. "And *you* won't? Promise, Daddy?"

"I definitely promise that." He lifted his arm to allow Alastair to snuggle closer. "We're all going to wake up tomorrow, but we all have to go to sleep. Nana wouldn't want you to be upset — she just wanted you to see your mum because we all miss her, that's all."

"She was very pretty. She smiled a lot," Madeleine said. And she was smiling now.

"You have her curls." Tom moved from the armchair to the edge of the sofa and stroked Madeleine's hair. Then he reached across Alex and stroked Alastair's.

"And you have her freckles," Alex told the little boy. "And she and Tom were very good friends and when Mummy found out how poorly she was, she —" He blinked rapidly, gathering in his emotions, containing them for the sake of the children. "She said to Tom, *I want you to look after my little monsters*, that's exactly what she said. So me and Tom would never let anything or anyone hurt you, and neither would any of the gramps. We all love you."

Tom smiled gently. "She said I had to make both of you — all three of you — happy."

"I love you, Daddy," Madeleine said. "I love you, Tom. I love you, Alster."

Once her brother had finished his own spirited rounds of *I love yous*, Alex said, "I love you all too, never doubt it."

"And I love all of you," Tom said. But that word took on a meaning now that he hadn't quite expected, and he avoided Alex's glance. "So, ready for bath time now?"

Alastair nodded, waiting for his sister's considered response.

"Yes, please! And soap crayons!"

Alex kissed her cheek, then ducked his head to kiss Alastair's nose. "It's a deal!"

Bath time ensued. Tom took a back seat, letting Alex run the show as lifeguard and scrubber both. The twins were soon giggling and squealing and Tom busied himself making sure the bath towels were warm and the talcum powder was ready. Eventually, amid much yawning and protestations that they weren't tired at all, the twins were scooped from the water and prepared for bed.

"I want Tom to carry me," Alastair decided. "He was a soldier."

Tom buttoned the neck of Alastair's pajamas and tickled him. "I could carry you over my shoulder like a fireman!"

"Yes please!" The little boy laughed. Alex finished brushing Madeleine's curls as she fussed with the sparkly puppy on her own pajama top then, to a squeal of excitement, slung her over his shoulder and carried her long the landing.

Tom hoisted the giggling Alastair over his shoulder, following Alex to the twins' bedroom. He let Alastair slither down from his shoulder and onto his bed.

"Night, Al!" Tom kissed the boy's forehead, and kissed Madeleine's too. Then he tried to perch on a tiny wooden chair that had been painted to resemble a toadstool.

"Read a story, Tom," Alastair asked. "Mad can choose."

Alex deposited Madeleine on her bed then settled on the beanbag and said, "Go on, Tom, do the honors?"

"Okay, Mads, what story would you like?"

She snuggled into her duvet and replied, "Mrs. Tiggy-Winkle. Al likes that one."

Tom took the little book from its boxset on the shelf, then balanced once more on the chair. He yawned behind his hand as he held the book at just the right angle, so that the twins could see the drawings, and he could see the text. The pall cast by Jenny seemed to have lifted a little, at least, and he felt the affection in Alex's gaze again as he read, but as the book went on and the twins began to doze, he saw his lover's eyelids growing heavier too.

Was the prime minister falling asleep to *Mrs. Tiggy-Winkle*?

Not, not falling asleep. He was out like a light.

Tom kept reading, but Alex's regular breathing was making him feel sleepy too. The children closed their eyes and Tom finally reached the last page. He stared at the illustration of the lush green Lake District hillside and had the oddest feeling that he was there, floating downstream toward Windermere.

Chapter Fifteen

Tom was in the car coming back from taking the twins to preschool when his phone chimed, heralding a text.

Client cancelled, gone into labour!!! — fancy coffee? Sx

Tom looked up from his phone. Should he? There were muddy clothes to wash from the twins' weekend away, but he couldn't turn Stuart down. *Old soldiers and all that.*

Yeah ok — you choose? Tom

In fact, a coffee would be perfect. Tom had woken up in the early hours on the floor of the twins' bedroom. He'd realized he must've fallen asleep on the chair and slipped off it. Alex, meanwhile, had been fast asleep on the beanbag — and Tom hadn't wanted to wake him, so he'd dug out a spare duvet and tucked him in. He'd looked rather comfortable in his nest, and Tom, on stiff limbs, had kissed his cheek before creaking back to his own room.

Make it oscars since we both know it and smoothies are the dogs ,,, i wont order without u x second date in as many days u must be sweet on me xxx

Tom felt a jab of guilt. Why hadn't he waited for Stuart the other day? And what the heck was he going to do if Stuart thought this was a date? No, he couldn't say anything by text—he'd have to tell him face to face. He'd met someone else.

OK Oscars it is! Ten minutes? Tom

Then he signaled to the CPO and the car pulled up, nearly at Whitehall. Tom climbed out of the car and turned up his collar. He was just another man on the street. Almost.

Tom had just reached Oscar's when he heard his name from along the road and there, jogging toward him, was Stuart. He was underdressed even for spring in Lycra jogging leggings and a vest that left little to the imagination. *Quite the Muscle Mary these days.*

And people had noticed, one or two passersby throwing him an admiring double take as he put his arm around Tom and said, "Hey, T-bone."

They went in and found a table. Tom ordered his coffee and Stuart looked excited by his smoothie as Tom felt his gaze pulled in the direction of the cakes. He tried to focus on what Stuart was saying, but the endless parade of anonymous celebrities who Stuart was bending into eye-watering positions was hard to follow and difficult to get too thrilled about.

"I know you want to ask the names." Stuart laughed as he came to the end of another anecdote. "But you can't twist my arm, so don't try."

"I probably won't know who they are," Tom replied. "Anything on the telly called *Celebrity This* or *Celebrity That* is full of people I don't recognize. Unless it's *Mr. Tumble* or *Peppa Pig*, I don't have a clue!"

"You know, if I wasn't a man of honor," he said in a low voice, "I could have a different dick every night. But I'm about the art of yoga now, I'm done with all that."

Tom raised an eyebrow, pantomiming a scandalized maiden aunt. "Sounds like Barcelona was fun, then."

Stuart shrugged. "More fun than breastfeeding the prime minister's kids, mate."

Tom paused, his mug halfway to his mouth. An image came to him of one of the infant twins lying in the crook of Tom's arm, gazing up at him as they suckled on a bottle because their mother was too ill to breastfeed.

"Oh, mate." Tom put down his cup. "At least I don't have to wear Lycra."

"Who'd believe you and me were ever soldiers, eh? Just look at us now!" He took a long suck at the straw, propelling the pond-like smoothie toward his lips. "But at least I kept up the training."

"You're very...ripped." It wasn't as if Tom could miss it. "But I love being a nanny. You'd be surprised how much of our training comes in handy! Heavy-lifting, strategy, cleaning up other people's mess..."

"But if your boss gets another bird, what then? Me, I'm building an empire. Here." From somewhere in those leggings — Tom didn't want to imagine where — Stuart produced a business card. It showed him in a pair of tight, fitted shorts and nothing else, his muscular body bent like a contortionist and in a too-cool-to-true font, the title, *StuDo Notting Hill*. "And it's working. I've already had had approaches from TV, one or two of the bigger reality shows, and I'm talking big-name clients. This body isn't just getting me laid, it's gonna make me famous. I worry about you, man, holding the baby and hoping your boss doesn't hook up and kick you out."

"My job's safe, no worries there!" A tingle of pleasure ran through Tom at the memory of his shower with Alex. *I'd say I get on pretty well with my boss.* "I'm part of the family. I mean…good luck with the yoga stuff, but I'm happy being a nanny."

Stuart shrugged and at the counter, Tom watched a woman tapping her chin as she considered the pastries on offer.

They do look good.

"So, what about the dating side? You seeing anyone just now?" Stuart stirred the straw.

"Yeah… About that." *Here is the moment.* Even though Tom couldn't say who his new man was, he could be proud of him anyway. "Yeah, I am actually. He's great. Really lovely guy."

Stuart nodded and lowered his voice. "One of the boys? Ex-army?"

"No, he's…a senior manager." Tom grinned. *Very* senior. "It's early days but…" *I've known him a while.* "It's good. I haven't dated anyone for ages, to be honest!"

"How's the body? Take the card— desk jockey might need it!"

Tom took the card. What supportive friend wouldn't? But he wasn't sure he could see Alex trying to bend backward.

"He's got a great bod... Not bendy, just...y'know, masculine. Broad."

"Fat?" Stuart screwed up his face. "You chasing chubs now? Dude, I'll give him a free training session — for old times' sake."

Are they the choices then, fat or ripped? And is that so important to Stuart?

Sadly, Tom suspected that it was. Personality could take a running jump so long as he were chiseled to high heaven.

Tom shook his head. "He's kind, caring. Okay, so he's handsome too, but I don't think yoga's his thing, really."

"Look at this place, though. They provide fuel if you know where to look." He gestured to the smoothie. "But everyone sits around stuffing sugar and fat into their faces like the world's ending. Not like you and me, we look after our temples, yeah?"

"Bet you have a sneaky cake every now and then, though?" Tom nodded toward the cabinet. It was more and more alluring by the moment, and — *are those lemon meringue tarts?* "The twins love those! Hang on, I'm going to grab some. I'll be back in a tick!"

Tom was out of his seat and in the queue in seconds. He hopped from foot to foot, hoping they wouldn't sell out of them, but it appeared to be the time of day when Oscar's was filled with people in Lycra drinking smoothies as equally unappealing as the one Stuart lauded, so by the time Tom reached the front of the queue, there were more than enough to spare. The server put them in a box for him, and he chose a caramel square for himself to eat there and then.

Tom sat the striped box on their table and tapped the lid. "Sorry, mate, but these are much better than a smoothie!"

Stuart laughed and shook his head. "Maybe *you'll* be needing that card, never mind your *broad* man! Your phone's been buzzing, mate. Someone's after your attention."

"Really?" Tom's first thought was of the twins, but then he dared to hope — had Alex been in touch? He picked up his phone and swiped to his messages.

There were two, both from Alex. The first was innocent enough and said simply, *I'll be home for supper tonight - lunch meeting with Mandy at HoC, Greg at 4 but will definitely be there. Sorry for falling asleep on you.*

It was friendly but not exactly affectionate. Were they flatmates again? Was he just going to pretend —

No. Not if the second message was anything to go by.

It's a week of meetings. All I can think of is how much I want to cuddle up with you again - in the shower and out of it xxx

Tom slipped his phone into his jacket's inside pocket. At that moment, it was all he could do to stop himself from running out of the door and back to Downing Street. Surprise him at his desk and — bring down the government. *Yes, that* would *be clever, Tom, well done.*

"Messages from my lovely man." Tom bit into his cake. The decadence of the thick caramel and dark chocolate suited his mood exactly.

"That's the sort of bloke you want." Stuart took another sip through his straw. "So, look, you've got your *broad* manager, but…you and me, we had a good thing, didn't we? Things you can do in the sack still keep me up nights and you know what I'm offering, 'cept now I'm the enhanced package, you get me? I'm not looking for love and dinners out, I can get that from a hundred people. I guess what I'm asking is… You can't be with the manager all the time, I can't be servicing my yoga peeps twenty-four-seven. What say you and me have a hook-up now and then, like the old days?"

Tom spluttered on his caramel square. He wiped the tears from his eyes and stared at Stuart. "Sorry — I am hearing you right, aren't I? You've just offered me — no-strings sex?"

"With this body," Stuart added. "No-strings, good times, hard-riding. You know I was brilliant, you haven't seen nothing until you see what I can do now. Half a million thirsty Insta followers don't lie, and I'm offering you a suck on *this* smoothie."

"Come on, I've got this new guy, he's wonderful — I'm sorry, Stuart, but I'm not looking for no-strings sex. Not with *anyone*." Tom was aware of ears at nearby tables waggling with interest at all this talk of sex, but he wasn't going to mince his words. And this was, after all, the man who had dumped him by text at the airport. "You're an attractive bloke, I'm sure there's loads of people who'd happily get bendy on a yoga mat with you, but no, thanks. I'm happy with the best guy for me."

Stuart shook his head and preened his waxed hair. "Mate, it's a hook-up, everyone's doing it. Don't tell me you're not looking at the fat controller and wishing he had a body like this!"

I'm bloody glad he doesn't.

Tom shook his head. "His body does things to me. When he holds me, his arms, oh, Stu, his arms… I could be happy for the rest of my life just kissing them. They're perfect!"

Tom looked down at the surface of his coffee, embarrassed by such an outburst in front of an ex. But every word was true.

He saw Stuart's head nodding as though in agreement, but when he spoke again, his voice had a sliver of ice running through it. "I can't figure you out, you know? Can't work out what you want. Back in the day you spent more time with your boss and his wife than your boyfriend, but I said, *whatever, she's sick, he's getting paid.* Then she dies and then I *never* saw you — like you loved them kids way more than you did me. You know you drove me away, and now you're turning me down?"

"They were babies, Stuart! Two small demanding babies — did you expect them to look after themselves? There was no one else to care for them — their grandparents couldn't be there all the time. And yes, it's my job, I get paid, but I love those kids as if they were my own. There. That's the truth." Tom's coffee had gone cold and his caramel square was a broken mess of crumbs. "Yes, I am turning you down, and I'm kind of shocked, really, that you even offered. I mean — we agreed to be mates, right? Not…not fuck buddies."

"A *nanny*? You were a soldier, mate, soldiers don't *nanny*!" Stuart looked incredulous, as though the very thought of it was absurd. "It's because of you that I got into hook-ups in the first place, if you want to know.

Always on my own while you were running around after Mr. Big-Man-Prime-Minister, what else was I supposed to do? Don't pretend you didn't know."

"You..." Tom ran Stuart's words through his head. And ran them through again. "Did you— What the—? You were shagging about behind my back?" Tom heard anger and hurt in his voice. But he didn't seem to feel it, as if he was already sheltering behind a blast-proof shield.

And Stuart shrugged. He actually *shrugged.*

"Had to get it somewhere."

"How...how many were there?" Tom was amazed at how blithely conversational he sounded, as if he was asking Stuart how many reps he'd managed at the gym.

"That's so you, Tom, keeping count. It was three years back, don't sweat it." He grinned, showing those porcelain-white veneers. "And before you ask, I'm clean."

"Gave yourself a good scrub, did you?" Tom only then realized that he had wound a paper napkin around his finger and was tearing bits off. "Bloody hell. Am I supposed to say thanks or something? *Glad you didn't give me gonorrhea, Stu! Ta!*"

"Jesus, you seriously need to lighten up. Everybody does it, Mary Poppins!"

"I've got responsibilities—two kids who lost their mum, and you could've... I can't even get my head round it. Bloody hell, Stu." Tom unwound the napkin and it sat on the table in front of him, a curved paper hull. "As it happens, I got tested after I broke up with the last guy I dated, but...but you know what, no, not *everybody* does it. Some people like the idea of cuddling up with just one person. One special person. And I'm sorry that wasn't you, Stu, because there was a time when I thought maybe you were."

"Then you should've put me first, not someone else's kids. End of."

"D'you know what? It would've been far healthier if we'd had this discussion when you decided to bugger off to Barcelona. If you'd just bloody well said all this to my face." Tom buttoned up his jacket, even though it was a warm day. "How dare you try to take the moral high ground—what there is of it—when you dumped me by text at the airport!"

So much for Zen.

And Stuart just didn't care. Tom could see it by the look on his face, that he had somehow convinced himself that *he* was the wronged party. Then he picked up his smoothie and sucked on the straw again, as insolent as a teenager in front of a disapproving parent.

"You know," Tom said, "when you got back in touch, I thought, maybe I shouldn't see Stuart, seeing as you hurt me. I still remember you getting shitty with me when I cancelled that date with you the day after Gill's funeral. Alex was in pieces, I couldn't leave him, and if you'd cared about me you would've known how impossible it was for me to go." Tom pushed back his chair. "But for all the times we ended up in a ditch on training, for all the times we wound each other up and said there were camel spiders in our boots—that's why I thought, you know what, I owe it to Stu to meet up. *Old soldiers, old friends. Comrades.* I wish you well, Stu. Hope the yoga stuff is a success. But you know it's probably best if we...if we leave things as they were."

Tom held out his hand across the table.

And Stu put another business card into it.

"Give it to your boss," he told Tom coldly. "I reckon he might enjoy it."

Tom gritted his teeth. He would've torn the card in half under Stuart's nose, but he wasn't that mean. Instead, he put it in his pocket.

"I'll pass it on, but don't bank on him booking a session."

"He gets a freebie." Stuart winked and grinned. "But don't tell everyone, Mary Poppins."

Tom sighed. He didn't say goodbye, but instead dropped some coins into the tip jar on the way out of Oscar's, waving at the server as he left with the twins' cakes under his arm.

Chapter Sixteen

Tom did his best to be chipper when he collected the children from preschool, and he was fairly sure they didn't notice how shaken he felt. He had to be happy for them. But memories from his time with Stuart were hovering at the corners of his mind.

How many?

And Stuart hadn't been able to answer. Could he even remember? Had he even kept count?

I've let him hurt me all over again. Idiot.

Alex was right to have been concerned about him getting in touch with Stuart again, but Tom felt like such an idiot that he couldn't bear to tell Alex what had happened.

Ready for a cuddle when you come home. Also — I have lemon meringue tart! T xxxx

The chance of Alex being able to read and reply to the text quickly was limited in the extreme, he knew, but it was enough to know it was there waiting for him.

In a week or so Alex's child poverty bill would be voted on in the House of Commons, the culmination of his time in office, the policy he had held dear to him for all this time, from his days in the charity sector before he even had the letters MP after his name. It had won the hearts of the public even as it had raised the hackles of his opponents for its reforming zeal. The welfare system was tottering, they seemed to agree, but better to shore it up than to try to renew its foundations. Yet Tom knew that it was his lover's passion. The father whose children had everything couldn't rest until the Child Poverty Action Bill had been voted into law, and by midnight next Tuesday, he'd know if he'd succeeded.

He should, of course, but Alex had always been too popular for his own good. With a general election looming, if there was an opportunity to cut him down to size and suggest to the public that his words couldn't be translated into action, then Tom knew that Alex's opponents in Parliament would seize it. Regardless of the fallout for the youngsters it meant to help, ambition and personal animosity could see it go up in smoke.

And it means everything to him.

The twins were happily engaged in some story writing when Tom's phone buzzed with Alex's reply.

I'm going to need tarts, cuddles and family, what a day! Xxx

Tom dropped into the armchair and replied. *You're a hero. T xxx*

This time, the reply was almost immediate.

I leave that to you. Lunch with Mandy now, see you tonight darling xxx

Tom quietly turned in the armchair and snapped a silent photo of the twins, writing at the kitchen table. Then he sent it to Alex.

All quiet at #11! See you later. T xxx

This was all he needed. Not the knowledge of Stuart's countless betrayals, of his selfish ego. This family and Alex's embraces. This mattered.

The twins were halfway through their tea when Tom heard the familiar sound of the key in the front door.

Both children looked up and bounded from their chairs, Tom in their wake as they hurtled toward the hallway in a chorus of "Daddy!"

"I'm so sorry I'm late!" Alex called as he swept the twins into his embrace. "Billy came to find me next door. You should've heard the ticking off she gave me. She chased me all the way home."

And there behind him was the cat, strolling into the flat as though she owned it.

Madeleine grabbed Alex's nose and tweaked it. "Daddy, Tom got cake!"

"Tom spoils us." Alex met Tom's gaze and smiled. "Finish your supper and maaaaaybe I won't eat your cake. Maybe."

"Please don't eat my cake, Daddy," Madeleine said. "I've been good *all* day long."

His arms laden with children, Alex nudged Tom with his elbow. "What do you say, Tom? Have they been good enough for pudding?"

"They have. They've been very, very good." Tom patted Alastair's arm. "Haven't you, Al?"

The little boy nodded and said, "Yep!"

"Finish supper first," Alex reminded them. "Then it's cake time, okay? And me and Tom need to eat too, unless you have already, Tom?"

"No, I haven't yet," Tom replied. "I'm all ready to go with a stir-fry when you are. Sounds good?"

"Perfect." He smiled. "Ready pretty much whenever you are. Should I supervise the mini-Harts?"

Tom heard in that question a sentiment. *I want to supervise the twins.*

Tom nodded. "They're all yours."

They went back into the kitchen and as Alex settled the children down to what was left of their tea, Tom busied himself with the stir-fry. He loved to see Alex with the twins, leaving behind the cares of his day, and in a funny sort of way it helped Tom too, because it reminded him that there was far more to life than the likes of Stuart.

"How was your day?" Alex asked once Alastair and Madeleine were eating again. "Anything exciting?"

"Had a coffee with an old — a former friend," Tom admitted. He wasn't sure how much he would tell Alex. It didn't seem fair to burden him, especially when he'd cautioned him about seeing Stuart again. "The best bit about that was bringing home awesome cake."

"A former friend?" Alex sounded thoughtful. Perhaps he'd already worked it out. "I've been ready for home since I left this morning."

"I bet you have. I hope lunch with Mandy wasn't too bad?"

He smiled and said, "She was fine. Wanted to know if we'd had a nice time on Friday night. Nothing gets past Mandy, does it? I told her we'd had a great night and recommended she get herself a table for the show."

"She'd love it!" Tom went on peeling a stick of ginger as he said, "So you didn't get a ticking-off for a night on the tiles with your manny?"

"Oh, you know…" The very casual way in which Alex ruffled his hair suggested that she might have been a *little* difficult, but that was Mandy. Tough, uncompromising, the scourge of the press everywhere. She was paid a fortune not only to know everything that was going on, but to make sure that the papers didn't hear the half of it. "Good ginger-peeling skills."

Alex drifted from his seat and pottered across the kitchen. Clearly well aware now of just how much Tom would enjoy it, he began the familiar routine of unknotting and abandoning his tie, his fingers nimbly unfastening the usual three buttons. Then came the cufflinks and finally, as he leaned back against the worktop where Tom was working, he rolled his sleeves to the elbow.

"You're looking relaxed," Tom said, trying to hide the husky timbre that had crept into his voice. Alex met his gaze and raised an eyebrow.

"It's being at home that does it. Can I help?"

"No, no, it's fine. Everything's under control." And it had to be, because Tom's gaze was wandering from Alex's arms to that flash of bare chest where he'd opened his shirt.

"You know you only need ask if that changes." Alex smiled. "Consider me all yours."

Tom took a courgette from the fridge and held it at waist height at an unmistakably phallic angle. He raised an eyebrow. "*All* mine?"

"Cucumber!" Alastair announced, as though there was a prize on offer.

Alex stifled a laugh and corrected, "Courgette," then he offered Tom a smile. "All yours, Captain."

"Every inch of you, I hope." Tom laid the courgette on the side and, ensuring the twins wouldn't be able to see him, stroked his fingertip down the vegetable's length. He heard Alex's breath hitch as he watched, a thrill running through him as a faint flush of desire colored the prime minister's throat.

"All of me," he whispered.

All of him.

"Finished!" Madeleine called from the kitchen table.

And just like that, in a wonderful whirlwind of childish enthusiasm, the stolen moment was over. Not that it mattered, because all of this was part and parcel of the family that had welcomed Tom with open arms. As the children ate their desserts, Tom and Alex dined on stir-fry, as normal as any other family. As normal as Tom's childhood had never been.

Bedtime followed bathtime as it always did, and Tom and Alex were left in the quiet flat.

"Drink?" Tom asked.

"Go and relax, let me?" Alex touched his hand. "You're allowed to sit down once in a while."

"If you insist." Tom wandered over to the sofa and flopped against the cushions. "I like being looked after."

"I've probably not done enough of it in the last three years, it's been... There's been a lot to process, as they say." Alex leaned over the back of the sofa and passed Tom a glass of white wine. "And I need to make a decision soon about another term."

"I'm here to look after you, though — don't feel bad." Tom took a sip of the cool wine. "Yeah — Jenny was inquiring about that when they collected the twins. *Have* you decided? But I don't expect you to tell me yet!"

Alex settled on the sofa beside him. "You'll be one of the first to know, but right now I'm still turning it all over. I want to do the right thing for the family but I don't want the public to say, *is that it?* But at the same time, I don't want to end up five years from now with people saying, *he should've gone years ago.* In some ways, I wish I'd never got the bloody job in the first place. I didn't count on Gill's cancer coming back or losing her so quickly... And I worry about the press picking your life apart if — *when* — we become public knowledge."

If.

"Better to leave on a high, I reckon," Tom said. "You don't want to get forced out by your own party, surely? And as far as I'm concerned, honestly, the press don't bother me. What do I have to hide? Captain Southwell, remember — I've got medals." Surely that would make up for Tom's less-than-illustrious start in life.

"It's easy to say that if they're not pointing a telephoto lens at you when you're standing at your wife's graveside with two babies." Alex took his hand. But Tom had been there with him. He'd lived through it and together they'd prevailed. "They'll take your life apart piece by piece looking for something to splash across the front pages, and I'm terrified that you'll end up blaming me. And resenting me."

"Why would I blame you? You're not a newspaper editor. It's ridiculous, some of the gossip they think passes for news. We've had all that manny nonsense, but that died down once they'd got bored of it." Tom squeezed Alex's hand. "I wouldn't blame you, that's all."

"I know you'll try not to but..." He put down his glass and took Tom's face in his hands, studying him. "How can you be sure?"

"Because..." Tom wanted to say it. *I love you.* But nothing happened when he tried to speak, until he asked, "What did Jenny say to you?"

Alex looked away on the pretense of picking up his glass, but it told Tom enough. Whatever she'd said, it'd had an impact. "Just mother-in-law stuff, you know how she is sometimes."

"Warning you off me, was she?" Tom couldn't help the brittleness in his tone.

"Tom, don't," Alex warned. "Please, darling—"

"*Are* we a thing, Alex? A couple?"

Alex gazed at him, saying nothing. After a few seconds he murmured, "I want us to be, I really do."

"But let me guess, *Nana says no*?" Tom was aware that he was starting to sound like a brat, but after that argument with Stuart earlier, it seemed as if what he wanted counted for nothing.

"Nobody's said— She's worried, Tom, that's all." Yet, since the children had returned, Alex had barely touched him, sweet text messages or no. "I told you that I might need a bit of time, how has that suddenly become a problem?"

"I'm trying, all right? But it's—you're denying yourself. Don't you want pleasure?" Tom covered his face with his hands. "You touch me, but you won't let me touch you. I'm trying to understand, Alex, but...I start to wonder if you really want this. If you want *me*."

"So *take all the time you need* translates as, *as long as that isn't more than three days*?" Alex's tone was sharp, but he put his hand on Tom's knee. Of course he did, because he wouldn't want Tom's hand on his, would he? What would people say? "I do want this, but — Tom, try to understand?"

"I'm trying my best, but one minute you've got your hand around my cock, the next —" Desolate, Tom stared down at Alex's hand. "Are you scared, is that it? Being touched by a man? I don't know — maybe you regret what happened and you don't know how to say so. And I feel like…like you don't want me. It's okay — we can stop. Just…stop."

"I'm scared." He shook his head. "I don't want to stop, but — I've spent years telling myself I'm straight. I've never been touched by a man, Tom. I haven't even kissed a man since uni. So — yes, okay, I'm scared, and I know it's pathetic."

Tom took Alex's hand. "It's not pathetic. I just — I don't want you to torture yourself over it. You've got such a beautiful body, and aside from that — you deserve to feel good. Everyone does. I just wish there was something I could do to help you. I don't want to see you struggle."

"I don't want to hurt you." Alex stroked his face. "I care about you so much, I — Look, I ought to go and do a bit more in the office. I've got the visit up north after Cabinet tomorrow, it's going to be a long day."

Tom gently touched Alex's hair. "I care about you, too. And I want you to be happy, Alex. Really, I do."

"I *do* care." He kissed Tom's hand. "And I promise you that I'll do better than this. But if you want to give up on me… I'd still think the world of you, but I'd understand."

Tom's hand rushed to his chest. It hurt to think of abandoning Alex. He couldn't do it. "No — no, I don't want to give up on you. You've got so much on your plate right now — you don't need this too. Would you like a hug?"

Alex nodded. "I could do with one."

Tom hung his arms around Alex's neck and rested his head on his shoulder. He closed his eyes, the scent of Alex's cologne comforting and familiar as he hugged him.

"I'll do better," Alex promised again. "Don't worry."

Chapter Seventeen

The twins were slowly waking up as they ate their breakfast. Madeleine was trying to show Alex the plastic figure that had fallen out of the cereal box.

"Daddy, look—is it a frog? Als says it's a rabbit."

Alex was rifling through the contents of his red box and barely glanced up when he said, "It's a frog." Then Tom saw the precise moment when Alex caught himself, the dismay in his eyes at the knowledge that he had dismissed his daughter's question. He put the papers down and asked, "Show me, Mads? Sorry, darling."

She leaned over the table and passed him the cheap little piece of plastic that had so enchanted her and her brother.

"Daddy?" she asked hopefully.

"Hmm." He made a show of considering it, as though it was an exotic new discovery from a strange land. "I think… I've heard of it but I've never seen it, I don't know for sure."

"What?" Alastair was enthralled, gazing at his father.

"This," Alex lowered his voice and leaned forward to impart his secret, "is a Madastair. I thought they only existed in legends, I never thought I'd see one."

"Really?" Madeleine said in a hushed whisper. "Where do they live? In cornflakes?"

"Only in our cornflakes," he whispered. "Tom introduced me to them, we're very lucky to see one."

"They're very shy creatures," Tom added. He crept over to the kitchen table and crouched down. "But very friendly if you're kind to them."

Alastair asked, "Do they just need a bit of time?"

"Yes, that's right," Tom told him. He glanced at Alex. "Sometimes not long at all, and sometimes a very long time, but in the end, they'll be friendly."

Alex said nothing. Instead he was gazing at Tom, his eyes filled with undisguised affection. Then he closed the heavy lid of the ministerial box and cleared his throat.

"Right, monsters, I won't be back for tea tonight, but even if you don't see me before you fall asleep, I'll come in and say night night when I get home." He kissed first Alastair then Madeleine. "Look after your new Madastair, won't you? And each other and Tom and Billy, and you can tell me everything I've missed at breakfast in the morning. Be very good and remember that I love you *stupidly*."

"Bye-bye, Daddy." Madeleine waved the Madastair at him. "We'll look after it! I love you, Daddy."

"Love you." Alastair beamed. "We'll all look after each other."

"That's the Hart spirit." He pulled the jacket of his dark blue suit on and put his hand on Tom's shoulder. "I'll see you in the morning, Tom?"

Tom patted his arm. And tried not to think of how he had rhapsodized about Alex's arms to his ex. "See you tomorrow. Good luck."

Alex let his hand linger then hoisted the battered red box from the table and left the kitchen. As he went, Alastair blinked up at Tom and asked, "What's more fun? Looking after us or being a soldier?"

"Looking after you." Tom smiled as he ruffled Alastair's hair. But how long he would continue to, Tom couldn't say.

Had Tom ruined everything last night? But he had had to say something. He didn't want to lose Alex, but at the same time his no-touching rule wasn't something Tom could easily understand. Perhaps he'd let Stuart bother him too much and that hurt had spilled over into his conversation with Alex.

Bloody Stuart.

And what would Tom do if he lost his job? Maybe there'd be other families willing to take him on as their manny, but would it be the same as it was with the Harts? He wasn't sure he could bear it. It was bad enough dropping the twins off at school for a few hours, but the thought of never seeing them again felt like a punch in the gut.

And Gill had handpicked him to care for her family. Before they were even born he'd been at her side, their friendship growing with every passing day. And she had asked him to care for them all when she was gone.

Tom didn't want to go back to the flat once the children had run through the gates and joined their playmates, so he busied himself shopping, carrying out his familiar duties with a new weight in his heart. He didn't even notice he had a text until he was on the way home, his little car filled with groceries and the radio turned up loud. But Alex was in Cabinet— it wouldn't be from him. It could wait until later.

Tom tidied away the shopping and decided to have a good rummage through the cupboards and make them as tidy as possible. He could sort the kitchen out easily, even if his life was more difficult.

Just as he was about to leave to collect the twins, Tom looked at his phone. And there it was, the text he'd left. It was from Stuart.

fancy coming out? X

Tom nearly threw down his phone but decided to reply. Short and to the point.

No thanks. T

A moment later the reply landed.

What about the boss,,, Whens HE coming out?

Did he really think Alex would be booking a yoga lesson with him? Was he as deluded as all that? Even if Alex didn't know a fraction of what Stuart had been up to, getting into Lycra and bending into unfeasible positions was about as far from his style as it was possible to get.

Not his thing. T

He didn't want Stuart to reply, but a second later he did.

Yea well we'll c x

Tom stared at his phone. He wasn't going to reply again. In fact, he was tempted to block Stuart's number completely. Stuart didn't deserve another moment of his time, not when Madeleine and Alastair were waiting for him. They mattered, *StuDo* didn't. Not anymore.

Once the twins were home again, Tom felt better. This was his job—and today it meant feeding lunch to children who were more interested in a plastic toy that had come with their cornflakes than eating sandwiches. Once they got down from the table, Tom's mobile rang. He had half a mind to ignore it, because if it was Stuart he might explode, but instead a different name flashed up on the screen. Mandy, the party's director of communications.

Tom answered. "Hi, Mandy, have you got the wrong number?"

"Not if this is Tom," she barked in her Guide Leader's tones. "And this is Tom, yes?"

"The very same." Why had she rung? The non-story based on the photo of Tom and Alex getting into a car on Friday—which seemed a long time ago now—had dropped like a stone. "Erm…my footwear isn't causing grief again, is it?"

"Not this time! Look, I know you keep out of party and political business, but a little bird whispered the word *burlesque* in my ear this weekend. Fancy a coffee later, Tom?"

"Yeah, if you like. Do you want to pop round? The twins are playing and they've got cartoons on — can't really leave but..." *Burlesque*? Jesus, was someone going to make a big deal about a man spinning pasties?

"Good stuff, Tom," she replied. She was apparently terrifying in full hairdryer mode, but even being friendly there was something about Mandy that said, *Don't cross me.* "I'll be there in ten minutes."

Christ, I'm glad I tidied the cupboards.

Even so, Tom dashed through the already immaculate flat, straightening duvets, closing wardrobe doors and lobbing toys into toy boxes. Then, as he wiped the twins' faces with a warm flannel, he heard a knock at the door.

"Right, Mandy's here." Tom grabbed the remote control and turned the volume of the television up just a little. Then he opened the door.

He knew Mandy Barker, of course — everyone did. And she was reputed to know everything about everyone who even came close to the government. Not that Alex made use of her supposed *dark arts,* — that wasn't his style — but her press contacts were second to none and they were more important than any outdated spin doctoring could ever be. She had once teased Alex for being *'too honest for two terms'.* It would be a sad indictment if she was right.

"Hello, Tom." She extended one perfectly manicured hand, the subtle silver tennis bracelet on her wrist glinting in the light. Mandy was a towering figure, from the pointed tips of her shoes to her glossy chignon, and Tom always wondered if there was a girl's school somewhere missing its headmistress. Or a women's prison missing its governor. "Sorry to call round when Alex is on the road, but needs must. How're you? How're the little ones? All good?"

"Yeah, we're all fine," Tom said lightly. *Fine – just messing up my life and everyone else's.*

Tom gestured toward the twins then pointed toward the kitchen.

"Shall we? Little ears might waggle," he whispered. Mandy nodded. She followed him past the sitting room where the children were happily completing a jigsaw with their *Madastair* and into the kitchen. There she sat at the table, her hands knitted before her, trying and failing to look like this was a social call.

"Tea or coffee?" Tom asked, clinging to the hope that this wasn't bad news. But what else could it be?

"Just hot water," she told him. "Don't look so frightened, Tom, I'm not here to attach electrodes to your extremities. I just want to get a feel for things in general since your name came across my desk this week. I know Alex doesn't like to mix domestic with business, but when it hits my blotter, it *becomes* business."

Visions of Tom's controversial trainers swam before his eyes. "Right...well..." Tom started to make Mandy her drink. "So you said on the phone this has something to do with burlesque?"

She nodded. "I've had a chat with Alex and he assured me it was nothing but a bit of a boys' night out. Is that right?"

Tom's mouth went dry. He was on the spot. "Yeah — we went to a cabaret in Soho. Had dinner. They have singers, performers. One of the acts was *boylesque* – stripped off his suit jacket and his shirt, and he had pasties underneath and he was twirling them and — We just fancied a night out, that's all."

"I've seen the show. So have a lot of journalists. Some of them were there on Friday night and I know you tried your best to keep a profile as low as a team on the arse end of league two, but these hacks know a government car when they see it. And they know the PM and his *manny* too, especially when they suddenly pop up out of nowhere and head for their tax-funded Uber." Mandy accepted the mug of hot water from Tom and took a sip.

The knowledge that she'd seen the show lifted Tom's anxiety, because at least she wouldn't have any visions of seedy joints and dirty raincoats. Instead she'd know it was as glossy as entertainment got, from its high-kicking chorus to the singers and specialty numbers. There was a reason every single London guide said that Colette's cabaret night was the hottest ticket in town.

"Nobody knows Alex as well as you, Tom," Mandy went on. "So was this a one-off or am I going to have to keep a lid on him heading off down the social every Friday night to watch oiled-up lads whipping their tops off? Mind you, not sure what social that'd be, but it'd make a killing in Westminster."

"Oiled-up lads? He's not going on a hen night." Tom picked at the cuffs of his hoodie. He was an idiot to have ever thought he and Alex could have had a relationship that ran deeper than what they'd shared for years. An image intruded on his thoughts of a garish headline — *PM BEDS MANNY*. It wasn't fair. "Look — he's so busy at the moment, I hardly think going on the razz is going to become a weekly thing for him. I hoped that if he socialized a bit, it might help him find a new partner."

And he had — for a couple of days, at least.

"A girlfriend? With election year looming?" She grimaced as if he'd just passed her a raw kipper. Then she laughed. "Not on my watch. You know how the public are — I'm not running an election with one hand and trying to delete pictures of some lass in a bikini with the other. When the election's done and he's got his second term, then...*maybe* we can think about his sex life. Until then I want him pushing his kids on the swings and eating carvery on a Sunday. Last thing we want is our blue-eyed boy losing the girls and gays because he's hooked up with a lass better-looking than they are. No offense with the gay stuff, Tom, you know I speak as I find."

Tom folded his arms. "Well, at least a lonely prime minister will win the pity vote." *Poor bastard.* "And I suppose you want me and my trainers to do our best to keep out of the media?"

"Look, the kids love you and so does Alex." She took another sip. "But next time he has one of these brainiac schemes, suggest more *family pub* and less *Moulin Rouge*? And run it past me first, all right? He didn't put it on expenses, did he?"

"Of course not." Tom clenched his teeth. *No, because Alex isn't a morally bankrupt arse.* "We'll take the twins down the Beefeater next time he has a space in his diary. Or maybe a Greggs café. Not much chance of a topless man there."

"Don't give me that face," Mandy warned. "And don't let anybody hear your talking Greggs down, it's stuff like that that gets people thinking, *Oh, that Alex, he thinks he's above a festive bake and a cheap cappuccino.* Greggs voters pay your salary and keep you in hundred-quid trainers."

"They do sell pasties, though." Tom shrugged. "Heaven forbid Alex goes in there and buys some, but I bet there'll be a reporter who tries to claim the pasties are of the tasseled rather than the Cornish variety."

She sat impassive then said, "Picture this then, splashed across every website, every paper, every sneering gob in every pub that hasn't closed down — *Prime Minister watches male stripper. But it's art*, I'll tell them. *His kids were with their gramps, it's burlesque.* Bollocks." She motioned with her hands as though knocking a nail in with a hammer. "*Prime. Minister. Watches. Stripper.* That's what they'll write on his coffin nails when they kick him out of Downing Street. Nobody wants that on their Wikipedia page. He's whiter than white, even the littlest stain's going to jump out. I can sell shit to shit shovelers, but the merry widower and the male stripper? All those lasses who go daft at his blue eyes aren't putting a cross in that box."

Tom rolled his eyes. "Alex was talking about moving into a monastery for the duration. And I've volunteered to go about barefoot. The kids have also promised faithfully to keep their toys tidy and to be as average as possible at preschool."

"Jesus, son, are you not getting it? The kids excel but they do it quietly, and you and Alex, you get no credit. You're Milli Vanilli, if you weren't too young to get the reference. The kids excel because this government's education policies are the second coming, and that's the message we ram up the opposition's pucker every time the twins come home with a gold star." She put her empty cup down on the tabletop. "While you live here, you don't get any credit, you don't get holidays that Mr. Average in Rotherham can't afford, and you don't watch strippers in cocktail bars. All of that helps me to help you, and keeps every rag from the *Sun* to the *Guardian* bashing Alex's metaphorical tambourine. And that means at least five more years."

Tom sighed. "It's a bloody boring way to have to live for another five years, though, isn't it?"

All Tom could see was his bed, and only himself in it. And Alex sleeping alone, torturing himself for his perfectly natural desires because of what complete strangers may or may not think of him.

"It's not boring, it's power. It's the game." Mandy rose to her feet. "Once he's safely got another five years, I'll have a think about a girlfriend. See if we know anyone who won't get the public's back up. Home baking and a nice little job rather than some Insta bint pulling her bikini out of her arse in Dubai. We can ease her in gently, get them used to her. People liked Gill, she was go-getting, plucky, never fazed even when she knew her card was marked. We've had Evita, now we want Delia Smith. She's a cook, Tom, before your time."

"Should this mythical girlfriend also be a big fan of Norwich City, though?" Tom raised an eyebrow. "Well, maybe after the election I'll hand round some fliers at the twins' preschool — I'm sure the yummy mummies will know the ideal woman. Like Nigella, but not as sexy?"

"Nothing like Nigella. We don't want rich dads, bad break-ups or any of that." As she crossed the kitchen she added with a grin, "And wash your fucking mouth out. Norwich City are dead to me. I'm relying on you, Tom. Keep our blue-eyed boy's eyes on the prize. Get the election called, get it won, and see where we go from there."

Tom went to the hallway and opened the front door for Mandy. "Yeah, he doesn't really need a girlfriend or a wife, does he, seeing as he's got me knocking about at number 11?"

She smiled again. "Now you're getting it. Give the kids a hug from me."

"Will do." *And I'll hug Alex, too, if he'll let me.*

* * * *

That evening, at the twins' request, Tom read a story about an astronaut on a long journey far from home. It took a while for them to drop off, but Tom promised them they'd see their daddy in the morning, and that seemed to soothe them.

Tom pottered around the flat until he felt tired, Mandy's visit uppermost in his mind. Any romantic relationship with Alex was going to be impossible. He knew that, and he busied himself with pointless tasks, trying to quiet the racket in his mind.

He read in bed until he fell asleep, then at some point in the night, he was aware of his bedroom door opening.

Small feet padded over the carpet toward him.

"Tom, we're awake," Madeleine informed him.

Tom sat up and rubbed his eyes. There beside the bed were Madeleine and Alastair, one with her ragdoll, the other with his toy duck, and tucked into the pocket of the little boy's pajama top was the Madastair.

"When's Daddy coming home?" Alastair asked, rubbing his eyes with his little fists. "Soon?"

Tom pushed himself up and switched on his bedside lamp. It was just after midnight on his alarm clock.

"He said he'd be late back. You'll see him in the morning." Tom turned back his duvet. "Come on, let's get you back to bed."

"There's monsters under the bed," Madeleine told him. "The Madastair said so."

Alastair nodded. "He says he'll keep them away but then he'll be too tired to play, so can we sleep in your bed tonight?"

"Well..." Tom knew that if he tried to get them to sleep in their own beds, none of them would get much sleep. Even if he did his best parade-ground bark at the monsters — because that only made the children laugh, and demand repeat performances. "Come on, then."

Tom lifted them into the bed and let the twins curl up on either side of him. "Mini-Harts in position? Ready for me to turn off the light?"

The twins pecked Tom on the cheek, a clear sign that they were happy. Just in case there was any doubt, Alastair informed them, "The Madastair says yes as well."

"Good! One, two, three—" And as the children joined Tom pretending they were blowing out an enormous birthday cake candle, Tom turned off the light.

Chapter Eighteen

Tom woke up to see the Madastair dancing a jig on his chest, operated by a small hand.

"Morning," Tom said, his mouth limp with sleep. When he tried to sit up, he was aware of a weight at the foot of the bed. Warm affection washed through Tom when he realized that there, lying across the bottom of the bed, was Alex. He was cuddled beneath Tom's duvet, his eyes closed and his expression serene. On the table beside the bed was the familiar vintage watch that Alex always wore, resting atop Tom's book.

"Shhh." Alastair pressed his finger to Tom's lips and whispered, "Daddy's asleep."

"Daddy!" Madeleine said excitedly, then clamped her hand over her mouth.

Tom glanced at the clock. It was time to get up. And who knew what time Alex had arrived home.

In a whisper, he said, "Let's go and have breakfast, as quiet as mice!"

"And the Madastair can stay here and look after daddy." Alastair put the little toy next to Alex's watch. "Breakfast time."

Tom brushed his fingertip over the watch's face, then herded the children to breakfast.

Once in the kitchen, Madeleine wanted to go back to Tom's room, keen to find out if the Madastair was looking after her father well enough.

Tom lifted her back onto her chair. "No disturbing Daddy — he'll be up soon."

The twins seemed to understand that quiet was the order of the day and their cheery conversations were in whispers, every dip of a spoon into a bowl of cereal done with exaggerated care and precision. When Billy wandered in and greeted the gathering with a gentle *miaow*, even she was shushed for her troubles. Not that it bothered her, of course, and she repeated her greeting before going to her bowl.

Amid the silence, as the children were spooning the last dregs of cereal from their bowls, Tom heard bare feet in the hallway. Despite himself, despite Mandy, his heart leaped in the moment before Alex ambled into the kitchen, bleary-eyed in his T-shirt and pajama trousers.

I wish I could hold you.

Tom smiled at him. "Morning. You look like you could do with a cuppa!"

"Daddy!" In her haste, Madeleine couldn't manage to get down from her chair, her legs apparently in a tangle. Luckily her father swept in, kissing her cheek before pecking at Alastair's too. He put the little figure on the table in front of them.

"Madastair told me it was breakfast time." Alex smiled. Then he lifted his gaze to Tom. "Sorry for crashing your bed last night. You all looked too snuggly, I didn't want to slope off on my own."

"It doesn't matter—I gatecrashed yours too, after all." *And what would Mandy make of that?* Tom grinned. "I'll get you your breakfast—take a seat. What time did you get in last night?"

Alex shook his head and admitted, "I stopped checking the time when it got to two. And PMQs today, just what you need after a late night!"

"I'll make your tea strong." Tom patted Alex's arm. Half his biceps was visible under the short sleeve of his T-shirt. Not that Tom was looking, of course.

"Do you know what I'm going to make for me and you?" Alex said it as though it was going to be a feast, something fit for an emperor. "Bacon sarnies. Fancy it?"

"Yeah!" Tom laughed. He hadn't expected Alex to offer to cook him breakfast. "Are you absolutely sure, though? You don't want to get a few minutes' extra kip?"

He shook his head and said, "Sleep or see the family before PMQs? No contest. Are you okay to marshal the troops while I do the extremely intricate and difficult cooking?"

"Yep—kids, bathroom!" Tom clapped his hands. "I want those teeth sparkling, Troopers!"

"Yes, sir!" the twins chorused as they climbed down from their seats. Once again the prized toy was in Alastair's pajama pocket, as precious as a jewel.

Alex watched them go as he opened the fridge door, then told Tom, "I meant what I said, Tom. I'll do better for you."

Mandy's words beat against Tom's brain like a remorseless rising tide. "You're a busy man—you don't have to apologize to me. Honest."

"They don't have a mum and the last thing I need to be doing as their dad is missing their bedtimes and— Yesterday, when Mads showed me that toy, I brushed her off, and that was something I swore I'd never do. You all deserve better than that."

Somehow, Tom managed to say around the lump in his throat, "I wish more parents were like you."

"No job's worth missing my kids growing up." He reached into the fridge, its contents sorted with Tom's usual military precision. "Have you got any plans for tonight?"

Tom shook his head. "Have you?"

"PMQs and Buckingham Palace when I didn't get into bed until past two is more than enough for one day." From the bathroom, the children called Tom's name and Alex glanced toward the door. "I'm going to be home by six. I'm not missing supper and bedtime twice."

"Followed by an early night—I mean, you'll be half asleep by the time you get home." And Tom took that awkward moment to hurry to the bathroom and wipe an enormous blob of toothpaste from Alastair's forehead. As he helped the children wash and dress he could hear Alex arguing with the *Today Programme* in the kitchen and smell the aroma of bacon cooking. Mandy *had* to be wrong. At its heart, there was nothing different about this family. She couldn't get when and who Alex had a relationship with— Maybe she could. Anything could happen in Westminster, after all.

Tom returned to the kitchen with the twins dressed and ready. There on the table was a fat bacon sandwich, made with thick slices of brown bread, and Alex stood beside the oven looking as proud as a man who'd just won a gold medal.

Tom sat down at the table while the twins crouched down to show the Madastair to Billy. "You should cook breakfast more often!"

"Sauce?"

"*Lots*," Tom replied with a wink.

Alex bought the bottle to the table and said, "That's what I like to hear."

Tom touched the back of Alex's hand, trying to bridge the gap between them. "Thank you. This looks great."

He sat down at the table with his own plate, taking the same seat which had become Mandy's imperial throne. "You don't let us look after you enough. So if I have to cook bacon to do it, I will. And even *I* can't get bacon wrong!"

Tom added a dollop of sauce to his sandwich and took a large bite. "Mmm!" And it *was* very good. But perhaps the best thing about it wasn't the soft bread or that the bacon had been done to a turn – it was because Alex, tired, overworked Alex, had wanted to make it for him.

"I might chuck an egg on it next time – I'm getting ambitious!" As Alex was speaking, he held out his sandwich, letting each of the twins take a bite.

Madeleine patted her stomach in a big circle, then held the Madastair toward the sandwich for a nibble. Alex, it seemed, had discovered a talent for bacon.

"Tonight," he announced, as the little toy monopolized his sandwich, "I'll be here for supper. And I want to hear all about our Madastair's adventures, monsters, but can I have my breakfast back?"

"He's finished now," Madeleine assured him, and passed the plastic figure to her brother. They played merrily as Tom and Alex dined, then swarmed around attempting to help their father load the dishwasher, but the morning couldn't wait forever and eventually Alex went off to shower and dress, ready to face the loathed circus of Prime Minister's Questions.

Chapter Nineteen

Tom put BBC Parliament on while he got the twins' lunch ready. His heart leaped as he saw Alex at the despatch box, but Tom wondered if everyone else watching could tell that Alex was tired. His rebuttals weren't quite so swift, his mastery of the minutiae a little labored and he was leaning on the despatch box not with his usual easy aplomb, but as though it was the only thing stopping him from falling. For the first time in four years of the circus, he wasn't the ringmaster.

Had something happened yesterday on his trip to the north?

But Tom couldn't imagine it was that—Alex had undertaken all manner of trips around the country—and much farther afield—during his time in office, and with little sleep had still ruled at the despatch box.

Tom caught sight of his own reflection in the chrome front of the fridge and recoiled.

It's my fault.

Because that was all that was different—Tom had kissed the man's neck. And he'd tied him in knots and forced him to confront his sexuality, and before them was a relationship that wouldn't work in a million years.

What the hell have I done? The Madastair sat on the table where the twins had left it for safekeeping, telling Tom that it'd keep an eye on him until they came home. He heard the opposition jeering from the television speaker, sneering at Alex, and he thought of Mandy's cold ambition and the twins and the toy and everything he stood to lose.

Because he'd ruined it all.

Alex, the consummate statesman, looked as if hadn't even brushed his hair that morning.

How had Tom ever thought this could work, this job? Stuart was right, it was a ridiculous job for a former soldier. And besides that, Tom was doing well following in his parents' footsteps. *Mess everyone else's lives up, because you're too selfish to see beyond the end of your nose.* He should have run a mile from the job—he wasn't up to it.

Seducing his boss. That's what he'd done, wasn't it? And he'd destroyed the man.

The consummate Southwell.

"An uncharacteristically subdued Alex Hart off to lick his wounds after that bruising encounter," the studio pundit said as the jeers from the Chamber died away. No, he didn't say it. He positively crowed it. "And by this time next week, he'll know if his cherished Child Poverty Action Bill has been approved by Commons. It should be a formality, but as we've just seen, anything can happen in the House of Commons."

All those children who went to bed hungry — and still would. And it was all Tom's fault.

Can't trust a Southwell.

Tom picked up the Madastair and turned it and turned it in the light by the window. He sniffed back a tear. Where on earth would he go from here?

He thought about Alex in his office even now, knowing that he'd been bested, tormented by the knowledge that in the last PMQs before his bill went to the vote, he hadn't had all the facts. In a decent world nobody would have any reason to cast their vote against it, but this wasn't the real world — it was the Palace of Westminster, a place where power-brokering and ambition could come ahead of even the welfare of children. There were people who didn't want reform, people who liked the status quo, and Alex had just exposed a dangerous chink in his armor to them.

Because of Captain Tom Southwell.

Chapter Twenty

Tom went through the afternoon in a daze. The twins ran around the flat, showing the Madastair every inch of the place. He should have been charmed at how they could find hours of entertainment in something so simple, but, after all, Alex had imbued it with magic.

And Tom had done an excellent job of destroying it.

As six o'clock arrived, Tom wondered what on earth he'd say to Alex. Surely he wouldn't want to be reminded of his disastrous PMQs. But didn't Tom owe it to him to say *something?*

This time the sound of the door opening didn't leave Tom breathless with anticipation, but filled with apprehension. Even though Alex didn't call out his usual greeting, the children flew off to meet him. He heard Alex's cheery salutation, his tone tired even as it sounded full of happiness to see them.

"Evening, Alex!" Tom called, trying his best to sound upbeat.

"Evening, Tom," Alex said as he carried the twins into the kitchen. "I'm getting too old for these late nights!"

"Me too!" Tom laughed, his mirth forced. "Tea or wine?"

"Tea, I think. I'll brew."

"Tea with tea." Alastair laughed. "Daddy's home for tea!"

"Lots and lots of tea!" Madeleine sang, punching the air.

"Are you sure, Alex?" Tom felt Alex's exhaustion draining his own reserves of energy. "Do you want to chill in the bath or something?"

He shook his head. "Can I do anything to help with dinner?"

"It's all in the oven, so you don't need to worry. Lasagne and a nice big heap of ciabatta."

"Maybe I will grab a very quick bath. How long have I got?"

"Half an hour." If Tom hadn't been so distracted with his own woes, he would've had the dinner ready earlier. *Failing once again.* It should've been ready close to six. "Time for a quick bath, I'd say."

"Bath and pajamas," Alastair said as he scrambled down from his father's arms. "Then tea."

And Alex seemed to agree, because twenty-five minutes after he had left the kitchen, he returned. Tom was ready to serve up and saw at once that Alex looked at least a little more refreshed. His hair was wet, his feet bare and he wore a pair of black pajama trousers and a bright blue T-shirt. The prime minister, it seemed, was home for the evening.

"You look more relaxed," Tom said. He pulled out a chair for Alex at the table. "Come on, sit down."

Tom would've offered him another shoulder rub, but as he knew only too well, it would only lead to disaster.

Instead he stuck to the safe topic of food and together the Harts and Tom dined royally, as though everything was normal. And to the children, Tom hoped, it would be. Their father was here, and that was all that should matter.

The twins sat either side of Alex, leaning against him, their eyes getting heavier and heavier as dinner went on. They had been awake in the middle of the night, after all, so Tom wasn't surprised. Bathtime wasn't as raucous as it sometimes was, and all too soon they were tucked up in bed.

Tonight there wasn't even a story, just two little people snuggled beneath their duvets, fast asleep before their heads had a chance to hit the pillow.

Now the night would be more strained than ever. Because now there was only Tom and Alex.

Tom poured them each a glass of wine. He couldn't bear the awkwardness a moment longer and said, "Alex, you don't seem yourself."

"We need to talk."

Tom's stomach knotted and he glanced away. "I know we do," he said, his voice quiet.

For a long moment Alex simply looked at him, and Tom waited, readying himself for the heartbreak that was about to follow. He hadn't expected his life with the Harts to end this way, so quickly and painfully.

And I deserve it.

But Alex didn't pull the trigger. Instead he reached out and caressed Tom's cheek with the pad of his thumb. Then he took a step forward and kissed Tom's lips, the touch soft as gossamer.

The kiss took Tom by surprise and he blinked at Alex. "Are you sure? We can't, Alex. We *can't*."

Because if he tried to touch Alex, he knew what would happen. And what if it never stopped happening? That wasn't a relationship.

"Don't you want—? Oh God, Tom, I'm sorry." Alex took a long drink from his glass. "The last thing you want is me lunging at you, isn't it?"

He couldn't be further from the truth.

Tom stroked Alex's arm, down to his wrist, and took his hand. "There's nothing I'd want more than you lunging at me, but...you wanted us to talk. Alex, are you okay? I watched PMQs—I'm sure you don't want to discuss it, but you didn't seem yourself."

"That was a bloody mess." Their hands linked, Alex led Tom to the sofa. When they were sitting he looked down at their entwined fingers and said, "I feel as though everybody wants a piece of me, Tom. Jenny thinks I'm trying to forget Gill, I'm asked half a dozen times a day when the election's going to be and what my plans are, and when I saw Mandy the other day, she as good as told me that my life belongs to the party until they decide otherwise. I'm ready for recess, because I need a break. Even if all I'm allowed is a week on the coast."

"She came to see me yesterday. I didn't want to bother you about it, but we're in trouble for going out the other night." Tom brought their joined hands to his cheek. "She said you're not even allowed a girlfriend until the election's over—Christ knows what she'd think if she knew we...we had..." *Whatever the heck it was.*

"She came *here*?" There was a hint of steel in his expression, a fight that hadn't been there in the

Chamber earlier. "She's crossed a line. My family—my private life—that's all off limits. I'm genuinely that stupid idealist who wanted to make a difference and all around me is ambition. They lose sight of what matters, they'll do anything for five more bloody years."

"Yeah... She rang me and the kids were back from preschool, so I said she could pop round. She sat there drinking a cup of hot water and pretty much told me off. For even existing, I think." Tom shrugged. "But after that, I could see why this—us—is so difficult for you. I don't know what we can do."

"We can do whatever we like. We're grown men. People like Mandy, they're out for themselves. She'll always rise to the top." He took a deep breath. "I want *us*, Tom."

"You—you do?" Tom stroked Alex's cheek. "I do too. And I thought I'd blown it."

"But I owe you an explanation, because how can I sit here and say *I want you* when I won't let you lay a finger on me?" Alex lifted Tom's hand and kissed it. "There's no big secret, no terrible revelation...there's just me. You've always been so honest about your sexuality, Tom, I didn't even know if it was okay to tell a gay man, *I'm bisexual.* Is it okay? Am I doing it wrong?"

"It's how you feel, isn't it? I'm not going to tell you to *pick a side*, or say you're confused, or any of that nonsense." Tom moved nearer and slipped his arm around Alex's shoulders. "If you fancy men *and* women, then it's fine by me. In fact, I'm pretty glad you do!"

"I've never done more than kiss a man," he admitted with a smile. "And I suppose I'm lucky that the few I did kiss haven't sold their stories. But I don't think that's the sort of thing High Court judges do, is it?"

Tom chuckled. "It was the gown and the wig, wasn't it? You couldn't resist!" He stroked Alex's back. "I wouldn't have known, by the way. You have a good *grasp* of what to do."

"I suppose I've got a bit of inside knowledge, since I'm a bloke." Alex shrugged, his smile mischievous. "And the judge and I were both twenty-one at the time, in case you were wondering. But when I met Gill, I knew she was the one I had to be with. And I never told her, and it's ridiculous, but now I feel as though I should have, as though I misled her."

"You adored her, Alex. You didn't mislead her. She knew you loved her — that's the most important thing." And perhaps, Tom wondered, the fact that Gill hadn't known was one of the biggest blocks in Alex's path. "You were happy with her, you weren't looking elsewhere. It didn't matter that you find men attractive too — I'm sure you weren't the least bothered about men while you were with her, right?"

"I wasn't bothered about anybody but Gill while I was with her. She was everything to me."

"There — so you didn't mislead her, did you? And do you know what, if she had known, I'm sure she wouldn't have minded at all. She loved every bit of you. Even the bits she didn't know." Tom smiled. "And you never know, maybe she even had an inkling but never said?"

"Maybe," he murmured thoughtfully. "When she was ill, she was so focused on us, on keeping her family together — and you were always part of that, you know. She thought the world of you, because you didn't look at her with the *sad sympathy face* that used to drive her up the wall. But you were just like me, she was Gill to you, not her illness."

"Yeah, she was *my friend Gill.*" Tom sighed. "I don't know how Jenny can think that you're trying to forget Gill. You never could, and neither could I."

"If we're going to make a go of this, Jenny and Malcolm and Mum and Dad need to know that nothing's going to change. That's my job, I know that." He kissed Tom's hand again, as though he couldn't quite believe he was real. "But I don't want you to think— I don't want you to think it's weird because you work here. Jenny was full of that employee and employer nonsense, I hadn't even thought about it until then...but I couldn't stop thinking about it afterward."

Tom looked at Alex in surprise. "I hadn't thought about that either! I don't exactly feel like your employee—your *friend,* really. Don't let that worry you for another second. If anything, I keep worrying that I took advantage of *you*—not the other way round. I hope to God I didn't. What a mess!"

"You took advantage of me? Bloody hell, Tom, that massage... I've not been able to get it out of my head!"

Tom raised an eyebrow. "Well, okay then—not so much *take advantage* as *recklessly seduce*?"

Alex opened his blue eyes wide. And they sparkled.

"I like the sound of that."

"I could always recklessly seduce you again, if you like?" Tom whispered.

"You could..." Alex slipped his arm around Tom's shoulders. "Or we could seduce each other? Recklessly, of course."

Tom leaned back against the sofa. "Each other sounds good. And what was it you were saying, about lunging at me?"

"Less of a lunge," his lover murmured, moving closer. "More a tactical lean?"

And he pressed his lips to Tom's, those gloriously fluttering fingers settling on his shoulder. Tom held him close, feeling the delicious weight of Alex against him, that sensation of Alex *having him*, of Tom yielding.

Their kiss was more passionate than Tom could've hoped — it had been days and Tom knew that Alex had been just as lost as he had been. But now they had found each other again, and Tom held Alex tight.

Alex's roamed his mouth over Tom's jaw and nuzzled his throat, filled with hunger. His hand rested on Tom's hip, and he nibbled lightly at his earlobe. When Alex spoke again, his voice was low with desire.

"Touch me."

"Oh, darling, I...where?" Tom reached between them, stroking Alex's chest. "Here?" he teased. Alex's hand closed over his and guided it lower, until their joined fingers were pressed to the heat of his erection.

"Here."

Tom closed his eyes as he caressed through the fabric of Alex's pajamas. "You're so hard, so big..." Then he gazed at Alex and whispered, "This is quite an honor — would you like me to...go inside?"

"Or would you rather we do this in bed?" Alex asked, breathless.

"Bed," Tom replied. "And I want your pajamas dangling off the lampshade."

"Yes, Captain." Alex laughed. "Can we take the wine? If we're going to be decadent, we might as well go all-in."

Tom winked at him. "Wine, nudity, and a handsome man in loose pajamas — sounds like my perfect evening."

"A handsome man?" Alex pantomimed a look of surprise. "I didn't know you had a guest over!"

"You're bloody gorgeous, Alex. And I'm not going to let you deny it." Tom rubbed the tip of his nose against Alex's. With a soft laugh Alex kissed Tom again, a sweet little peck on the lips. Then he took his hand and together, they made their way through the flat to Alex's bedroom.

And of course they forgot the wine, but with that enormous bed waiting for them, neither Alex nor Tom was in a rush to go back for it.

Between the bedroom door and the bed, Tom had managed to lose almost all his clothes, and he had started to peel Alex out of his pajamas. Tugging up the hem of Alex's T-shirt, Tom said, "Your body does things to me, Alex. I won't lie."

"It's not quite burlesque, but..." Alex took a step back and for a second Tom's heart plummeted. As Alex peeled the T-shirt higher then cast it aside, though, the jolt of anxiety disappeared with it. This time there wouldn't be any timidity, that much was clear.

Tom smoothed his palms appreciatively over Alex's firm, broad chest. His skin was so warm, and that lovely scattering of hair... Still stroking with one hand, he slid his other down to the waistband of Alex's pajamas. "Ready?"

"Ready," he said. "More than ready, I think."

Tom kissed him, slow and deep, as he slid Alex's pajamas down. He traced the revealed skin of Alex's buttocks and onward to his the top of his legs, then, gazing into Alex's eyes, stroked down his stomach. "Lie down?"

He settled back onto the pillows wordlessly, his expression tender as he watched Tom. Tom's breath hitched as he ran his gaze over Alex's body. He was exquisite in every way.

Tom slipped out of his shorts and lay down beside Alex, kissing Alex's chest as he stroked his stomach, then he brought his lips back to Alex's as he closed his hand around his erection.

"Would you like to guide me?" Tom asked. In reply Alex slipped his arm around Tom's shoulders and held him close as he entwined his fingers with Tom's around his own erection, stroking slowly.

"You feel really good," Tom murmured. "You're very big. Really good to hold."

"That night we spent together... I was so desperate for you and so mixed-up." Alex touched his forehead to Tom's. "I thought I'd wrecked it."

Tom seemed to fall into the depths of Alex's blue eyes as he gazed at him. "You didn't. And don't be shy. You have absolutely no reason to be."

"I'm going to seem very naive and clueless to you for a bit," he smiled, moving their joined hands a little faster. "But I'm very keen to learn."

Tom looked down at their hands. A frisson tingled through him at the thought of seeing Alex climax. "All you need to do is tell me what you'd like. *Anything*, Alex."

"*This*. Just you, really..." Alex admitted breathlessly. Then he kissed Tom again, *kissing him into the pillows*, as he had said bashfully just a few days ago.

Like Scarlett O'Hara.

It was as if Alex somehow knew that Tom wanted him to do it, as if he knew that Tom had tried so hard not to gaze at him and imagine just that. Had Alex daydreamed about it? Alex might be new to this, to taking a man to bed, but his intuition seemed more finely honed than some of the men who had spent years building up their repertoire. Tom was so wonderfully aware of him, of the strength of his embrace, the touch of their skin, the heat of his erection beneath their joined hands.

Against Alex's lips, Tom whispered, "I want to taste you."

"Please," Alex breathed, the word filled with desire.

Tom helped Alex roll onto his back, and he moaned as he kissed his way down Alex's body. Perhaps he should have teased, taken his time, but Tom could sense Alex's need as keenly as he could his own. He felt every tremble of Alex's body as he moved lower, and he locked his gaze with Alex's as he kissed the tip of his erection.

He saw a shudder of pleasure run through Alex's muscles and as it did, a moan slipped from his lips. It was filled with need and heat and promise, filled with everything Tom now knew that they both wanted. Alex reached down and stroked his fingers through Tom's hair, then whispered, "You're absolutely beautiful, you know."

"Not too bad yourself." And he showed Alex just how beautiful he thought him by taking him in his mouth. As Alex's hips rose to meet him, Tom saw him clutch at the bedcover, another moan escaping his lips. For a moment his head tipped back into the pillows, then he looked down at Tom, his expression caught between pleasure and wonder.

Tom didn't break their gaze as he rose and fell on Alex, tasting him, enjoying him, and knowing from every gasp that he was pleasuring him. What an honor to be in bed with this majestic man, to be trusted and held close.

Every sigh, every moan made Tom's heart pound faster, and when Alex's hand closed on his shoulder, the suggestion of contained strength sent fresh darts of excitement through him. In the pale light he could see the tensing of his lover's muscles as his climax approached, the rise and fall of his chest growing faster with every second.

Tom's heart seemed to open at that moment, affection flooding him. He held Alex's hand where it rested on his shoulder, and they were joined, their once-separated bodies at last bridged.

A shuddering gasp of Tom's name announced that Alex had reached the peak. His body bucked as his orgasm swept through him and his eyes closed in an obvious transport of pleasure. He surrendered to Tom at last, giving in to the need to *feel*.

Tom slowed, tender now where he had been carried away with lust. Then he crawled up the bed and brought Alex into his arms as he kissed him.

"It was worth it, wasn't it?" Tom asked. Alex nodded and held him tight, silent for a time, other than the sound of his breathing as it slowed from the pitch of pleasure. He clung to Tom, kisses taking the place of words.

Tom caressed Alex, a sheen of perspiration contouring his body. He was so desirable, but more than that, Tom was drawn to his strength and his tenderness. And Tom wanted to look after him, to give him love.

"Oh God," Alex whispered, touching his fingertips first to one eye then the other, as though worried he might find tears there. "That was wonderful, Tom. I feel like I should probably say thank you."

"And I would say you don't need to, because you deserve it." Tom kissed him, then lay still, just looking at him. His handsome, glorious lover.

"I'm..." He smiled and shook his head. "I'm a little bit overwhelmed. In the best way."

Tom propped himself up on his elbow and drew circles on Alex's chest with his fingertip. "You of all people? I didn't think that was possible!"

"So after four years living in a very snug flat together, I can still surprise you?" Alex reached up and brushed Tom's hair back. "I've surprised myself tonight."

"You surprised me when you first dropped your drawers in front of me!" Tom laughed gently. "You're a fine figure of a man."

Alex nodded, his cheeks flushing. "I creak along well enough."

"You're all broad and strong and when you kiss me into the pillows—" Tom chuckled. "How did you know I'd like that?"

He smiled bashfully and admitted, "I didn't. Perhaps we just go together really well?"

"I think we do. Alex and Tom. Tom and Alex." Tom assumed a silly voice. "*Hello, Alex and Tom, get yourself a babysitter, we're all going to Collette's.* Sounds good, doesn't it?"

"It does, actually. *Tom Southwell, the Prime Minister's boyfriend, arrives for the State Opening of Parliament.*" Alex grinned. "Sounds better than, *the State Opening is bereft of handsome former soldiers who look like shower gel models. Again.*"

Looks like a shower model? Tom wasn't too sure about that, but he laughed and said, "Should I wear just a towel around my waist?"

"Now I'm thinking of that massage again." Alex closed his eyes and drew in a very contented breath. "I think *just a towel* would be perfect. Let the *Mail* publish that!"

"And what if I accidentally drop it?" Tom leaned forward and kissed Alex's chest. "You'd have to defend my modesty with your jacket."

"Would I have to roll my sleeves up too?" The tone was pure innocence and all the more teasing for it. He drew one fingertip down Tom's back. "What about unfastening a few shirt buttons?"

"Unbutton them all except the last three, and that election's yours." Tom chuckled. "And my erection, too. Sorry, obvious joke, but I had to say it."

Alex looked down rather pointedly. "Bearing in mind that I'm new to all this... What would you like me to do about it right now?"

"You could stroke it, or..." Tom put his finger in his mouth and slowly drew it out, but he laughed at how silly it must look. "Whatever you'd like. As long as you're doing it, I'm happy."

But Alex didn't look as though he thought Tom was silly. Instead he kissed him, starting at his lips and slowly working his way down his jaw to his neck, easing him back against the bed as he went. With tender care he danced his lips down Tom's chest, pausing at his nipples to stroke and tease with his tongue.

"Alex..." Tom sighed as he caressed Alex's hair. "Darling..."

Some things only needed instinct, not experience, and Alex seemed to have instincts to spare. He lingered at Tom's chest for a while before he kissed his way lower, circling Tom's navel with his tongue, and all the time they were gazing at each other.

Tom gripped the bedsheet with his other hand, a shiver of anticipation trembling through him. Alex's lips felt so warm and sure, so caring against him.

Then he went lower, low enough to draw the tip of his tongue along the length of Tom's erection. It sent a blaze through his blood, a heat that increased as Alex gently kissed the very tip. Tom pushed his hips down, trying not to buck against Alex.

"Yes," Tom murmured. "That's wonderful."

"If I get it wrong, I want you to tell me," Alex murmured. He put his hand on Tom's hip then took Tom's erection in his mouth, moving with gentle care.

Get it wrong? He couldn't if he tried.

"You won't...you can't..."

Tom had never been to bed with someone he cared for so much before. Everything was more intense, as though tingles of electricity were shooting through him.

At first Alex was tentative, but as the minutes passed Tom sensed a new confidence in him. He rose and fell, his tongue swirling, his lips tight around Tom's body, and as he did, Tom could hear gentle groans of pleasure in his lover's throat.

It was those sounds that sent Tom over the edge, his body pulling taut with bliss before pleasure swooped through him. He shuddered, moaning Alex's name. And if any of this took Alex by surprise, he didn't show it. Instead he slowed his movements as the waves of Tom's ecstasy subsided, bringing him gently back to Earth.

Tom reached his hand to Alex. "Come here and hug me, you lovely man."

Alex returned his head to the pillow beside Tom and embraced him. He pulled the covers over them and they cuddled together, wrapped in each other's arms. They fitted together so well.

"That was amazing," Tom said.

"What do you think, Captain?" Alex propped himself up on one elbow, cradling his head on his palm. "Can you work with these raw materials?"

Tom ruffled Alex's hair. "Oh, yes. We can have lots of practice — we'll enjoy that!"

"And...I don't want you to think that I'm trying to keep us under wraps." He drew his fingertip down Tom's chest. "Mum and Dad are back from holiday next week. When they are, I'm going to tell them and Jenny and Malcolm and the kids about us. If we're together, it's not going to be some secret."

"Look, if it's going to affect the election — I don't mind it being between us just for a while," Tom said, his voice soft. "I'd just hate for it to be a secret forever, that's all. Although the twins might work it out, and any more talk to Nana about tickling in bed — they'll all guess anyway!"

"The election isn't — Before any of this happened, I was already doing a lot of thinking about that." He shrugged. "I haven't quite made my mind up yet, but I'm tired of seeing the kids for an hour, two if I'm really lucky. Gill and I always said two terms maximum, but I don't know if I want another five years of missing my children grow up."

"What would you do if you weren't prime minister?" Tom tried to picture Alex going through a different door — not number 10 or number 11 or into the Houses of Parliament, but a glass office block where nothing remotely governmental went on. "I know that sounds weird, it's just I've only ever known you as the prime minister!"

"I'd take a very long holiday, and then, who knows? I loved what I did before, with the charity. Maybe I'll go back to that. It didn't take four years to make something happen." Alex snuggled down on the pillow again. "But whatever it is, I'll take my time to decide. People seem to think I've done a decent job, but…it's been exhausting. I wonder if it's time to leave the stage."

"Decent job? You've been *fantastic*." Tom stroked his arm under the covers. "And, well, you haven't had the easiest time of it, and you carried on anyway—I think the country owes you, you know. You've been great."

"If the bill goes through next week, I can do so much more actually out in the field than I can behind a desk in number 10. And I can do it without working twenty-hour days." He kissed Tom's shoulder, his voice thoughtful. "And we can all have a normal home again with just the occasional CPO to remind us we used to live here."

Tom was silent for a moment. The image he had in his head of Alex stepping into that office building became clearer. Then Alex was at a youth club, surrounded by interested kids—not for a photo-op, because there were no cameras there, but because he was there, listening to kids who few grown-ups bothered with. "Then I hope it goes through."

"Until then, my diary's manic. But I'm coming home to my family, that's all I need."

"We'll be ready with dinner and the continuing tales of the Madastair." Tom kissed Alex then lay back and looked at him. *Admired* him. Alex's blue eyes were dancing, and Tom said, "I've loved you for so long in a…well, a brotherly sort of way. But it's changing. Maybe it's already changed. Alex… I love you."

"You must know how I feel about you." Alex's words were a whisper. *'You must know.'* "I love you, Tom."

Tom smiled broadly, every wish he'd had suddenly realized. "Then that's just perfect, isn't it?"

"Perfect," his lover echoed.

Chapter Twenty-One

Tom wasn't sure if he was dreaming or if he really was floating. He was in love. And it was like nothing he'd ever felt before. Perhaps being with such a wonderful man helped, and not someone who was just passing through and looking for a bit of fun. This was real, and deep—but above all, it brought Tom a happiness and lightness that he didn't recognize.

The twins seemed to have picked up on a lightened atmosphere in the flat, and were even more contented than usual. Madeleine had insisted that Alex join them in a dance around the lounge with Billy on Tom's shoulder—the poor man had only just come in from a long day, but Tom knew he wouldn't fail his child.

"It's the weekend!" Madeleine had said, and together the little family had danced around the living room as Alastair turned every surface in the room into part of his own impromptu drum kit.

On Saturday morning Alex would be out again for one of his morning constituency surgeries, but for now, it was Friday night. And on Friday night, even the prime minister didn't work late.

Tom and Alex took turns reading the bedtime story, Tom providing steam train sound effects. Finally, the twins fell asleep, and Alex and Tom settled on the sofa with a well-deserved glass of wine each.

The evening couldn't have been more peaceful. Phones were silenced, dinner had been eaten and everything seemed almost perfect.

Until the knock at the door.

"Not expecting anyone, are we?" Tom rose from the sofa. "Billy's in, so it's not her."

"It's nine o'clock on Friday night, who's still here?" Alex stood too, instinctively protective. "It's not Greg, he headed up to his constituency after lunch. You wait here, darling. I'll see who it is."

Tom didn't sit down again. He picked up his glass, clutching it, wondering what was happening. *Please, not a disaster* — not because it would take Alex away from him, although it would for a few hours, but because Tom couldn't bear the thought of heartbreak and tragedy existing in a world where he and Alex could be so happy.

"I've been phoning you," he heard Mandy say, as though she were accusing Alex of something. "Can I come in?"

And moments later, she was there in the living room with Alex at her elbow.

"It's Friday night," he warned. "And the kids are asleep, so keep your voice down."

"Tom." Mandy nodded a greeting. "I need to talk to you both. It can't wait."

"Both?" *Why?* Tom sipped his wine then put the glass down on the table. He folded his arms then remembered something about *hostile body language,* so he sank his hands into his pockets. "We're not back to the nipple tassels again, are we?"

She settled onto an armchair and took out her phone, glancing down at the screen for a few seconds. "I've had Doug from the *Mail* onto me tonight. He says they've got something on you. On the two of you."

"*Something?*" Alex's tone was guarded and he stood a little closer to Tom, as though he could shield him.

"He's got an exclusive from someone who says he's got photos of a sexually explicit message from the prime minister to his nanny." She looked from one man to the other. "And his source's claiming it's an affair that's been going on for years. He's not saying for sure that it was happening before Gill's death, but he's not saying it wasn't. It runs tomorrow and I want to know how far up Doug's arse I'm going to ram this phone when I tell him he's been sold a bag full of horseshit."

"*Sexually explicit?*" Alex asked, disbelieving.

She looked at the phone again, then held it up. There was a photograph of Tom's phone, showing the messages from Alex.

I'll be home for supper tonight — lunch meeting with Mandy at HoC, Greg at 4 but will definitely be there. Sorry for falling asleep on you.

It's a week of meetings. All I can think of is how much I want to cuddle up with you again - in the shower and out of it xxx

A photograph taken in Oscar's.

Years ago, Tom had been given training in how to survive interrogation without giving anything away.

Mandy may not have tied him to a chair, and she wasn't literally punching him, but Tom still smarted.

Fuck you, Stuart, you bendy fucking bastard.

Showing as little emotion as he could, Tom replied, "Yeah, looks like horseshit to me. It's just some messages on someone's phone."

"That's what I said, but then I checked my diary and I did have a meeting with Alex for lunch. We arranged it on the hop." She slid her phone back into her jacket. "So if that message's for real, how do I tell them that the other is bollocks?"

Tom forced himself not to look at Alex. He needed to hold his hand, but it would only prove that the text was right. "It's a text. Isn't that an invasion of privacy?"

"Oh, well, I don't know why I was worrying then! Why've I come up here rather than going home with a box of wine and a bag of crisps?" She shrugged, as though all her cares had deserted her. "I'll just tell Doug it's an invasion of privacy and he'll pull the story. He'll probably even send over a bunch of daffs to say sorry. Bloody hell, Tom, thank God you're here!"

"Just a minute—" Alex warned, but the director of communications was in full flight.

"If this is real I need to know. Because we can put a lid on it here and now. We hit the *Mirror* hard with a rebuttal—they love going up against the *Mail*." She jabbed a finger toward Tom. "We'll get their photographer up here tonight, get the kids out of bed, grab some photos of the four of you. We'll tell them it's nothing sordid, nothing seedy, just two blokes playing happy families. *Glad to be gay*, all that. All they've got is a mucky text, so we take your *I have two daddies* spiel and we slam it up their arses with both hands. What do you say, Tom? Fancy being the wronged mate who carries a torch for the boss?"

"What—? This is *horrible*." Tom shook his head. "We're not getting the kids up. We're not—all right, *I'm* not pandering to the media. It's not mucky, it's a text, and it's *private*. It's got sod all to do with anyone else."

Mandy drew back her nude-painted lips, revealing caffeine-stained teeth. "I think you'll find it's got a great sodding lot to do with a bloody huge number of people, Tom!"

Alex crossed to the door and closed it, then returned to Tom. "You've stepped out of line, Mandy. First, you don't come up here trying to sniff out scandal from Tom when you know I'm not around. This is home. Home's off limits." She opened her mouth to speak, but he was in the sort of form he usually reserved for ranting at *Newsnight*. "The text's real. Tom and I are a couple and nobody's coming up here to take photos of my family tonight or any other night. Tell the *Mail* to print their exclusive. I don't think most people get too het up about a couple of single blokes falling in love these days. You can also let them know that if they make even the slightest suggestion that I was unfaithful to Gill, I'll sue. They won't care, but at least they'll know what's coming."

"Of course they won't care," Mandy replied, tapping her foot. "This is gold for them, you realize that? Your nice, cozy *tragic dad* act has rather fallen apart, hasn't it?"

"I think you might be losing your touch, Mandy." Alex sounded too calm, always a sign that he was furious. "The Mandy I used to know wouldn't have let the *Mail* walk over her. Here's your rebuttal—Downing Street has no comment, but if they need *an anonymous source* to say something, he says that same-sex relationships haven't been shocking for decades. Even the *Mail* knows that."

With effort, a deflated Mandy tried to draw herself up to her full high-heel-augmented height. "Right. Well. I shall pass that onto them. I just hope you survive this, that's all. Both of you. And your relationship, too."

"Look, Mandy, we've always worked well together, but I've got this little family and I'm spending more and more time away from them." The warning note had gone from Alex's voice, Tom realized. "I'm thinking about my future a lot, I have been for months. After the vote, I'll have made a decision. Let them run their story, but let's not dignify it by pretending there's anything dirty or sordid in it, okay? That's what a rebuttal would do, just fan the flames."

Mandy nodded. "You've been a good man to work for, Alex. I'll do as you wish. But I'd move to Churchill's bunker for the next few days, if I were you."

"You know the official line." he smiled. "Unofficially, this is all going to be public knowledge pretty soon anyway, because we don't plan to hide it. But let's not announce ourselves with a photo spread in *Hello!*?"

"That will come." Mandy smiled as she pulled out her phone. "Shall I arrange something? They book a few months ahead."

"Let's play it by ear." Alex held out his hand to Tom. "I think we're probably a bit too dull for them!"

Tom took Alex's hand and rested his head on Alex's arm. The first person to see them together and it was Mandy, of all people.

"I don't know," Mandy said. "You do make a *gorgeous* couple!"

Alex gave a bashful laugh and said, "That's Tom's doing, I just bask in his good looks."

"Nonsense!" Mandy wagged her finger at him, but this time it wasn't admonishing. "It's all right. I'll see myself out. *Out!* Don't worry, I'll keep quiet."

"Night, Mandy. I wouldn't want anyone else dealing with this but you."

Mandy shone them a smile, then the door closed softly behind her. Tom still leaned his head against Alex, and only now that Mandy had gone did he say it, his voice small. He wanted nothing more than to curl up and hide himself in a corner.

"This is all my fault. I'm so sorry. The last thing you need is a scandal — right before the bill. You warned me and I thought, *old soldiers won't let each other down.* I was so wrong. So fucking wrong."

Alex wrapped his arm around Tom's shoulders and together they sank down onto the sofa. His silence was worse than any angry outburst could be and for a few seconds he said nothing. Then he sighed and admitted, "This isn't how I wanted people to find out. But we've done nothing wrong."

Yet could it really be worse than this? The prime minister outed over a cheeky text message just days before the vote on a bill he'd put his heart and soul into? And he'd barely found the courage to admit his feelings to himself, let alone a public that they both knew could be vicious if the mood took them.

How will we survive this?

"I should never have trusted Stuart. Even after I'd said I was dating, he — " Tom paused, deciding on a polite way of putting it, " — propositioned me. And I turned him down. I bet this is why he's done it. He doesn't need the money, it's just spite and hurt pride."

"How did he get the photo?" It could have been an accusation, but it didn't sound like one. "I'm guessing you left your phone on the table and nipped to the loo or something like that?"

"I bought cake. That was all I did." *Bloody Stuart.* "I left my phone for a second because they had lemon meringue tarts and the twins like them."

Alex gave a slow nod. Was he thinking of tomorrow morning, trailing round the streets of his East London constituency with the press pack baying at his heels? It would be a nightmare. "It's going to be all right. I'll give Jenny and Malcolm a call first thing, though. They need to be prepared."

"It shouldn't have been like this. Why didn't I think? After working for you all this time — why didn't I *think?*"

"Because you spend your days with two children, not with the conniving, backbiting, ruthless lot that work down the road." He kissed Tom's hair. "We'll weather this, Tom, I promise. I'm not ashamed of you and me, but I won't have them even *suggest* that we cheated on Gill. If I have to give a statement... We'll cross that bridge if we come to it."

Tom had seen enough of those statements to know how they went. An embattled politician, his family around him, standing at the gate of his beautiful home. A prepared speech, one that nobody believed, and then what? Sometimes, for the lucky ones, a quick slide into obscurity. For others it was infamy, years of mockery and ridicule.

But Alex had done nothing wrong.

"Should I speak to Stuart? See if he'll back down?" Tom was clutching at straws now. Even if Stuart *did* retract his story, wouldn't the newspapers be curious now and on the lookout for anything juicy about Alex's private life? And he didn't want to talk to Stuart anyway, because he couldn't trust himself not to fly into a rage and make the situation even worse.

"No, definitely not that. You're going to have friends getting in touch to be nice and to be nosey and — I know you're going to want to talk to your mates and get some perspective, but please, darling, just be careful who you trust? It's not for long, just until we see how this is playing out. Is that okay?"

Tom nodded. "I'm so sorry. He — he's such a git. He even told me that he went behind my back with other men while we were dating. And he didn't seem to care. Couldn't even remember how many. He's callous. So much for *old soldiers*."

"I'm sorry he did that," Alex whispered. "If it's any consolation, he's lost the best man he could ever have."

"He was jealous that I spent time with you and not him." Tom stroked Alex's jaw and added, "If he hadn't seen that text, I think he would've guessed in the end who my handsome new man was."

"In the history of scandalous texts, it's a pretty weak effort." Alex managed a smile. "Only *my* sex scandal could involve cuddling. It's not quite whips and chains, is it?"

"There might have been stripping in Soho, though!" Tom was halfway through laughing when he realized that was the last thing he should have reminded Alex about. "Ahh...oh, dear."

He felt Alex draw in a deep breath before he heard him sigh it out again. "Collette's, though? That's like accusing Harvey Nichols of being a sex shop for selling underwear."

Tom chuckled. "That's true. And Stuart was there too, for heaven's sake. He's such a hypocritical shit — goes with countless men behind my back, then tells the paper you had an affair while Gill was still with us." Tom bit his lip then added, "But don't worry, I've been tested and all that."

"Honestly, that thought never even crossed my mind." Alex picked up his glass of wine and took a long drink. "Don't take this the wrong way darling, but… What the hell did you see in him in the first place?"

"We were similar. I know that sounds silly, but we'd been through some tough times together when we were serving, and he was a laugh, good company, and when Stuart told me he was gay, we dated. If I'd known he was shagging around behind my back — " Tom shrugged. "I should never have met up with him again. I know that now."

"I just… I hope he's thought this through. There's always a backlash." Alex shook his head. "Still, he'll probably get a reality TV career out of it if he wants one, but I don't think I'd sell my soul to the papers for that."

"I doubt he has. It's revenge, pure and simple. Thing is, I worry about the twins, but out of everyone, they're the people who will mind the least. There's kids in their class who have two dads and others who have two mums — it's not a weird concept to them." Tom squeezed his arm around Alex. "And in a way, they've always had two dads, haven't they?"

"They have," Alex agreed and kissed his hair. "It's going to be all right, darling. I promise."

Chapter Twenty-Two

Tom sat at the kitchen table, hearing only one side of Alex's conversation with Jenny. Alex's laptop was open, showing the story in the *Mail*. They'd raided their archive and even the dreaded £100 trainers had made a reappearance, along with photos of Gill and Alex together when he had first been out on the campaign trail. The tone was barely factual, gasping at scandal everywhere. They even managed to make it sound as if a nanny living in with the family they cared for was strange and obviously a ruse for Alex and Tom to carry out their *gay affair*.

Tom no longer felt nauseous — he'd seen the story now and it was the worst thing that could have happened. His phone kept pinging with messages but Stuart was suspiciously silent. At least his friends cared — even some casual exes he'd known got in touch.

I'm jealous of both of you — what a lovely couple. Nice trainers too! <3

He tried to fix his thoughts on his friends and their well-meaning messages, and not the sense of dread in the pit of his stomach or the nagging voice in his head.

Just like a Southwell to mess everything up.

And Stuart's face, flat and straight at the top of the story as he told of the moment that, *PM sexted MY date — how can I compete with the blue-eyed boy who runs the country?*

It didn't sound as though Jenny was convinced. Alex was calm but there was an edge to his voice, an exasperation as he went through the facts again and again, as though being interrogated. Did she think the story might change? That he might forget his cover?

It's the truth.

Eventually Alex said, "Well, I appreciate it, Jenny, thank you. No, no, they're fine. I do understand but they're better here with us."

Tom gaped at him in open-mouthed alarm. So Jenny wanted to take the twins? *Bloody Stuart.* At that moment, Tom could've tied his bendy limbs together in a bow like the ribbon on a birthday present.

"No," he said in reply to whatever the question was. "They're on holiday until later this week but I've left a message. Bit hard to get hold — Exactly, that's right. Better to hear it from me, that's precisely why — Jenny, please."

Alex looked at Tom and rolled his eyes. When he spoke again, his voice was rather more decisive than it had been. "*Stop it.* You know all there is to know. Tom and I are together now, since last week. There's been nothing *going on*. Do you really think we could've kept a secret like that for four bloody ye — I'm not swearing at you, I'm frustrat — Well, I need to go as well, so perhaps we can talk later when it's a bit calmer? All right, bye."

Tom hopped up from his seat and put his arms around Alex. He held him tight.

"I love you," Tom whispered. "This is such a bloody mess."

Alex threw his phone down with a clatter. He closed his eyes and sank into Tom's embrace with a murmur of, "I love you."

"Did she really believe that crap — that we went behind Gill's back? And was she really going to take the twins?"

"She's upset, that's all." He gave a long sigh. "She doesn't want to take them away from us, she just wants them to be where the media *isn't*, and to her, that's the farm. It's a lot for Jen and Malcolm to deal with, don't think badly of them."

"I'm being protective of you, that's all. And the twins." Tom kissed Alex's cheek. "This is such a horrible way for you to come out — we just have to weather it, don't we? And do we dare even look to see if any other papers have picked it up?"

"It's too early. They'll all have their own angle on it soon, I'm sure." Alex shook his head. "Meanwhile, I have a constituency to look after. This is exactly what I didn't want to happen, Tom, it's what I was frightened of."

"They think you're ace, though — they wouldn't have voted for you otherwise." At least, so Tom hoped. What if Alex's visit today was nothing but intrusive questions about his private life? "I was going to take the twins to the park but... I can't, can I? It's a shame to be indoors in weather like this."

"Would you mind, just for today, taking them into the garden? I don't want them upset." He kissed Tom's cheek. "I just don't want them to notice anything off."

"Okay—we'll do that. Kick a ball about with the Madastair." Tom couldn't help but feel sorry for the twins, though—no ducks to feed in the Serpentine, no ice-cream seller on a bicycle. And all because Tom had trusted the wrong person.

"I'm doing my best," Alex said quietly. "Could be worse—you could be doing a door-to-door this morning like me."

"This shouldn't have happened." Tears pricked the back of Tom's eyes. Some big, brave captain he was. "I'll make it up to you, I promise."

Alex stroked Tom's hair. "It's not much of a break, but as soon as the kids get out of preschool on Friday let's head to Chequers and have a long weekend? We'll eat bacon sandwiches and turn off the phones."

"That is a brilliant idea!" Tom brushed his lips against Alex's and, just as they were about to kiss, the twins' footsteps hurried along the corridor. Tom broke away. "Incoming small children. Should we?"

We should. But it's not up to me.

"Let's," Alex decided, slipping his arm around Tom's waist as the children burst into the room. There in Alastair's pocket was the Madastair, seemingly a permanent fixture nowadays. "Good morning, minis. How were your dreams last night?"

"I met Mrs. Tiggy-Winkle," Madeleine told them.

Hadn't she noticed?

"I bet she was pleased!" Alex scrubbed her hair. "Me and Tom have got some news—"

Alastair looked at his sister with undisguised triumph and announced, "Told you!" Then he asked, "Are you getting married?"

Madeleine gasped, as if she only now realized what her father's arm around Tom's waist meant. "Can I be a bridesmaid?"

"We're not getting married yet." Her father laughed. "But...Tom and I are a couple now, properly. We love each other."

Madeleine nodded, her smile growing. "Like Bertie's daddies at school?"

"Yeah, just like that. It doesn't mean that we've stopped loving Mummy or you two or any of the gramps, it just means that we love each other too."

"Or Billy?" Alastair asked, looking to Tom for his answer.

"*Everyone* loves Billy!" Tom said.

"And I love breakfast," Madeleine said with an earnest nod, and Tom laughed.

Alex scrubbed her hair, then Alastair's too. He looked a little less tense, Tom thought as his lover kissed his cheek, though perhaps that was wishful thinking. Yet as Tom prepared breakfast and Alex got into his regular Saturday casual-but-not-casual clothes, the flat felt oddly lighter. The story was out and, there was nothing they could do now other than show people that they were nothing more special than two men in love.

"I forgot to tell you," Alex told the twins as he pulled his jacket on. "Yesterday morning, I caught Gregory feeding Billy scraps of ham. He's a secret cat fan!"

Tom laughed. "See, like I said, everyone—even Gregory—loves Billy."

Madeleine paused at her cornflakes long enough to say, "Billy is a famous cat. Like Mog."

"Just like Mog." Alex kissed each of the twins on their cheeks then, apparently without a second thought, kissed Tom's cheek too. "I'll be home this afternoon and we're getting pizza and ice cream. Love the lot of you, have a lovely morning!"

Tom took the twins into the garden to play. They didn't mention the park, but the presence of Billy, sunning herself in a flowerbed, must have made up for the lack of ducks. Tom turned off his phone—he was working, after all, and the twins were his priority, not replying to texts and phone calls from friends. Once it was switched off, he lost the temptation to look online and see what people were saying.

But Alex was never far from his thoughts and Tom wondered what sort of welcome he had been met with. He hoped that the constituents Alex had represented for nine faithful years would remember all the work he'd done for them, but what if they didn't? What if they let Stuart's rotten story and the scandalous hints in the article sweep all of that good work away? What if being gay was more important, more distasteful, than any benefit Alex had brought them?

It's not the 1970s.

Once the twins were flagging in the heat, Tom took them upstairs and gave them squash to drink in front of the cartoons. He switched on his phone and sent Alex a text.

How's it going? T xxx

For a couple of minutes there was no reply, and no matter how many times Tom checked his phone, it remained resolutely silent. He had just decided not to check it again when it rang, Alex's name flashing up on the screen.

Tom swiped the screen at once. "Alex? Are you okay?"

There was a huge amount of noise behind him, so loud that Alex had to raise his voice to be heard. Had he stumbled into a carnival?

"Darling, I'm fine. I thought you might've been wondering how it was going." He heard another voice, muffled, prompting Alex before his lover went on. "Do me a favor, just get on Twitter and check for a hashtag? Love is love."

"Okay!" Tom brought up the app and when he looked he saw—he saw what looked like a parade. With Alex at its head. "What on earth is happening, Alex?"

"I'm not entirely sure! I think we've become a bit of a cause." He laughed, disbelieving. "People are taking this muckraking business very seriously on our behalf!"

"You're kidding! But see, I told you—your constituents think you're great, Alex!" *And so do I.* And if people were actually out in the streets giving Alex an impromptu parade of all things to show their support, then Stuart and the newspaper who'd swallowed his gossip had made a dreadful error of judgment.

"Not everybody's happy about it," Alex told him. "But I'd say we've got a lot more friends than enemies!"

Tom sighed. "I'm so bloody relieved, Alex. I can't tell you how much!"

"Look, I don't think I'm going to be able to escape this without saying a few words, there're TV cameras here." From somewhere behind Alex Tom heard the sound of whoops and cheers, as though it were a party.

"But I'm not going to talk about us, okay? I think this is all a bit bigger than that."

"You're probably right," Tom said. "I'll put the telly on in the kitchen—the kids are watching their cartoons in the lounge. Break a leg! Or don't."

"I'll see you in a couple of hours, darling. Love you!"

"Love you too!"

Tom flicked through the channels, and soon found a live news report which seemed to be taking place where Alex's parade had been happening. Even the reporter looked delighted to be covering a story like this as behind her, a crowd filed past filled with people of all ages and genders, creeds and classes.

"—think we've *ever* seen anything quite like this," she said, gripping her microphone in rainbow-gloved hands. "It's completely impromptu and appears to be the public's reply to stories in the press this morning regarding the prime minister. It's safe to say he's as surprised as all of us at what's happening at his regular constituency walkabout today!"

"And so what's the mood of the crowds, Penny?" the studio anchor asked. "Are they largely supportive of Alex Hart?"

She put her finger to her earpiece, listening intently, then nodded. "Oh, it's like a festival. We've found one or two dissenting voices, but people are telling us very clearly that they've had enough of press intrusion, and that they're really ready for change."

The anchor, who evidently had to argue such things to avoid accusations of bias, asked, "Is there not an argument to be made that the prime minister's sexuality is in the public interest? What would the people gathered there today reply to that, do you think?"

A small crowd had assembled behind Penny and she glanced back at them. Then she smiled down the lens and asked, "Would you like me to ask them?"

"Yes, they are the public, after all!"

Tom was beginning to think that the anchor would've quite liked to have been outside with Penny.

"You've all come out in support of the prime minister." Penny took a step back, closer to her little audience. "Do you think his sexuality is a matter of public interest, or doesn't that matter to you?"

A woman with her hair in intricate plaits pointed at the camera. "No! It doesn't matter! He's doing a good job, we all love Alex around here—and if he loves a man, why should that matter? The newspapers need to stay the hell out of people's private lives. They wouldn't like it, so why do it to someone like Alex?"

Beside her an elderly man in a porkpie hat nodded, waiting until the microphone was in front of him to say, "He no more did the dirty on his wife than I did. Let the man be happy, we've had enough lying bastards in the job, he's one of the good lads!"

Tom smiled at Penny's efforts to look disapproving. "I do have to apologize for the language just then, we are live, these things happen."

The news anchor wore a wry smile. "Erm...yes, thank you, Penny! We'd like to apologize to viewers for any language heard on this live broadcast of what appears to be a monumental occasion on the streets of East London."

"And they're saying in the crowd that other demonstrations are happening across the city under this *Love Is Love* banner and—" As one Penny and the crowd turned, peering at something the lens couldn't see. Then she set off at a clip, chased by her camera.

"Alex Hart is about to make a statement, we're going to try and catch it!"

The anchor took over for a moment as the outside broadcast camera jogged about in the corner of the screen. "We're live in East London at an impromptu parade—some might call it a protest—in support of Alex Hart, the prime minister, whose private life has received comment in the press this morning. Mr. Hart is going to make a statement. Penny, can you tell us what's happening now?"

The children pottered into the kitchen and gazed at the television as the camera panned to show Alex, standing on what looked like a pile of market crates. At the sight of their father they cheered, and Tom felt a rush of affection for him, the pride and love he felt almost overwhelming.

"I've served this constituency for nine years," Alex announced, "and it's been a privilege. I don't have a speech, I don't have anything prepared because I wasn't expecting anything like this. I think we're all in agreement that we're tired of muckraking and press intrusion into private lives, but for now all I really have to say is…you're right. Love is love!"

Tom clapped just as the crowd burst into applause and the twins joined in too. He punched the air and said, "Go, Alex!"

"Go, Daddy!" the twins chimed in, their small hands raised too. As the reporter handed back to the studio Alastair took off on a lap of the kitchen, cheering his approval and waving his hands above his head. It was as he was on his third circuit that a message from Alex appeared on Tom's phone.

I'm coming home xxxxx

Chapter Twenty-Three

Tom woke up in Alex's bed the next morning — the whole country would know, and in a way, Tom was glad. Having to creep about, hiding who you are, was something Tom had had to do in the past, and he was glad that was all over. Now they weren't creeping, they were somehow at the head of their very own march.

Metaphorically speaking.

Their phones had been switched off last night when even the well-wishers had become a bit much, and though outside the city was awake, the prime minister was sleeping. Tom lay there, watching him, knowing he wouldn't have to slip out before the twins woke up. If they found him in their father's bed, they wouldn't think it odd at all. And no one now would raise an eyebrow even if Madeleine reported that Tom had tickled Alex's feet again.

But what would #*LoveIsLove* mean for Alex's decision about the future? It hardly mattered, if they'd be spending it together.

Alex shifted slightly in bed, just enough to put his arm around Tom's waist. Without opening his eyes he whispered, "Hello, Captain Southwell."

Tom kissed his eyelids. "Morning, Prime Minister!"

"I had a dream that we all ate far too much pizza and watched cartoons until way past the children's bedtimes." He opened his eyes. "Or was that exactly what happened last night?"

"It was indeed." Tom yawned. "Then we had a good kip. Seems to me like an excellent way to celebrate."

Alex stretched his arms above his head, lifting his back from the mattress for a few seconds. Then he turned onto his side and kissed Tom, softly murmuring, "I love you."

"I love you too." Tom danced his fingers over Alex's back, enjoying the warmth of his body against him. "I hope there won't be anything else in the media about us. I didn't have an easy time as a kid, so I don't want to be the reason for you getting more crap flung at you."

"You look worried." He propped himself up on one elbow and blinked down at Tom. "You can talk to me, darling, you know that."

"It's just...do you think they'll dig about for scandalous stuff? Even the smallest thing about me?" Tom's throat was tight—he didn't want Alex's opinion of him to change, but maybe he'd find out anyway once the press were tipped off. "It's my fault Stuart went to the *Mail* in the first place, and it was all so long ago, and I've put it behind me, and I've changed—I don't talk about it, it don't even really think about it. But..."

"You're a decorated soldier." Alex kissed his forehead, but Tom's stomach plummeted. There was so much *before* all of that. Stuff that was from another lifetime, but now...now he was public property. "You went through every security check known to man to get this job. Tell me what's bothering you?"

"I just don't want you to think badly of me." Tom winced, closing his eyes as he went back through his memories, to the places he never liked to return to. "You know how I looked after my brothers and my sisters—I told you my mum was ill, didn't I? Thing is, she drank. And I'm so scared I'll end up like her. I nearly did. When I about fifteen, I suppose—by then I'd been caring for my brothers and my sister for years, and I sort of…snapped. I'd go out with this crowd, they just hung out at a bus stop and drank cider, but…some of them ended up in prison. *I* didn't, but some of them were dealing weed and did a bit of vandalism. Bored kid stuff. But if that got in the papers—that'd be pretty shit, wouldn't it?"

"No." Alex shook his head. "Why would it be shit that someone who raised his siblings—raised them well, mind—looked after his mum and served his country with distinction had a few moments of teenage madness? I don't mean this to be patronizing, darling, but you're a bloody amazing example of what you can achieve."

"I joined the athletics club at school—well, I told you about that, didn't I? But that was why. I was running—literally *running away* from all of that. From that hazy, comfortable feeling when I had cider in my stomach, because otherwise I knew I'd end up like my mum. From the kids in the gang breaking windows. From all of that." Tom stroked his toe against Alex's foot. He wished to stroke all of him, all at once, because it was better than returning to his memories of the past. "By the time I went to Sandhurst, my siblings were old enough to look after themselves, and now…well… David's in Australia, Kaz is stationed in Gibraltar, and who knows where Rob will fly off to next! I just feel sad, you know, that Mum never saw us achieve what we have. Drank herself to death. I don't want any of that in the news. Not a word of it."

"If I were an editor, and I've known a few, and I was planning to run a scandal story about — what're they calling us? Rolex? *Tolex*, isn't it? Well, I'd take a look at the way public opinion went yesterday and I'd spike it." He kissed Tom, letting the touch linger. "Because who wants to be the only one at a party telling everyone to turn the music off and go home?"

"Do you think so? I hope you're right. I'm sorry I didn't tell you about all that." Tom's frown melted as he said, "Even got a text from Dad yesterday — there were so many, I forgot to mention it! Him and his regulars at the taverna all giving a thumbs up. He's mellowed in his old age. We'll have to go and see him on his Greek island one day — the twins will love the beach."

"Do you know, I'm prime minister and I've really achieved nothing against you. I've been extraordinarily lucky — I didn't realize just how much until Gill got sick. I've never had to struggle, never had to fight… Maybe *you* should be running the country?"

Tom laughed. "I'd be rubbish at it. I'd challenge the opposition leader to a duel if he pissed me off! I mean, I know the Duke of Wellington did, but steady on."

"That's not very *Love Is Love*, Captain Southwell! Shouldn't you be handing him a daisy and a cup of green tea instead?"

"See what I mean? I'd be *rubbish!*"

"I'd never think badly of you." Alex gathered Tom into his embrace. "You should be proud of everything you've done, darling. I love you."

* * * *

It was shaping up to be a fairly average Sunday, despite the drama of yesterday. Breakfast was late, and Tom hadn't been able to get the twins out of their pajamas before midday. Late in the afternoon, the Madastair was driving the fire engine across the floor, Billy batting at it, when someone knocked at the door.

It'll be nothing.

"I'll go?" Tom offered. Alex was too busy trying to find the corner pieces of Madeleine's jigsaw to be disturbed, surely, and he greeted Tom's suggestion with a smile.

"I'll make you a cuppa when you get back," he promised. "Or once we've found the corners."

Tom whistled a tune as he went to the door. He saw Jenny and a CPO through the spyhole. What the heck was she doing turning up unannounced?

Tom's stomach clenched as he said, "Jenny?"

"Hello, Tom." She pushed her hands into the deep pockets of her cardigan and pursed her lips. "I take it you're going to invite me in? It's you I've come to see."

"*Me?*" This didn't sound good. She must've traveled all the way from Hereford just for this. "Come on in. Cup of tea?"

"I'd love one, I've had quite the drive!" She followed him into the flat, leaving the CPO with a polite farewell. As soon as the door closed Jenny shouted, "Where're my favorite grandtwins?"

"Nana!" Madeleine shouted and ran at a Jenny's legs to hug them. "I'm going to be a bridesmaid!"

Tom bit his lip as he put the kettle on. From the hallway he could hear Alex's voice, the words indistinct beneath the excited chatter of the children, but even though he couldn't make out the words, he could discern the frost in the air. A minute or so later Alex joined him in the kitchen, leaving the twins and their grandmother to settle down in the sitting room.

"Are you okay?" he asked.

"Surprise visit," Tom remarked under his breath. "To see *me*. Why?"

"If you want me to wade in and do the protective boyfriend bit, I will. Tactfully." Alex kissed his cheek. *Alex Hart is* my protective boyfriend. "Jenny can't make demands of you, but I'm not entirely sure that she's come all this way to be unreasonable. She's quite willing and able to do that over the phone."

Tom raised an eyebrow. "Maybe she's made a special visit just to throttle me? Okay, I'll speak to her, but if I call you, will you come in?"

"You've known Jenny a long time and the two of you've always got on." Alex put his arms around Tom's waist and kissed him. "But if you need me, I'll come in."

Tom returned his kiss. "Can we use your study?"

"This is your home too. You don't have to ask."

"Thanks, Alex." Tom glanced toward the hallway where the twins were chattering to Jenny. "I'm scared, you know. Going into enemy territory, I was at least trained and prepared. Had my men with me and — now it's me and an unhappy Nan and I really don't know how to deal with that."

"Do you want me to talk to her instead?"

"No, it's okay. I'll do it." Tom patted Alex's arm. He went into the hallway with a mug of tea for Jenny — made how she always took it. "So you want to have a word?"

She took the mug and nodded. "I didn't drive for three hours for a cup of tea, Tom. You and I need to have a conversation."

Tom led the way to Alex's study. He pushed the door open, only then remembering that this wasn't the best room for them to talk in, as it was easily the untidiest in the flat. Files and toys, thick reports and children's books carpeted the floor and covered the desk and every chair. Tom cleared a space for Jenny on the sofa, and on the desk chair for himself, hoping it would grant him an air of authority even if he hadn't brushed his hair yet. He took a round fluffy ball with googly eyes from Alex's desk and gripped it.

"Alex says geniuses make a mess. I think that's just an excuse, though!"

"Ah, that must be where Malcolm heard it." She put her mug on the arm of the sofa and wrapped her fingers around it. He felt as though he were in a job interview. *So much for authority.* "So. Where does one begin, Tom? *How* is my son-in-law suddenly gay?"

"Jenny, it's probably not for me to say, but people aren't suddenly gay. Or bi. Or trans. Or…whatever." Was that a big enough hint? "We love each other, and it's changed from a supportive, fraternal sort of love to…well, romance."

He saw her jaw tighten, the movement reflected in her fingers that gripped the mug. "He and Gill were devoted to one another. Next year would've been their twentieth anniversary. This is a lot for Malcolm and me to take in." She took a quick sip of tea, as though to steady herself.

"I know Gill adored you, but… He nursed her when she was ill. The first time, when we all thought she'd beat it, and at the end. There was never a moment that Alex wasn't a rock for us all, even *after* he became PM. It's important that I know…truthfully. How long has this been going on? Did he go behind her back?"

Tom was silent for a moment. It felt as if Gill were in the room with them, her vital energy, her refusal to listen to stuff and nonsense. Her presence was so keen that Tom was sure he could've put his hand out and touched the woollen fabric of her skirt.

"Just over a week," Tom finally answered. "That's all. Alex didn't—would never have gone behind her back. You know how devoted he was to her. Just as devoted as she was to him. He would never—it would never even have occurred to him to go behind her back. I know what people say about bi men, but it's not true. *Bisexual* isn't code for *sex maniac*."

Jenny studied him, as though satisfying herself with the veracity of his words. Then she nodded and said, "I've been so afraid of Alex meeting someone new, Tom. Of course he should be happy and he deserves to be, but...what about Gill? The children were so young when she died, they won't remember her and—" She took a tissue from her sleeve and dabbed at her eyes. "Everybody moving on like this. I'm terrified we'll become just a necessary evil. A trip out to Hereford once a year just because you think you should."

As she spoke, the sound of childish footsteps could be heard passing the study. They paused and Alastair said, "But we want to show Nana!"

"She's talking," Alex told him, their voices growing distant again. "Show Nana and Tom when they've had their chat."

"You'd never be forgotten—the twins adore you, and so does Alex. And I see you more than I see my own father." Tom rolled his chair a couple of inches nearer to the sofa. "We've known each other for four years, Jenny. And Gill became such a good friend of mine, I'll never forget her. And I'd hate the twins never to know her. They love hearing stories about her, and seeing photos. She's alive to them in a way I couldn't ever explain."

And now I'm going to cry.

"It's funny, really. When the French fellow visited last year with that terribly glamorous First Lady and the press were saying, *Oh, isn't it time Alex met someone new?* and obviously I didn't know that he was —" She gestured helplessly, then leaned forward a little and patted Tom's knee. "And I looked at Malcolm and I said to him, *It's a shame Tom's not a woman, he'd be perfect for Alex.* I did, you can ask him."

Tom laughed, even as he brushed away a tear. "Well — your wish came true. Not exactly, but..."

"I can't help but think that Gill would've been delighted by this," Jenny admitted. "And the children love you, and children do tend to have a sixth sense, don't they? When I said that Alex was there for us all, I should've said that he wouldn't have been able to do any of it without you. I suppose even a rock needs a rock sometimes."

"Gill asked me to look after them all, and I have," Tom said. "When I came here to work, it was just another job, but before I knew it — it wasn't a job, it was a duty. And I was part of the family." Tom rolled his chair forward again and stopped beside the sofa. He reached for Jenny's hand. "Do you know, I was convinced that Alex would find a new woman and she'd throw me out on my ear! I'd've missed the twins and Alex so much. I suppose we've all been worrying about the same thing, haven't we? Losing the ones we love."

She dabbed her eyes again and smiled. "It seems as though we have. Welcome to the family, Tom, and thank you for keeping the twins smiling and Alex's feet on the ground."

He felt that presence again, as if Gill were in the room with them — no-nonsense, but happy.

"Hug?" Tom asked. It was a risk, he knew, but it was a risk worth taking. Jenny put her mug down and nodded.

"I think Gill would like that."

"I think she would." Tom wrapped his arms around Jenny, his chin on her shoulder. After a moment she returned the hug, patting his back very softly. And in some ways, this felt like a bigger win than the march yesterday. Jenny wasn't easily swayed, he knew, just like her daughter.

"Thanks, Gill," Tom said. There was a suspicious silence from outside, punctuated only by the sound of the twins laughing. His nannying instincts must have been more finely honed than ever, because often, silence meant mischief. More so when their father was with them.

Tom chuckled. "I think we better check on the twins…and their dad!"

They emerged from the office and made their way to the sitting room just in time to see Alex closing his laptop, the twins sitting one on either side of him. At the sound of their arrival he looked over his shoulder and said, "Mum and Dad have found Wi-Fi in Nepal. They're at base camp or something, I'm not quite sure where exactly!"

"Have you…" Tom couldn't think of the best word to use and described a circle with his hand. "Told them?"

Alex nodded, then asked, "And you two are…?"

"Thick as thieves," Jenny told him with a wink. "So you'd better watch out!"

Tom draped his arm around Jenny's shoulder. "Yeah, Nana and manny! There'll be no mucking about on *our* watch."

"Mum and Dad say hello." Alex scooped the merry twins into his arms and stood. Alastair pressed the Madastair to his cheek and made a spirited smooching sound. "And congratulations. Jenny, you're not driving back to Hereford tonight, surely? You'll stay here, I hope?"

She shook her head. "I wasn't sure I'd be invited. I was having a bit of a silly moment. I'm staying in Wimbledon with Auntie Di."

"Not before dinner, you're not," he said. "In fact, not before you've helped put the terrible two to bed, I hope!"

"Will you read us a story, Nana? Tom does train noises," Madeleine told her.

Alex settled the children on the sofa and clapped his hands. Then he crossed to the door and said, "And while you're doing that, Jen, Tom and I can get supper ready. How does that sound?"

"It sounds very sensible," Jenny smiled. "I'd love to."

Once Jenny had taken the twins to their room, Tom said to Alex, "So Jenny is Tolex's first dinner guest?"

"Unexpected but fitting." Alex took his hand. "How did it go? Was she angry?"

"At one point I thought she was going to crack her mug, she was holding it so tightly!" Tom chuckled. "She was just worried we'd forget about her and forget about Gill. And that's the last thing that'd ever happen."

"It's never going to." Alex shook his head and held Tom's hand that little bit tighter. "Mum and Dad were delighted, if a little surprised. Apparently they always thought you'd end up with someone as ridiculously good-looking as you, rather than a middle-aged dad."

"You're a babe, though." Tom tweaked Alex's cheek. "I'm glad, I really am. They'll have to come over when they get back from Nepal. And I will make sure to tell them that their son is gorgeous and thousands of people across the country are madly jealous of me."

As their lips met, the sound of Alex's phone ringing sounded through the flat. He gave a resigned groan and asked, "Should we ignore it?"

Tom bumped his forehead against Alex's. "I'd like to say *yes,* but I suspect I'll have to say *no.*"

Alex sighed and murmured, "Wouldn't it be something to have a job where the phone didn't ring on a Sunday night? I'll be as quick as I can, darling."

Tom tapped Alex's bottom. "Quick, march, Trooper!"

"Yes, sir." He winked, throwing his hand up into a smart salute as he crossed the room and picked up his mobile. "Oh god, Mandy."

At almost the same moment, Tom's own mobile buzzed with an incoming message. Tom groaned as he took his phone out of his pocket. "What now?"

"She's going to tear me off a strip for something, the only question is *what?*" He put the phone to his ear. "Mandy, hello!"

Tom looked at phone. It was Stuart.

Hey tbird. Soz about papers no hard feelings mate. Gotta make coin xxx

Tom inhaled, counting to ten in his head, then breathed out, counting to ten again.

Then he told himself, *Calm. Be calm. Nice and calm. Don't reply. Don't, whatever you do, reply.*

"You utter bastard, Stuart," Tom said at the phone. "You utter, traitorous git."

"I don't think it's for—" At Tom's words, Alex turned to face him and mouthed, "*What is it?*"

"Stuart's texted me," Tom whispered. He held out his phone to show Alex.

"Just a minute, Mandy." Alex pressed his phone to his chest and looked at Tom's screen. His jaw grew tight the moment before he murmured, "He's got some bloody nerve. Do you know what I'd do, but you don't have to?"

"What's that, chuck him in the Thames?" Tom was only half-joking.

"Block his number, let him get on with *Big Brother* or wherever the road takes him, and forget him." Alex raised his eyebrow. "Mandy wants me to do the British Morning Show tomorrow. They want to talk about the marches and this *Love Is Love* thing. My instinct's to say no, but after that…what do you think?"

Tom considered for a moment, then replied, "I think you should. You're the first male PM to have a boyfriend he's not shy of admitting to—that's a big deal, and if people see you as a *Love Is Love* figurehead then, why not?"

"Do you think? I'm not rolling out our private life to the nation, but…" He looked thoughtful. "Pierce Cowell, though. He's an odious little bugger, but it'd be nice to thank everyone that came out in support of *not* being odious little buggers, wouldn't it?"

"Yeah—yeah, it would!" Tom hugged Alex. "It hit a nerve—there's a lot of people rooting for you, and you've become a spokesman for people who didn't have one before. That's so important and so awesome."

"An accidental spokesman." Alex shrugged and put his arm around Tom, then returned the phone to his ear. "I'll do it, Mandy. On a couple of conditions. First, Tom and I are off limits, we're not up for public discussion. Second, I want a charity donation from the channel. Well, it might be unorthodox, but so is having the PM on to talk about impromptu street parties." A few seconds passed before he grinned. "Wonderful, I'll ask my office to pass on the charity — No, Tom *won't* be on the sofa. Yeah, well, I'm sorry about it too, but — Mandy, text me the details and let me eat my supper. Okay, night."

Tom clapped. "Excellent. This is going to be *brilliant. You're* going to be brilliant. Can I come to the studio? I'll lurk in your dressing room. *This is your five-minute call, Mr. Hart!*"

"They want you on camera. Apparently you've got *box-office looks*! I'd love you to come to the studio, but I didn't think you'd fancy being on camera. It's a seven o'clock call. Is that going to work with all things mini-Hart?"

"Box-office looks? Certainly not at seven in the morning!" Tom chuckled. "I'm not sure I'd want to go on telly in front of that many people live. Erm...seven o'clock isn't great for getting them to preschool. It's okay — I'll stay here. It's more important they're washed, dressed and breakfasted and ferried off to lessons than it is me faffing about in a TV studio."

"Isn't that what grandmothers are for?" Jenny asked casually as she joined them. "Two children out like lights and no supper cooking. What time do you need me here? Alex? Tom?"

"Would you?" Tom clasped his hands, pleading. "It would be such a help, and they'd love to show their Nana to all their friends. I mean, not like show-and-tell, but you know what I mean!"

"I get up at the crack of dawn on the farm, it'd be a pleasure to help." Jenny smiled. "But since my son-in-law's the prime minister, is it too much to ask you to send a car to Di's?"

Alex laughed. "Not at all. You'll travel in luxury."

Chapter Twenty-Four

Jenny seemed extremely pleased to be ferried off in a limo.

"I was worried, I'll admit it." Tom shrugged. "But all's well that ends well. And you need to get a good sleep so you look dashing and fab on telly tomorrow morning."

"Is that your way of telling me it's bedtime?" Alex looked more relaxed than he had in a long time, as though the final hurdle of telling the various parents had been all he needed to lift the last weight from his shoulders. "Did you block Stuart's number in the end?"

"Yes, I did. And I enjoyed doing it!" Tom kissed Alex. "Your bed or mine?"

"Where do you fancy?"

"I don't mind, as long as you're in it!"

"Mine's bigger." Alex smiled, perhaps recalling that first night together. "Ours?"

"Ours." Tom had already moved in anyway, having transferred half his bedside table to the one on his side of Alex's bed. But he liked to ask him which bed he wanted to sleep in, as if they were dating and living in separate houses. "Would you like a back rub? Make you all nice and relaxed for tomorrow?"

"I'd love one." He kissed Tom's hand, chivalrous as ever. "Do I get to take my shirt off this time?"

"Yes, please. I even have some nice oil." Tom grinned as they went into the bedroom. "I couldn't help it — the bottle just leaped off the shelf into my shopping basket!"

Alex said nothing, but took Tom's hands and guided them to his shirt, kissing him as he did. He teased his tongue against Tom's, letting the kiss deepen. How he loved Alex's kisses, so loving and heated, as elegant and assured as he was. As each button fell away, Tom stroked over Alex's chest and stomach, feeling his muscles tense then relax under his touch. Then he broke from the kiss as an image came into his mind.

"Alex…would you wear a towel around your waist as I massage you?"

If that was a surprise, Alex did his best not to show it, but there was a look of affectionate amusement on his face when he said, "If that's what you want, darling, of course I will."

"I know how cheesy that sounds, but when I was rubbing your back before, I pictured you with a towel around you, and me…" Tom combed his hand through his hair, awkward. "Would you like me to keep dressed, or…?"

"When you pictured it, me in my towel…" Alex took Tom's hand and returned it to his chest, holding over the spot where his heart pounded. "What were you wearing?"

"I had a towel as well," Tom replied. He slid his hand up to Alex's nipple and rolled it between his fingers. "And nothing else."

It took a moment for Alex to breathe a reply of, "Wear that." Then he dipped his head to nuzzle Tom's throat, murmuring a soft gasp of pleasure as he did.

Tom stroked Alex through his trousers, his erection firm and long beneath his hand. "I'll go and get changed in my bathroom, shall I?"

"Do you want me waiting on the bed when you get back, Captain?"

"Yes, I'd like that… Ready for your massage." Tom kissed him then, looking back at Alex over his shoulder, he went to his bathroom. He knew he probably shouldn't have chosen the smallest towel he could find, but he hoped he wouldn't be wearing it for very long.

Stuart would never have played along with Tom's silly fantasies — Stuart's idea of a fantasy was *having sex* and that was about it. But Alex seemed to enjoy indulging Tom's playful side, and that made Tom happy.

And when he went back into their bedroom, Tom was very happy indeed to see Alex smiling at him as he lay on the bed wearing nothing but a white towel around his waist. He had pillowed his cheek on his folded arms, and Tom leaned against the doorframe for a moment, admiring how the soft glow from the bedside lamps perfectly accented the curves of Alex's shoulders, the small of his back and his firm, round bottom clad in its towel. The backs of Alex's muscular legs looked very inviting, and after Tom had closed the door behind him, he got onto the bed and clasped Alex's calf.

"You're so firm, so muscular…"

"I just hope I measure up to the fantasy." Alex glanced over his shoulder, his smile filled with mischief. "And you can interpret that however you like."

"You exceed the fantasy in every way." Tom leaned forward and kissed Alex's shoulder. It was only then that he realized what a sight he must look in his towel that was on the verge of indecent. He reached for the drawer by the bed and took out the bottle of oil, rubbing it on his palms as he got into position, straddling Alex's thighs.

This is real. This fantasy – all of these fantasies – they're all coming true.

"I feel relaxed already," Alex murmured, his voice content. "You're magic like that."

"Magic? Would you like to see my wand?" Tom leaned down and kissed Alex's nape, kneading Alex's shoulders. The reply was a low moan, Alex's muscles yielding and relaxing beneath his touch. In the lamplight the oil defined the planes of his body, just as it had in Tom's wildest dreams, mapping the contours of his sculpted back.

Tom caressed and stroked, then kneaded out the knots in Alex's muscles before caressing again, smoothing away any soreness there might be in Alex's body. And there were those gentle sighs and groans again, each one sending fresh pulses of desire through Tom. How different this was from that first massage, and how wonderful.

Tom worked his way down Alex's back and finally reached his waist.

"Would you mind losing your towel?" Tom asked, his breath hitching.

"Not at all," Alex told him. "Whip it off."

Tom reached around Alex's waist and drew the sides of the towel apart before taking it away with the swift movement of a magician pulling away a cloth from a table set for dinner. He bowed his head and kissed Alex's buttocks, then threw aside his own towel.

Tom began to rub Alex's bottom, running his palms up from the top of Alex's thighs to his rounded arse.

"This country is very lucky to have such a lovely bum sitting on a chair at number ten," Tom said.

"I've never had my bottom kissed before." Alex's voice sounded somewhere between disbelieving and heated. "I can't remember the last time I felt quite so...*admired*. And what a man to be admired by!"

"I'll kiss it a lot, if you don't mind—you deserve to have lots of kisses." Tom slowly ended his caresses and began to wipe the oil from his hands on his discarded towel. "Now, I bet there's a part of your anatomy that you'd *really* like me to stroke by now?"

With a soft laugh, Alex propped his chin on his hand and looked back at Tom.

"What I'd really like, if you don't mind giving me a few pointers, is to make love to you."

Tom nearly dropped the towel. They'd stroked and caressed, kissed, but they hadn't gone any further. Tom clambered off Alex's legs and knelt on the bed beside him.

"That'd be amazing. You mean...all the way, right?"

"If that's all right? We can wait if you'd rather, darling."

"Alex, I'd love it." Tom ruffled Alex's hair. "I just so happened to buy some other bits and bobs when I was buying this. Can't blame a man for being hopeful, can you?" He held up the massage oil and nodded toward the bedside table. Alex followed the direction of his nod, then signaled his own understanding with a slight inclination of his head.

"So…how do you fancy teaching the prime minister how to make love to his boyfriend?" Alex gave a very somber look. "I'm a fast learner, don't worry."

"Well…" Tom lay down beside him, his hands crossed casually behind his head. "You know how awesome it is when you kiss me into the pillows? Just think about that, but using your hips as well… Yeah?"

"I'm hoping that being with the man I love is going to make it all pretty instinctive." Alex turned onto his side. He drew the tip of his finger down Tom's body, then took Tom's erection in a gentle grip. "I've been thinking about it a lot."

"Really? You saucy man." Tom grinned as he reached for the drawer again. "It's…yeah, instinctive. But there's something we need to help us on our way."

Tom took a tube of lubricant from the drawer. "Give me your hand."

Alex held out his palm obediently, all the time watching Tom through those bright blue eyes. There was such trust there, and such love, as he squeezed some of the tube's contents onto his fingers.

Tom kissed him then said, "So…would you like to stroke me, between my legs?"

Alex pressed his lips to Tom's and kissed him as his hand moved very tentatively to follow the instruction. He was inexperienced with his own gender, perhaps, but in every other respect Tom knew him to be a man of the world, and, as the kiss grew deeper, he slid his hand over Tom's buttocks, caressing him. Tom murmured encouragement through their kiss, moving in time with Alex's touch. He had once thought that such intimacy between them was only an impossible fantasy, but somehow — somehow — he was lying in Alex's bed, with Alex tenderly exploring him.

The very tip of Alex's finger teased the curve of Tom's buttocks, just slipping between them. He broke their kiss and asked in a voice that trembled with desire, "Can I?"

Tom nodded. "Yes, go on… I want you, Alex."

"I've wanted you for so long… I imagined us like this." Alex kissed Tom's jaw, dotting his way down his neck, his lips soft. As he did, he let his finger slide between Tom's buttocks, stroking him tenderly. "Oh God, you feel wonderful…"

"So do you," Tom replied, as pleasure began to course through him. "Just perfect."

And Alex's kisses didn't stop at Tom's throat. Instead he ducked his head lower and drew Tom's nipple into his mouth, licking and teasing the hard nub with his tongue. As he did, he stroked a second finger alongside the first, his confidence clearly growing.

"Pointers? You're one man who doesn't need pointers!" Tom bent his knee and lifted his hips a little, beyond pleased to be so abandoned with Alex. As his hips moved, Alex's fingers slid a little deeper, his mouth becoming hungrier. He murmured Tom's name against his chest, his voice a low growl of desire.

"A third," Tom whispered, pleasure growing in him to such a pitch that he almost couldn't speak. Alex had hit his sweet spot and Tom had to bite his lip to hold back. "Try another, Alex, please… Oh, this is so good…"

Alex obliged, sliding a third finger into Tom's body. He seemed to intuit exactly what Tom needed and focused all his efforts on the center of that delirious pleasure, stroking and caressing and teasing out every second of ecstasy. His free hand closed around Tom's erection, just adding to the heady whirl of joy as Alex drew the tip of his tongue over Tom's chest then kissed him again, fierce and hungry.

Tom knotted his fingers in Alex's hair, holding him close, his body moving with Alex's rhythm. He grasped for Alex's nipple, tweaking, so much pleasure washing through him that for a moment he struggled to reach farther down and stroke Alex's erection.

"I want you," Alex gasped, his voice hoarse. "I want you so much…"

"Then have me." Tom moaned. He brushed away the strands of hair that had fallen into Alex's face. "I want to be so close to you that I don't know where either of us begins or ends."

It was a few more seconds before Alex finally took his hands from Tom's body and reached into the drawer again. Tom watched Alex, his oiled back catching the soft light.

"Would you like me to put it on you?" Tom asked.

Alex nodded. "I'd love you to."

Tom plumped up the pillows and gestured toward them. "Just sit back."

He watched as Alex settled into the pillows, his gaze never leaving Tom. Once he was comfortable, he reached out and put his hand on Tom's thigh, the gesture as easy as it was affectionate. Then he knitted his hands behind his head, giving every impression of a man who wouldn't rather be anywhere but here.

"Now there's a sight I'll never get bored of." Tom straddled Alex's legs, admiring his naked, aroused lover. He tore the condom packet open with his teeth, then rolled the condom down onto Alex. "Is that comfortable — have I got the right size?"

"I think so." Alex smiled. "So...sorry, darling, I'm not usually so naive. How do you— is there... Do you have a position you prefer?"

Tom slicked lube onto Alex, his hand trembling at the thought of their union being so close. "There's loads, apparently, and I really want you on top of me. Sorry...I've lain in bed some nights just imagining how good that would be. But seeing as this is all new to you, I'll straddle you—get you used to how it feels, then...we can see where the night takes us."

"I've thought about it a lot too," Alex admitted. "So...I'm ready if you are, darling."

Tom rested one hand on Alex's waist, the other stroking his nipple. He kissed him, then asked, "When you think about us together, what do you see?"

"I know it's a terrible cliché, but...maybe it's all that shower model talk." His face flushed and he admitted, "I've thought about us making love in the shower a *lot*. And face to face, kissing you into the pillows, I suppose."

"The shower? Alex, you wonderful sauce! I'd really like that." Tom grinned as he rose up on his haunches, the tip of Alex's erection just below him. He rested his forehead against Alex's, bringing one arm around Alex's shoulders, the other still on his waist. Gazing into Alex's fathomless blue eyes, Tom asked one simple word. "Ready?"

Alex put his arms around Tom's waist and whispered, "Ready."

Tom brought his lips to Alex's and gently lowered himself down onto him. He tightened his arm around Alex as their bodies met, a moment of discomfort followed by a wonderful sensation of bliss as they were joined as one. He heard Alex's breath grow faster, felt the arms around his waist grow tense for a moment before he relaxed and whispered, "I love you, Tom."

"I love you too, Alex." Tom waited a moment, staying still, imprinting on his mind just how good it felt. Then he began to move, gently at first, little thrusts of his hips against Alex's. He felt Alex's body moving with him, matching his pace and rhythm. Then Alex tightened his embrace, bringing Tom to him for a kiss.

Tom murmured Alex's name against his lips, shivers of bliss coursing through him with every movement of their bodies. Alex took Tom's erection in his hand and stroked him, catching every moan in a kiss.

Tom sighed. "That's it, that's it... Alex, you're fantastic."

He had lost count of how many times he'd imagined this, thought hopelessly of being in Alex's arms, of the two of them making love. Even his wildest dreams hadn't come close to the reality, to the sense of love and exhilaration that their every move only increased.

And he really wanted Alex to kiss him into the pillows.

Tom felt daring and saucy and incredibly naughty as he asked, "Darling—do you want to go on top now?"

Alex's nod left him in no doubt. "I'd love to."

Tom put his arms around Alex. "Let's roll over—slowly!"

"Slowly," Alex repeated, the word filled with merriment. He put both arms around Tom's waist to steady him, and together, with some laughter and maybe just a touch of accidental elegance, they completed the maneuver. Tom was beneath Alex now, just as he had dreamed of being, yielding to him.

He ran his hands across Alex's chest, his breath catching with desire. "I've wanted this for so long — you're perfect."

"I'm doing okay, then?" his lover teased, grazing his teeth against Tom's earlobe. "You feel wonderful."

"So do you." Tom lifted his legs and crossed them around Alex's waist. Alex was deeper inside him now, and Tom moaned. "Isn't that great?"

"It's perfect," Alex breathed. He took Tom's erection in his hand again and began to thrust just a little harder, their bodies joined more deeply than ever now.

Tom smoothed one hand through Alex's hair and, the other across Alex's strong shoulders. All those nights he'd lain awake running this scenario through his mind and hating himself afterward for daring to think such things about his decent, kind boss. And he'd never for one moment thought that Alex could want him too, could long for him just as Tom had longed for Alex.

There'd be no longing anymore, no impossible crush or guilty fantasies. Only pleasure and their bodies combining as one.

For all his shyness, all his anxiety, Alex didn't need any instruction. They were soaring on instinct and love, caught in this encounter that was theirs alone. They were all kisses and sensation, surrendered to each other.

Tom's breath grew ragged, his hips moving faster, every touch more intense. "Alex... I love you," he whispered.

"I love you," Alex gasped, catching his lips in a kiss. "Always, darling..."

Bliss captured Tom, a pleasure so deep that he could not escape it. It ran through his blood, heated and intense, and he held Alex tight, his body shuddering with his climax. He felt Alex's muscles grow taut in the moments before his orgasm claimed him. Then Alex gave a low cry of pleasure and clung to him, gasping Tom's name. Tom kissed Alex's face, traveling down to his neck, holding him as trembles still went through them both. Alex sank down into Tom's embrace, nuzzling his lips against Tom's shoulder. They lay together in silence for a long time until Alex lifted his head and blinked down at him.

"I love you, Tom," he whispered. "And I really don't care who knows it.'

"You're so brave, Alex. I adore you," Tom replied. Life had changed forever, and he wouldn't have had it any other way.

Chapter Twenty-Five

Tom stood in the shadows, just behind the line of the cameras in a spot marked out with tape. He wasn't sure if Alex could see him or not, but even if he was only an outline in the gloom, Alex would know he had the support of the man he loved.

And it wasn't as if Alex hadn't done this before.

Pierce Cowell sipped a glass of orange juice, sharing an anecdote about his children. Tom was far from being the man's biggest fan, but watching him chat with Alex now, Tom suspected that the badass act was all put on. He seemed...nice.

"Can I grab a photo for my Insta?" Burnished brown as a nut in her white bodycon dress, Pierce's co-host, Kelly Naylor, appeared at Tom's shoulder with her phone held out. "Me and my very own manny? I caught Alex in makeup, but I haven't got you yet!"

She looked even more tan than she did on *Strictly*, if that were possible.

"Yeah, okay!" Tom leaned closer to her to fit them both on the screen and he grinned. He'd mostly managed to avoid the limelight over the years, but if it helped Alex, he didn't mind. On the screen Kelly beamed, her veneers bright white against her tan skin, her blonde hair almost glowing under the lights.

"Perfect!" She kissed his cheek and tripped off across the studio floor as the ten-second countdown began. By the time they were on air again she was safely on the sofa, beaming her immaculate smile into millions of homes over the breakfast table.

Alex'll slay. He always does.

"Welcome back." Kelly grinned, crossing one leg over the other, demure as she was bubbly. "We are *honored* to have some of the cutest blue eyes I've ever seen on this sofa next, isn't that right, Pierce?" She looked at her co-host and reached out to touch his hand. "Or are you feeling a bit like one of the ugly sisters sat in between me and our next guest?"

"I can't say I've ever thought of a man that way myself, but the same can't be said for our very special guest, whose private life came into the spotlight over the weekend." Pierce grinned as he brushed his lapel with the back of his hand. "Isn't that right, Alex Hart?"

"Smoothly done, Pierce," Alex told him with a smile. "Especially for a Monday morning."

Tom bit his lip, trying not to laugh.

"Only two days ago," Pierce went on, "you found yourself in an impromptu parade through East London. Under the slogan *Love Is Love,* is it true that these people were voicing their feelings regarding the press and how it homes in on the private lives of people like you, Alex, who are very much in the public eye?"

Alex. No Mr. Hart for Pierce Cowell.

"That's exactly what they were doing," he replied. "I was doing my regular constituency rounds and they gathered to join me. It was completely unexpected and rather wonderful. I think it really says a lot about what matters to people."

Kelly nodded and said, "Well, I've had my own run-ins with the papers. They're obsessed over my tan lines, you know! I had a long lens pointed in my hotel window in Thailand."

Pierce tutted, shaking his head, before asking, "So, Alex, you think that the public *aren't* interested in things like — Kelly's tan lines, or who you're dating?" He was wearing a frown that seemed to say, *I'm a serious journalist, asking the important questions of the day.*

"I live in the real world, Pierce. I'm sure people're interested, but I think there has to be some measure of privacy, don't you?" Kelly was nodding firmly, her expression now composed into something resembling serious as she listened. "There are plenty of opportunities to indulge in a bit of celebrity gossip with the full consent of the celebrities involved. I think people are a little bit tired of the old-school way of doing it. And this weekend they were very clear that they don't consider someone's sexual orientation as anything other than private."

"Totally." Kelly nodded.

"But *isn't* it, if the person concerned is the *prime minister*?" Pierce put everything into his pantomime of offended morality.

Alex looked utterly comfortable despite the question. He frowned and asked Pierce, "Why?"

"You would be our first gay prime minister," Pierce said slowly, as if Alex was rather dim. "And I'm sure there's lots of gay and lesbian voters out there who would be pleased to know that the prime minister is one of them."

"I think that people are more interested in a government that delivers on the things that matter, regardless of their private lives." This wasn't the man who'd looked so tired at PMQs, Tom could see. This was Alex as he'd always known him. "We all care about health, education, employment. There are a hundred more important factors than my sexuality, and that's what we're focusing on. It's what's behind my bill, it's what the electorate voted for."

"But surely, Alex, you must know that people are intrigued by what goes on behind the door of number 11." Pierce folded his arms, as if he was bored. "You and your late wife hired a male nanny, a choice that went down well with the politically correct. And now, you're apparently *sleeping* with the man. We have a gay relationship in Downing Street, but you don't want the public to know."

For a moment Alex was silent, then he asked, "Why would you think I didn't want the public to know? Do you think I'm trying to put the lid on my sordid little secret?"

Yet he sounded as pleasant as ever, like a man chatting with friends in the pub.

Pierce held out his hands, pouting. "So you, yourself, would call it sordid?"

"Oh, Pierce, come on—how long have I been doing this? I'd call you prurient, but I wouldn't call my domestic situation anything but settled and loving." Alex smiled, all placid charm. "Sorry."

"Aw, that's lovely." Kelly beamed. "You should be happy, you've had some tragedy since you got the top job!"

Pierce nodded, adding, "Losing your wife only a few months after the birth of your children must've been very difficult. Finding comfort in the arms of a nanny wouldn't be unusual were it not for the fact that *your* nanny is a man."

"Do you want to talk about this weekend or are you absolutely set on my love life?" Alex smiled. "We can do either, Pierce. It's disappointing, because I really want to talk about the wonderful groundswell of support and the way people came together, but you're the ringmaster."

Kelly laughed. "He wishes."

"But what happened this weekend came about *because* of these revelations about your sexuality." Pierce shook his head and sighed. "So yes, it *is* a relevant part of this interview."

"Okay. You're a journalist, you want your scandal, I get it." Alex nodded, then glanced into the studio darkness toward Tom. "When Gill died, I couldn't have got through it without a huge amount of help. Our family and friends were amazing, and so were people we never even met, people who got in touch just to say how sorry they were and to remind us that we weren't alone. Gill chose Tom to look after the kids, and when she knew she wasn't going to make it, one of the most important things to her was that he was there for all of us. And before you jump on that, I don't mean as anything but a friend. And he's been there ever since. If you want your scoop, this is it. Until last week we were best friends, and it took us until then to realize that we'd fallen in love with each other. And I'm not at all ashamed to admit it."

And just like that, Alex told the world, not a hint of embarrassment or timidity about it.

Tom wiped his eyes on the sleeve of his jumper, then he blew Alex a kiss even though he didn't think Alex would see.

"Last *week?*" Pierce spluttered, incredulous. "The report in the *Mail* suggested that this had been going on for much longer than that. In fact, before your wife passed away. There's nothing wrong with being gay these days, and although it's not unusual for politicians to have affairs, it's still scandalous stuff. Are you claiming you've only been in love with this manny—who apparently is very attractive, although I wouldn't know—for a week in order to hide the fact that it's actually been for very much longer?"

"While Gill was here we were rather preoccupied with dealing with her terminal illness and two newborns." Alex shook his head. "Tom and I have been together a week and I'm happily singing it from the rooftops because I can't quite believe it myself. I know *you* weren't suggesting I'd had an affair, of course, I can almost hear the show's lawyers clenching at the thought of it!"

"Oh come on, Pierce, you know he's gorge!" Kelly nudged him. "Stop pretending you don't. You can still be straight and think a bloke's good-looking, you know!"

"I really don't know if a man is attractive or not. I'm not gay!" Pierce protested. Tom heard a note of desperation in that tone—was Pierce trying to hide something about himself? Even if he was, though, Tom wouldn't delve. Unlike Pierce. "Alex, when you first met your manny, then, did you think, *cor, he's gorgeous,* or didn't you notice until a few years had gone by? I'm just curious, really, as to how this works, going from being a straight man to a gay bloke."

"I don't think sexuality has to be quite so rigid, do you?" Alex asked. "I didn't notice anybody other than Gill because I was married and very, very happy. You're trying so hard to get an angle, but it's called bisexuality. It's pretty common."

"Oh, hang on." Kelly pushed her finger into her ear. "Oh, Alex, your mum-in-law's on the phone, she wants to have her say. Funny, Pierce, the gallery said they've been telling you for five minutes!"

Jenny. Tom wasn't sure exactly what he thought about this new development.

"My earpiece must be on the blink!"

The man evidently wasn't an actor, because that was the least convincing fib Tom had ever heard. Even three-year-olds could fib better than that.

"Hello, Jenny!" Kelly exclaimed. "You've got something to say to Pierce, I think?"

"Hello, Kelly," Jenny's voice said. She sounded incredibly posh, Tom thought, like a woman doing her very best phone voice. "I'd just like to give our perspective on it really, as grandparents."

"Please do." Kelly smiled, positively beaming at Pierce.

"Right, well. Alex was a marvelous hubby to Gill and he dotes on the twins, they're his life! But Gill thought the world of Tom and so do we all. I know you're trying to be shocking, Mr. Cowell, but really, shame on you. We couldn't be happier for Alex and Tom. They're perfect together."

Pierce laughed, a dismissive bray which didn't quite disguise a creeping sense of horror that was visible on his face. "*Trying* to be shocking, Mrs....erm...Jenny? I'm merely asking the questions that the public who weren't parading through London on Saturday want the answers to!"

"I'm the public," Jenny pointed out. "I have a very personal stake in Alex's domestic situation and even *I* didn't ask such intrusive questions. It's Monday morning, for heaven's sake. What must you be like by Friday?"

Pierce folded his arms again. This time it looked defensive. "But surely you were tempted to ask? Weren't you? Weren't you curious about such an unusual domestic set-up right under your nose?"

"Would you have expected me to pry if the nanny in question had been a lady?" Jenny asked. "I hope I'm wrong, Mr. Cowell, but this has a distinct whiff of prejudice!"

"Prejudice— That's just— I'm not prejudiced!" A faint squeak of panic had entered Pierce's voice. "Some of my best friends are gay, although I don't want to go to bed with them—just want to make that clear. Heavens, no."

"I bet you listen to Freddie Mercury too." Jenny chuckled, and, on the sofa, Alex gave a bark of laughter. "Because you're very modern, Mr. Cowell!"

"Jenny," Alex warned with a smile. "Pierce can't help his fragile masculinity!"

"Look, now that's—that's pretty below the belt, Alex, can I just say?"

Tom snorted with laughter. He couldn't help it, and Pierce glared into the shadows, almost right at him.

"In case viewers are wondering, Pierce is giving the lovely Tom a Paddington Bear hard stare." Kelly grinned. "He's going to turn to stone if you keep glaring at him!"

Tom glared back, but Pierce couldn't possibly see, so Tom moved nearer. He'd eyeballed enough new recruits in his time to know he could give a terrifying stare if he needed to. Tom came farther and farther forward, one military marching step at a time, until a floor manager appeared beside him, waving a clipboard at him. Tom turned and found himself staring down a camera lens. He had crossed the *cordon sanitaire*.

Oh shit.

Tom waved. "Erm… Morning, people of Britain!"

"Darling!" Alex gestured to Tom. "Come and sit down!"

"Hello, Tom, darling," Jenny said. "I'm off to have coffee with Di now. I'll see you both later!"

"Bye, Di!" Tom waved again, he and Jenny apparently using a television studio for a Skype session.

Tom sat down on the sofa and put his hand on Alex's knee.

Pierce bristled, but seemed to be attempting to regain control. "So joining us on the sofa with the prime minister is his — what do we call you? Boyfriend?"

"That'll do." Tom had no idea if he was doing this right. A boom microphone swung overhead and it occurred to him he hadn't been miked up. Had anyone heard him?

"Panic over, we can do it the old way." Kelly passed a handheld mic across to Tom. "Tom, we're just flashing up some tweets on the monitor for viewers and I think it's fair to say, Alex and you have caused a sensation all over again. *Love is love* is trending and — " she laughed. "Oh, Pierce, a few people are saying Jenny might make a good anchor!"

Pierce laughed, his teeth revealed from his drawn-back lips like a horse's. "Yes, I'd like to see that. Now — Tom, we've put to bed, if you'll pardon the pun, the rumors about you and Alex having a gay affair while his lamented, lovely wife Gill was still with us. But is it the case that *you* have had an affair in this relationship with Alex? The story broke thanks to Stuart Donnelly, your boyfriend."

Tom's throat dried up. *Is this right? Are telly presenters allowed to do this?* Tom glanced at Alex.

"The same Stuart Donnelly who moved to Spain nearly three years ago?" Alex looked at Tom and squeezed his hand. "Unless he's got a TARDIS, I'm not sure how the timelines match up!"

"The same Stuart Donnelly who said in the *Mail*..." Pierce riffled through the papers on the table in front of him and found the *Mail* open on the relevant page. He held it up to the camera. "Who said that Tom was his date. Which implies that — Tom, were you having an affair?"

Pierce was staring again, so Tom stared right back.

"Stuart and I were soldiers together. I trusted him with my life. Once we were civvies, we dated, and Stuart got the hump because Gill was ill, I was caring for the twins, looking after Alex." Tom took a moment to compose himself before continuing. "And Stuart went off to Spain and dumped me via text — while he was at the airport. He must've been in the tunnel going onto the plane. Maybe he was even in his seat, reading the inflight magazine? And I didn't hear from him or see him until the other week. And do you know what he told me? He told me he'd been seeing other men behind my back. If you want scandal and affairs, Mr.

Cowell, *there* they are. But I've never done the dirty on anyone. I never would."

Pierce's mouth opened and closed like a beached fish's. He glanced at Kelly. She looked utterly serene as she said, "I think you make an adorable couple, I really do. And I think 'love is love' is the message we all need just now. Alex and Tom, we've got to go to break, but thank you for sharing your story with us."

Tom nodded dumbly. Should he have said all of that? But he felt calm now. He'd said his piece.

"That was brilliant." Kelly stood and took the microphone back from Tom. She stepped past Pierce as though he wasn't even there. "You're both brilliant. And you're a gorgeous couple."

"Thanks," Tom said.

Pierce, his face rather red, had his finger in his ear, nodding. His earpiece was finally working, it seemed.

"It's been a pleasure," Alex assured them. He was already unclipping his microphone as he stood. "I'm flat out until the division tomorrow, so we need to run. But thank you both, it's been...exhilarating."

Pierce was on his feet, grabbing Alex's hand for an energetic handpump. "It's been great, cheers, thanks for coming on the show. Hope you didn't mind my line of questioning, but you you know how it is, we can't court editorial bias or the keyboard warriors take off on Twitter!"

"I imagine your timeline's going to be busy." Alex shook his hand graciously. "For all sorts of reasons."

"My PA will already be dealing with it, I'm sure," Pierce replied coldly. "Tom, do you shake hands?"

"Erm...*yes.* I can also drive a tank."

"Ha ha, that's it, fella!" Pierce now shook Tom's hand, and Tom gave his firmest army grip in response. "Careful, I quite like that hand!"

And now they were very official indeed. And everybody had better be happy for them, because otherwise Jenny would have plenty to say about it.

Chapter Twenty-Six

In bed that night, Tom recounted his moment on television.

"I didn't even mean to go on camera," he told Alex as he stroked his fingertips over Alex's chest. "I just kept striding forward and suddenly — there I was."

"And you were amazing." Alex snuggled him close. "Mandy's been fending off calls to interview you all day. You know you don't have to turn them down, darling. The decision's got to be yours."

"I don't mind doing a few." Tom kissed Alex's shoulder. "I just — I don't want to say the wrong thing and make it difficult for you."

"While I was sat on that sofa trying not to punch Cowell's lights out, I came to a decision." He blinked, stroking Tom's hair. "About the second term."

Anxiety crawled into Tom's stomach and lay there like a serpent waiting to strike. "And...and what did you decide?"

"I had a good run, but I'm a father and a boyfriend now, and I think we'd all benefit from getting out of the city, don't you?" Alex smiled. "I'm leaving Parliament at the next election. I'm going back to the charity sector and we're going to have a *long* family holiday."

Tom stared at him. "But — you're such a good prime minister. I mean — I'd love to see more of you, the kids would too, but are you sure? You're so popular, even after all this, you'd win the election easily!"

"I don't want to look back in five years and say, *when did my kids reach nine*? I'm leaving the country in a better state than I found it and if the bill goes through tomorrow… Well, there's nothing more I'd ask for than that. Are you okay with not being the PM's boyfriend, darling?"

"Well, I *was* looking forward to wearing Jackie O pearls and those boxy skirt suits that prime minister's other halves always wear." Tom chuckled. "But maybe they wouldn't have suited me anyway."

"Don't worry, I'll still roll up my sleeves and unfasten one too many buttons." Alex stroked down Tom's chest. "I think you deserve the credit for the morning's interview, you know."

"No, no, you put Pierce in his place! So did Jenny!" Tom laughed. "That was brilliant. What a fantastic mother-in-law."

"But after last night, I was floating above the clouds. And that's all down to you." He drew his fingertips over Tom's erection. "Captain."

Tom purred with delight. "It's amazing what a good old-fashioned roll in the hay can do."

"I've got a mad day tomorrow. Cabinet in the morning, and it's my bill in the evening, I'll be lucky to be home before ten." Alex sighed, then asked casually, "So how would you feel about another roll in the hay tonight, to keep me going tomorrow?"

Tom saluted. "Captain Southwell at your service, sir. Always ready to do my duty for the country. And my lovely PM." He kissed Alex, then said, "So…any requests this evening, my love?"

"This might be a bit twee, but…you're so nice to cuddle up to. I wondered—" He flushed and asked, "How do you feel about a bit of old-fashioned spooning?"

"Now that's definitely something I can get behind— I mean, *you* can get behind!" Tom rubbed the tip of his nose against Alex's. "I do love being held by you, and I do love feeling you inside me, Alex. That's not crude, is it?"

"No." Alex shook his head. "Not a bit."

"Good." Tom kissed him again, then kissed his way down to Alex's chest, stroking the scattering of hair there. Beneath his lips he felt Alex's heartbeat quicken, a soft sigh slipping from his parted lips. "Would you like a treat first?" Tom asked.

"I'm never going to say no to that." Alex combed his fingers through Tom's hair. "I'd love a treat."

So Tom kissed farther, down Alex's body until he reached his erection and took it in his mouth. Alex was hard and sizeable, and it had brought Tom so much pleasure last night—and would do again tonight, Tom was certain.

"God, I love you." Alex gasped. His hips lifted from the bed toward him, his fingers tightening in Tom's hair.

Tom looked up. "Alex, do you want to try something? If you're in a raunchy mood?"

"Only if it's suitably prime ministerial," was the answer.

Tom raised an eyebrow. "Well...you work at number 10. We live at number 11. What other well-known two-digit number can you think of?"

The thoughtful look that descended over his lover's expression was a picture, especially the moment when Tom saw the penny finally drop. Alex's eyes widened and he said, "Ah. *That* number."

"Yeah, *that* number." Tom paused for a moment, trying to read Alex's expression. "So...do you want to try it?"

"I'm always one for new skills." Alex winked. "Let's give it a go."

Tom turned around on the bed, looking over his shoulder at Alex. "This feels so debauched—I love it!"

Alex gave Tom's bottom a playful tap. "Probably not one to discuss on breakfast telly."

Tom rolled onto his side and grinned at Alex over the lengths of both their bodies. As he stroked Alex's erection, he said, "Yeah, this is definitely post-watershed entertainment."

"A *new politics*?" Alex winked then kissed Tom's thigh and drew his finger along the length of his erection.

Tom trembled at his touch, then brought Alex's erection to his mouth again. He felt Alex follow his lead, his lips soft and slow as they slid down the length of Tom's cock. Tom stroked his tongue around Alex, moving up and down on him. Trying to focus wasn't easy while Alex did the same for him. He held Alex tight around his hips, steadying himself as he pleasured him.

They seemed to fall quite by accident into the same rhythm, each mirroring the other's pace. Alex slid his hand over Tom's buttocks, stroking his fingers just between them as the pressure of his lips grew tighter. Tom moaned, glad that his lover was so instinctive in bed. He wondered how Alex would react to the same touch, and slipped his finger between Alex's buttocks.

Alex's hips jolted forward and Tom felt the effort it took him to contain himself. One thing he couldn't hold back was his groan of pleasure, and he pushed his own finger deeper in reply, his tongue laving Tom's cock. Tom moaned again, then took his mouth from Alex. Looking between their bodies again gave him a gloriously debauched sight.

Tom's voice was soft with desire as he asked, "Darling—do you want to spoon now? I'm not sure I can hold on much longer, you tease."

For a few moments he thought Alex hadn't heard, then he met Tom's gaze and slowly released his erection from his lips.

"I was in another world," he admitted gently. Then he kissed Tom's thigh and said, "Come here?"

Tom moved back up the bed and put his arms around Alex, kissing his shoulders. "That was fun, wasn't it?"

He murmured his agreement. "We should do lots more of it. Lots more of everything."

"When we have that long holiday…" Tom grinned. "The things we can get up to!"

"Where would you like to go?" Alex opened the drawer and reached inside. "Anywhere you want."

Tom hugged himself. "Somewhere warm. Beaches for the twins to play on, and for us to have romantic moonlit strolls."

"Somewhere away from the world." Alex tore open the condom wrapper, apparently as confident now as he had been bashful just a few days earlier. Maybe it was love that did it. "Just for us."

"I love the thought of that." Tom stroked Alex's stomach, enjoying the shape and feel of his body. "And once we've left number 11, where will we go and live?"

"We'll move into the constituency house while we decide. It's not quite Downing Street— it's a lot nicer, for starters." Alex looked thoughtful. "I'd like to get away from the city, but I don't want to cause too much upheaval for the twins. We'll find somewhere perfect, just for our little family."

"They seem to enjoy the countryside. All we need is a donkey in the garden and they'll be happy!" Tom had never had a conversation like this before while naked in bed with a man. But then, he'd never loved the men he'd been with until Alex.

Alex kissed his cheek and promised, "I'm going to spoil all of you rotten."

"You already do—" Tom raised his eyebrow as he looked down at Alex's body. "Especially with that lovely big cock of yours."

He watched as Alex slicked lube onto his erection, anticipating the moment when their bodies would be joined. As Tom lifted his gaze it met Alex's and his lover asked, "I'm doing okay for a novice, then?"

"Look at you, prepping like an expert." Tom nuzzled close to him. "You're everything I ever wanted."

"I told you, I'm a quick learner." He kissed Tom's cheek. "And maybe I've imagined this moment a few times too."

"While you were lying in bed and I was only at the other end of the corridor?" Tom turned onto his side, reaching behind him to caress Alex's stomach again.

"Or were you at your desk in number 10, and I was only on the other side of the wall?"

"I told myself you might as well be on another planet. I couldn't tell you and even if could, I'd hardly be your type." Alex kissed the nape of Tom's neck and laughed softly. "Happily, I was wrong on both counts."

"You were — fortunately!" Tom turned his head and smiled. "You know what to do, don't you?"

With a deep kiss, Alex teased his fingers between Tom's buttocks. When he withdrew them he put his arms, those arms that Tom had fantasized about a thousand times, around his waist and pressed the tip of his erection closer.

"One little thrust, darling." Tom's voice trembled with anticipation. He heard Alex's breath catch as he made the move, their bodies tight together. Then Alex's lips were nuzzling his neck, his fingers encircling Tom's cock.

Tom reached back one arm to loop around Alex's neck. "Is this how you'd hoped it would be?"

"Everything with you — " He began to move his hips and hand, losing the words in another kiss. "It's all better than I could've dreamed."

Tom began to move with him, following his rhythm exactly without really trying to. "We fit together perfectly," Tom whispered.

He wasn't a man who believed in fate, but this was enough to make him wonder. Maybe they were meant to be, two people thrown together as friends, enduring through the years to end up here, wrapped in each other's arms, perfectly in tune. Alex and Tom, Tom and Alex, each suited to the other. Tom recognized now when Alex was nearing his climax — he sensed it, something in Alex's muscles, his breathing. And as

Tom's climax approached, he knew that Alex could tell, and Tom sighed his name as bliss coursed through him.

We were made for each other, Tom knew as they soared into bliss. *And always will be.*

Chapter Twenty-Seven

Tom had done his best to explain to the twins why Daddy wasn't going to be tucking them in that night.

"He's going to try his best to make life really, really good for other boys and girls too. You just need to share him for one evening, that's all."

They went into a hushed and huddled discussion with the Madastair and some assorted other privileged toys on the kitchen table, a little Cabinet all of its own, and were still engaged in delicate negotiations when Alex pottered into the kitchen, fastening his cufflinks. He joined Tom at the fridge and whispered, "What's this?"

"I was trying to explain why you wouldn't be here at bedtime," Tom replied. "I think there might be a vote on that. Sorry — all you need today is *another* one!"

"I thought we might go to Chequers this weekend," Alex told the children, who looked up as he added, "Or because it's a bit dull there sometimes...how about the seaside instead?"

"The seaside, Daddy!" Madeleine clasped her hands. "Please! And it must have sand, for sandcastles."

"And ice cream," Alastair exclaimed. "And donuts?"

Alex turned to Tom. "Which do you fancy, darling? The country pile or fish and chips on the beach?"

"Fish and chips on the beach? Chuck in candy floss" — Tom laughed as the twins cheered — "and I'm there!"

"You're on. Right, breakfast, then I'm off to Cabinet and *the* day." He looked at the children again. "Wish your daddy luck?"

"Good luck, Daddy!" Madeleine passed him the Madastair. "The Madastair wants to go with you."

Alex knelt between the chairs and puts his arms around the twins, the Madastair clutched in his palm. With a kiss to each of the children, he assured them, "Well, I don't think I can lose then. You two, Tom and Billy at home, the Madastair in my pocket. I'll make sure I feed him plenty of biscuits too."

"He does get very hungry, but he's a useful chap to have around!" Tom said. He kissed the top of Alex's head. "Good luck, darling."

"We should win." He looked up at Tom. "But who knows how the *Great British Morning Show* went over? The public's one thing — parliament could be feeling bloody-minded, though — too populist, and all that."

"You've done everything you can — I'll be thinking of you all day." Tom added in a whisper, "I do anyway, but you know what I mean!"

Alex caught Tom's hand and kissed it. "I can't wait to be home."

* * * *

Tom couldn't relax. After he'd come home from dropping the twins at school, he'd managed to make himself a cup of tea twice, and both times he'd forgotten he'd made it and they'd gone cold. He sent Alex a text.

Thinking of you – how's it going? T xxx

As he waited for the reply to land, he switched on the television and there, on College Green, a sizeable crowd had gathered and was growing all the time. Dressed in a rainbow of colors, the young and the old had come together again under their *Love Is Love* banner, holding an impromptu picnic and singalong. For a moment he smiled, until he heard what the reporter was saying.

" – are asking whether this might be the proverbial red rag to the bull. In Westminster, this sort of support isn't a common sight, and being too popular could prove costly when it comes to Members making their feelings known at Mr. Hart's bill tonight."

Tom turned the television off. As the picture blinked out, his phone buzzed.

Everyone's being far too smiley and nice. I'm not sure what it means but I don't like it. Xxx

Tom replied, *Have you seen the crowd outside? Even if you lose the vote, you've still won. T xxx*

A few seconds later, Alex replied.

I've got the three of you, Billy and the Mad. I've won at life. Love you xxx

Tom sent his reply. *I love you, Alex. Good luck! xxx*

He tidied the flat then tidied it again, remembering as he plumped the pillows on Alex's — on *their* bed, their encounter last night. Filled with a new warmth, Tom let himself think not of the vote, but of their little family, of Gill's friendship and the warm support of the public. He couldn't do anything to influence the way the MPs would respond to Alex's child poverty action bill, but he could make the day fun for Alastair and Madeleine, and when they were home from preschool that was exactly what Tom did.

The day passed in a whirl of painting and storytelling, with some pasta-making thrown in for good measure — always a winner with the mini-Harts. Despite their tender years, they seemed to sense that important matters were afoot and carried out their sous chef duties with care and calm, reverential as they helped. They'd grown up here in number 11, and no matter how hard Tom and Alex had tried to give them a normal upbringing, life as the children of one of the most important people in Britain would never be ordinary. Soon enough, though, no matter how well the vote went today, they'd be adjusting to a different life.

Tom read a Noddy story at bedtime, but all the while he wondered how Alex was faring. It was a different world from this bedroom, an innocent haunt for children with its mobile of elephants hanging on the ceiling. By now the division bell would be silenced and in the lobbies, the fate of Alex's legacy would be decided. Whatever deals still had to be made had missed their chance. Now it was down to each individual Member of the House and their own conscience. They could vote no and nothing would change. But if they voted yes, the supertanker would turn and the system, creaking and rickety, would begin the process of reform. Years from now, the proof of reform would be felt as those children Alex sought to help became adults and perhaps even followed Alex Hart into politics, bringing something more than cynicism and ambition with them.

Just before ten his mobile buzzed with a message from Alex, sent in haste.

Into chamber for results. Will be on 10pm news xxxx

Tom sat in the lounge, his untasted glass of wine on the table beside him. He switched on the television and leaned forward in his chair with all the tension of a football fan waiting to hear the results. He was just in time, it seemed, as the screen was filled with an image of the Commons Chamber, as busy as it was at any PMQs, despite it being past ten o'clock on Tuesday night. In the bottom of the screen was a banner that said simply, *LIVE*, and there on the packed front bench was Alex, his head bowed in conversation with Gregory.

"Come on!" Tom shouted at the television. "You bunch of total pillocks, vote for Alex's bill!"

A curious *miaow* came from somewhere in the room, and Billy appeared. "Are we voting for you as well?"

The cat leaped up onto the chair and kneaded Tom's lap. "Look—there's Alex," Tom said. "Can you see him?"

The cat purred loudly as it turned itself into a furry cushion on Tom's lap. He stroked Billy's back and turned up the sound in time to hear the Speaker's familiar bark of "Order!", as though calming a yard full of unruly children. At a repeat of the instruction the hubbub died down and Tom almost held his breath as the results were read out.

"The ayes to the right, six hundred and three." And the roar that went up was deafening, so loud that Tom could barely hear the paltry two dozen who had voted no.

Love Is Love had done nothing to dent Alex's dream. It wasn't so much a landslide as an avalanche.

"The ayes have it!" the Speaker declared, and as he bellowed, "Unlock!", the camera showed Alex and Gregory again, each smiling as widely as the other.

Tom hugged Billy to him. "He did it. He only bloody did it, Billy!"

Tom hopped from the chair and danced around the room with the cat in his arms. What a way for Alex to finish his time in Downing Street.

So busy celebrating was Tom that he didn't hear any of the pundits who came after, or pay much attention to the breathless wonder at the results. In fact, he was still waltzing Billy across the sitting room when he realized that the scene on the television had changed. Where the studio had been was now an exterior shot of Westminster, a place that had become as familiar to him as his own home. The last person he expected to see was Alex, but suddenly there he was, strolling out of the Palace as though he were a tourist on a daytrip.

"This night is going from one unexpected event to another," said the anchor. "It's unheard of, but a jubilant Alex Hart is going to make a statement not only to this growing crowd of supporters, but to the country."

Tom froze. Was Alex going to thank them all for their support? Or was he going to — was he going to tell them, tonight, at the moment of his victory, that he was leaving number 10?

"I've had an extraordinarily privileged few years at number 10," Alex told the crowd as behind him police officers gathered, hawklike as they watched the mass of spectators. He was clutching something in his fist, and though Tom couldn't see it, he knew what it was. The Madastair was making its public debut. "And tonight, everybody in the United Kingdom can rest assured that Parliament has united to ensure a better future. Not just words, but actions, backed up by a pledge of funding and a pledge of caring. And it's this, all of this."

Alex gestured toward the cheering crowd. "Because this started out as a simple message of tolerance and respect and love. And I know that might sound a bit simplistic to some people, but it's a bloody good start, isn't it?"

With tears of joy in his eyes, Tom nodded, even though Alex couldn't see him. "Yes, darling, it is — it *is*."

"And in these four years, there've been times when I was lower than I thought I could ever be, but Gill, my late wife, taught me that you don't give up because things get too hard. And look at what we can achieve!"

The crowd answered with a roar, though Alex silenced them with a gesture of his hand.

"But I need to be there for my family now, for Tom and my children, whether it's for a hug or to stick a plaster on a graze or just dance around the kitchen and collapse onto the sofa with a takeaway. And that's why this will be my last year in Parliament. But this work we've started here, this outpouring of love, that will go on. And *Love Is Love* should be all our missions. So, I want you to have a party tonight, celebrate this victory, and I'll go home to my family. Goodnight!"

Tom hugged Billy and kissed her velvety head. "What a bloody gent."

And he was on his way home.

Chapter Twenty-Eight

Tom didn't have long to wait for Alex. He'd put the champagne in the fridge, just in case, and he'd only just put the glasses out on the kitchen table when he heard the front door. Alex's footsteps were jaunty as they danced along the hallway. He stopped in the kitchen doorway then, as though he were Steed with his bowler hat, threw his tie through the door and onto the table.

"Well...we won!" Alex beamed. He crossed the kitchen to take Tom in his arms, as though they were about to dance. "We *really, really* won!"

Tom rested his forehead against Alex's before settling into a kiss. He broke from it to say, "*You* are the best prime minister ever. No contest."

"I thought we might just edge it after talking to the waverers today, but...bloody hell, Tom, I feel like I've been drinking!" He kissed Tom, taking his face in his hands. "This is going to make a difference. No politician is ever going to dare to turn around now and say these reforms had no mandate. We did it!"

"You did, you did, *you did!*" Tom danced Alex round in a circle. Then he grabbed the bottle of champagne. "You do the honors, darling!"

Alex didn't take the bottle immediately. Instead he put the Madastair carefully on the table and unfastened those tantalizing few buttons on his pristine white shirt. Next he discarded his jacket and cufflinks, before rolling up his sleeves with deliberate care. Only then did he reach for the champagne.

"I thought you might appreciate the full effect," he teased, tearing off the foil and removing the cage. He offered Tom a mischievous wink and said, "I'll tense them just for you."

"You know what I like." Tom watched Alex's arms tense, and those large, square hands clutch the bottle. "Sexiest and most deserved champagne bottle opening of all time, I'd say."

With a decisive twist, the cork popped free. A fountain of champagne rushed toward the bottle's neck and Alex quickly lifted it to his lips and drank before the overflow could escape, like a man who had just claimed the laurels at a Grand Prix. With a cheer of celebration, he decanted the bubbly into the waiting glasses, filling them almost to the brim.

Tom picked up a glass. "Link arms?" It was cheesy, but Tom didn't care. Besides, things that felt cheesy with other people didn't feel the same with Alex. With him they felt silly and playful— *sweet* in fact.

"Arms again?" Alex joked as they entwined their limbs. "This is it, you know. Everybody knows about us, the bill went through, everybody knows I'm off. The future's whatever we want it to be."

"I want our future to be happy—I want us to be together." Tom sipped his champagne, feeling the pull of Alex's strong arm against his.

"The world's changed, hasn't it?" Alex took a sip from his glass. "And it's…it's amazing."

"And you've made it happen, Alex." Tom kissed him.

Alex shook his head and murmured, "You were the one giving the massage, darling."

Tom grinned. "So, we really owe all this to Gregory-not-Greg, seeing as your thrilling meeting with him made you all tense."

"Gregory-not-Greg shared my car back to Downing Street. You'll never guess what he asked me." He took another sip of champagne. "He wants to know if there's any chance we could be convinced to leave Billy. You've got to love that man's confidence—he's already appointed himself PM before we've even called the election!"

"Billy? He'll have to ask the twins about that!" Tom touched the tip of his nose to Alex's. "But then, Billy is a civil servant and she's not old enough to retire yet. She's got a fair few years left of patrolling Downing Street."

"If Bill stays, Mad and Al will have to be carried out under protest." Alex kissed Tom. "But I did say I'd let him know the rescue she came from. I think that's Greg's version of coming out, you know!"

"He wants a cat—he can't be so bad after all." Tom drained his glass. "Top-up? Bet you could do with a back rub, right?"

"I'd love a back rub and I *need* a shower. It's been a long day."

"Back rub *in* the shower?" Tom suggested. "I'll wash your hair for you—that'll relax you."

Alex murmured his assent into a kiss and whispered, "You spoil me rotten."

"You deserve it—especially today. And don't forget the champers!"

Champagne in the shower at Downing Street with the prime minister in his arms was, Tom decided, a fairly unique experience. Every day with Alex seemed like another chance to make one of his fantasies come true, and as the warm water cascaded down over them, he and Alex lost themselves in lingering kisses.

What a man, and what a body to cling to.

Tom lathered Alex up, washing away his strain, rubbing out the knots in his muscles. And, in between sighs and kisses, spilling champagne over them both.

The man who kissed him into the pillows yielded to Tom's ministrations, trusting and loving as he gave himself over to his lover's touch. He ran his hands over Tom's body in reply, caressing his skin through the steamy shower bubbles and murmuring the sweetest sentiments he had ever heard anyone utter.

"How are you feeling now, darling?" Tom asked as he curled his hand around Alex's erection. "A little more relaxed?"

"I feel wonderful," he admitted, putting his empty glass on the shower shelf next to the supplies they had brought in from the bedroom. Alex's arms were around Tom's waist a moment later, holding him close. "What about you? You do so much for me, darling."

"Wasn't there something you'd been thinking of us doing in the shower?" Tom blinked away the water as it splashed over them. "I think we'd both enjoy that."

Alex nuzzled a kiss to his throat as he reached up for the packet on the shelf. His mouth roamed Tom's shoulders and jaw, leaving a trail of heat before his teeth nipped gently at Tom's earlobe.

Tom cupped Alex's face. "When you thought about us in the shower, what did you see?"

"It was pretty..." Alex laughed and admitted, "Raunchy, I think is the only word for it. Then I woke up and had to sit at the breakfast table with you and pretend I hadn't dreamed about us wildly making love in a steamy shower."

"Alex, you bad boy!" Tom kissed his chin. "So if I turn around like this..."

Tom turned, his arms folded against the tiles. He looked at Alex over his shoulder. "The prime minister's very own shower gel model?"

"You're perfect, you know. Every bit of you is just *gorgeous*." Alex stroked an admiring hand over Tom's buttock. "You're better than any shower gel model."

"I'm real, and I'm here, and Alex Hart has his hand on my arse." Tom tensed his buttocks, just for Alex. "You gorgeous man."

Alex stooped and pressed a very gentle kiss to Tom's bottom. He kissed his way along the length of Tom's spine to his nape as he rolled the condom over his erection, then slipped his arm around Tom's waist and whispered, "Ready, darling?"

"Very," Tom replied, reaching his hand behind him to touch Alex. "More than you can imagine."

All of Alex's timidity was gone now, a far cry from the bashful man with whom he had showered in what felt like another lifetime. Their bodies joined so easily, so instinctively, and he felt Alex's chest pressed to his back, his hand moving on Tom's erection.

Tom thrust against him, their bodies finding their own rhythm. He turned his head, trying to catch Alex's lips for a kiss. It felt like flying, like being weightless, here in Alex's arms. The kiss went on and on, as filled with hunger as it was with love. Tom wasn't sure he knew where he ended and Alex began, only that they needed each other.

Tom's future would be with Alex, and in a way he'd only ever hoped for. This wonderful, kind, loving man — gorgeous and sensual, attentive and warm — was his.

How Alex could ever have doubted himself, Tom didn't know. In fact, he knew nothing but pleasure and love as they clung to each other, loved and loving. As joy claimed them, Alex pressed his lips to Tom's ear, gasping, "I love you…"

"I love you, too," Tom whispered, leaning back against Alex as his body trembled with answered need. They stayed there in each other's arms for what felt like a long time, exchanging gentle kisses, their bodies intertwined, sated and content. The air was filled with steam even when the water stopped and Alex dried Tom with a fluffy towel, every touch reverential, fluttering kisses punctuating the strokes.

"Bet you're *very* relaxed now," Tom said. "I could get used to having a man like you around to look after me."

"You should, because this is your life now, Captain Southwell." Alex stroked his thumb over Tom's cheek. "I'm going to look in on the minis and put their Madastair to bed. Will you come with me?"

"Of course I will." Tom reached for one of the soft bathrobes on the back of the bathroom door. He tied it on and asked, "Do I look respectable?"

"Eminently so." Alex fastened his own robe and together the men made their way through the flat, pausing only to collect the Madastair from the kitchen. They trod lightly into the bedroom that the twins shared and paused just inside the door, watching the peaceful slumber of the children.

Tom slipped his arm around Alex's waist. For all the raunch that he and Alex were capable of, they still had their innocent family moments.

The children must have sensed their presence in the doorway, as Madeleine blinked herself awake and Alastair stirred.

"Daddy and Tom?" Madeleine whispered, rubbing her eyes.

"Back to sleep," Alex told her gently, crossing the room to put the little toy on the table between the beds. "We're just putting the Madastair to bed. He's had a busy day."

"Did you win, Daddy?" Madeleine asked as she glanced at the toy. "Did the Madastair help?"

"He was the best help I could've dreamed of. We won, darling, and the Madastair kept me company all day. I made sure he was well fed and looked after."

"Yay, well done, Daddy!" Madeleine sat up in bed, her arms extended to Alex. "And all the other boys and girls will be okay now, won't they?"

He nodded, leaning in to hug her. "They will."

"Can we sleep in your bed?" Alastair asked sleepily. "Because you won."

"I think that would be nice," Tom replied as he crouched beside Alastair's bed. "Alex?"

"Come on, you two." Alex scooped Madeleine into his arms, waiting while Tom lifted Alastair from his bed. "The Madastair can keep your toys company tonight."

Madeleine waived to the toy. "Bye-bye, Madastair!"

Tom lifted Alastair onto his hip. The little boy was mostly half-asleep but he was smiling. "Come on, you two, off to the big bed!"

The family made their way to Alex's bedroom and there the men settled the children, Madeline and Alastair already asleep again before their heads hit the pillows. It took just a couple of minutes to exchange bathrobes for pajamas, then Alex and Tom climbed in beside them, lulled to sleep by the sound of their gentle breathing.

Epilogue

Tom slipped a biro between the pages of the hotel brochure to keep his place. Gregory-not-Greg was on the television. He was standing outside 10 Downing Street, a plump ginger cat cradled in his arms as he waved its paw at the horde of cameras. The new prime minister and his companion gazed at one another with ill-disguised devotion, then Gregory addressed the reporters.

"Well, I have big shoes to fill, and so does Mateo. So if you'll excuse us, we have work to do."

With that, he turned. The black door of Downing Street opened and Gregory and Mateo disappeared inside. Alex nudged Tom and whispered playfully, "He's not as good-looking as the last bloke, is he?"

"No, he doesn't get my vote." Tom chuckled.

Billy had come in and, perhaps recognizing her old haunt, stood on her hind legs and batted at the screen.

"Billy, naughty!" Madeleine chided. Alastair laughed and Billy, as though enjoying the audience, batted the screen again before she strolled over to the children and lay down in front of them, right across Madeleine's comic. Alastair put the Madastair beside her, as though the two were about to cook up some mischief together.

"Right, that's enough telly," Alex decided, linking his arm through Tom's. "We've got holidays to book, donkeys to feed and sunshine to enjoy. Who fancies a walk if there's ice cream at the end of it?"

The children leaped up. "Me!" they both shouted.

"Dodgems on the pier?" Tom suggested, and the twins zoomed in excited circles. "That's a yes, then!"

"Come on then, family." Alex kissed Tom's cheek, then rested his head against his shoulder. "Let's go exploring."

Want to see more from these authors? Here's a taster for you to enjoy!

A Little Bit Cupid: The Dishevelled Duke
Catherine Curzon & Eleanor Harkstead

Excerpt

All the champagne cupcakes had gone. Only a few slices of red velvet cake remained, sharing a plate with the last three heart-shaped cookies. Imogen had said that Billy could take them home with him. What a way to arrive. Ten years in London and Billy would appear on his parents' doorstep with leftover Valentine's Day cake and hundreds of unsold photographs.

At least I tried.

For the last time, Billy loaded the café's dishwasher. In a couple of minutes he would turn the sign to closed for the last time, shut the blinds for the last time and leave The Chelsea Bunn forever. He would lug his case through the crowds, clamber onto a packed train and say goodbye to London.

But he wouldn't say goodbye to Charlie-who-has-no-surname, who came in five times a week for a cup of tea and a bun for the two wolfhounds that dragged him around like slightly undersized donkeys. Charlie with the peppery hair and laughing eyes and the lines that crinkled around them when he smiled. And he smiled a lot.

Billy wouldn't say goodbye to Charlie because for the last two weeks, his shifts had changed to fit around the shop's new hours and he hadn't seen him since. For the Bunn to be busy enough for extended hours was great, but it meant no more Charlie. Charlie didn't come in late, it seemed, only for that mid-morning tea and cake.

Not having seen Charlie for a fortnight had made Billy realise how much he would miss the friends he had made in London. People from art school, and Imogen, who had given Billy enough shifts to eke out his life in London for just a few more months, even a place to sleep when his love life had turned sour. And most of all Charlie, who always had a smile for him, who always found the time to speak to him.

Billy's favourite customer.

Not that Charlie would have missed him. Billy was only a server in a café, a barista if he wanted to make his job sound fancy. But he already missed Charlie, and as he wiped down the counter one last time, his gaze fell on the table where Charlie usually sat with his dogs beside him. He'd read the newspaper or fill in a crossword with his silver-barrelled pen, but more than anything he'd just chat to Billy or fuss the dogs that so clearly adored him. The table was empty now and the next time Charlie and the dogs came in, Billy would be long gone. *And we never got a chance to say a proper goodbye.* Billy drew in a deep breath then crossed to the door and turned the sign to closed.

He buttoned up his coat and, looping his scarf around his neck, he glanced outside.

A light snow had begun to fall, bringing a romantic sparkle to Valentine's Day that Billy's life was completely devoid of. He'd enjoyed nothing but romantic failures in his time in London, and spending his last day in the city in a café filled with every kind of Valentine's-themed cake imaginable had merely reminded him of how little success he'd had in the big city.

It was time to go home.

He pressed the light switches and the shop fell into darkness, only the bulbs in the kitchen illuminated now. With a last look back at the street he flipped the lock down and shut out the world, then turned away and walked back towards the counter. It seemed right that his last night in the city was spent clearing up the mess of other peoples' Valentine's Day whilst the rest of the world had fun. Hadn't that pretty much been the story of his failed adventure in the metropolis?

He jumped at the sound of a sharp knock on the glass door. Someone rattled it, someone who was too late for coffee. *Don't I deserve an evening off too?*

"We're closed!" Billy called.

He saw a figure still there at the door and felt immediately guilty. A slightly shambolic figure. If it was a rough sleeper, Billy would give them the leftover cake. He took the bag from the counter but as he headed to the door, he realised that it was Charlie.

He didn't have the dogs with him tonight, but carried something large and flat under one arm. With one more knock at the door Charlie turned away, about to be swallowed into that ceaseless tide of Londoners that coursed along the pavement.

Billy nearly snapped the lock off in his haste to open the door. He hoped Charlie would hear him over the noise of the street.

"Charlie!"

For a moment Billy thought he hadn't heard, then Charlie turned and beamed that smile that had always brightened Billy's miserable mornings.

And this is the last time I'll see it.

"Billy!" Charlie raised his gloved hand and began to make his way back towards the shop, gripping the brightly wrapped parcel precariously beneath his arm. It was a vivid red against his dark blue greatcoat, the same shade of red as the scarf he always wore, and the silver ribbon that ended in a flamboyant bow around the paper seemed brighter and more cheery still next to that sensible greatcoat. A light dusting of snowflakes rested on Charlie's shoulders and in his hair but he didn't seem to notice, nor was he troubled by the slushy mess that was already building on the pavement.

"I thought I'd missed you, today has been rather a nightmare. I've been running here, there and everywhere." Posh Charlie, his accent as cut-glass as his clothes were creased. "And now I'm keeping you from going home!"

"Are you dashing off somewhere?" Billy asked. "I've got to get my train in a couple of hours from Waterloo, but..." Billy gazed at Charlie, trying to imprint every last facet of him into his mind. He'd thought he'd never see Charlie again, but luck had given him one last chance.

"Well, there's an invite to see the brother and his brood at the weekend, but this particular chap's rather hoping that the snow might save one from that fate," he admitted mischievously. "What about you, off home to the promised land? Will you be back before the twenty-eighth? I'm having a bit of a do for Nigel and Delia's birthday—there'll be cake, of course—and I thought maybe… They're not littermates but so much easier to have the one doggy party!"

Nigel and Delia. A birthday party for the wolfhounds is so you.

Snow was settling on Charlie's hair as he spoke. It made him look even more festive, a Mr Tumnus in Chelsea. Billy wished he could say yes to his party. He wished he were coming back. A shiver went through him, and it wasn't from the cold.

"Will you come in, Charlie, please?" Billy asked. "There's something I didn't tell you—I didn't get the chance. And now you're here… There's cake if you'd like some?"

PUBLISHING

Sign up for our newsletter and find out about all our romance book releases, eBook sales and promotions, sneak peeks and FREE romance books!